"Remarkable . . . An often brilliantly interpretive work of fiction. With a coolness more effective than indignation she shows the making of a psychopath."

—Julian Symons, *Sunday Times*

"A crisp inventory of the horrors of growing up privileged in England between the wars . . . It is an ordinary family household, but seen from the underside it is a Renaissance court with its own rituals, threats and dagger-play . . . Brooke writes clinically and simply in the historic present. She convinces us that accidents are rarely accidental—and that they happen especially in the best-regulated families."

—A. Whittane, *Times Literary Supplement*

"Compelling . . . Astonishingly direct. For those who don't mind wandering with [Brooke] down the corridors of erotic adventure, there will be some squalid and startling experiences in her company. She uses the historic present like a club."

—David Benedictus, *Daily Telegraph*

"Dinah Brooke's sentences are short, harsh, nervously tense; she writes with concentrated and possessed fury."

—Anthony Thwaite, *The Observer*

LORD JIM AT HOME

LORD JIM
AT HOME

DINAH BROOKE

WITH A FOREWORD
BY OTTESSA MOSHFEGH

McNally Editions

New York

McNally Editions
52 Prince St., New York 10012

ISBN: 978-1-946022-64-6
E-book: 978-1-946022-65-3

Design by Jonathan Lippincott

1   3   5   7   9   10   8   6   4   2

FOREWORD

When *Lord Jim at Home* was recommended to me, it came with no introduction. I'm glad. I wouldn't have wanted the effect of the novel to be mitigated in any way, so I'm reluctant to introduce it now. But I will share with you my experiences: I read very slowly at the beginning, studying Dinah Brooke's uncanny descriptions and syntax, squinting hard to see around the curves and outcroppings of the story, stepping back in astonishment to watch a sentence unfurl like some wild plant, surreal in its beauty and dangerous in its intelligence. Like this child's bedtime:

> The curtains are drawn, the door shut, and like a rubber duck held down at the bottom of the bath and suddenly released he shoots up to float bouncing gently, turning and twisting dizzily between the floor and the ceiling. Swooning in space with the darkness velvet under his hands his body takes on strange shapes, huge, liquid, swelling head and knees, hands like a giant's, fingers grasping from corner to corner of the room, then suddenly shrinking,

wizened, like the inside of his mouth when he has managed to put a thumb painted with bitter aloes into it.

It took me about three weeks to make it through the first seventy-five pages. I kept having to put the book down and get up and look around. "Where am I?" On a train. In a hotel room. On the sofa. In my room. That hadn't happened to me since I was five, when I'd get hypnotized by the television. But now there was also the unsettling question, "Am I still the same person?" Not really. As I got to the middle of the book, I had the sensation that I had aged about twenty years. Then the sensation reversed, and as I neared the end, I got younger again. I grew new nerves, as if it had altered my anatomy and sense of time.

When *Lord Jim at Home* appeared, in 1973, Brooke was thirty-seven, living in London, married to an actor, and raising twins. In a later autobiographical essay, she would list the main events of her life in the early seventies: "Became ardent feminist, then ardent encounter groupie. Turned house into commune. Husband left."* A time of inner discovery, I suppose. An encounter group (for the uninitiated) is a form of psychodrama therapy in which individuals concentrate on and express their innermost feelings. The idea is that you encounter yourself more honestly by confronting others honestly. I wonder whether Brooke spoke of *Lord Jim at Home* in those

---

* "An Obsession Revisited," in *Fathers: Reflections by Daughters* (ed. Ursula Owen). London: Virago, 1983

groups. Did people understand anything she said? Or maybe she studied the others, took notes on their limitations and delusions, and fed them to her book like mice to a snake. Perhaps she also fed her book the traumas of people living in her commune. There is a lot of pain in *Lord Jim at Home*. And a lot of humor. And a lot of another thing that I can't properly name. And almost no analysis, not really. It is too cool a book for that—cool in temperament as well as in attitude.

To describe the plot here would be to ruin a surprise, so I will only say that the novel is largely a portrait of one Giles Trenchard, born in Cornwall between the wars, a son of the British middle classes, and that apparently it is based on a true story (something I didn't know when I read it). Giles suffers a horrible and privileged upbringing, goes away to school, joins the Navy, comes home, and attempts to begin a life as a grown man. The novel ends when he is twenty-something and has done something very unexpected, but not altogether shocking—except to the people around him, who ask how someone so "healthy and clean-limbed," with such an "honest, reliable, open English face" can have acted the way he did. The situation and language echo the Joseph Conrad novel *Lord Jim*, about a young English sailor who disgraces himself at sea, then spends his life in the South Pacific, trying to escape his cloud of shame. In Brooke's novel, as the title suggests, escape is not an option. ("Patusan," the island paradise that Lord Jim makes his own, has become the name of a Navy destroyer.) And the moment of public disgrace isn't a catalyst, it's the outcome of a life.

Although we meet Giles as a newborn baby, we never grow to love him. This is not an emotional novel, although it is concerned with the vulnerability of a child's mind. It is a strong, impermeable book. The narrator's mind sticks to the facts of subjective experience. If it weren't such a pleasure to read, I'd say that *Lord Jim at Home*—read by a novelist, like me—was an instrument of torture. It's that good.

It takes enormous control to write well about a baby, for one thing, and from a baby's point of view. A reader naturally feels threatened by that perspective. Ego barges into the mind and says, "What about me? I was a baby, too." At least that has been my experience. In the same way that we might not want to hear the details of another person's dreams, we don't want to hear about their experience being a baby. Nobody should get credit for having a certain kind of dream. And nobody should get credit for being a certain kind of baby. Babies don't create themselves. They don't make any decisions about how to be. They don't know how. And yet we project onto our baby-selves the wisdom of a Buddhist sage. Case in point. My first memory is of being in the crib at my babysitter's house, waiting for my mother to pick me up. It was night and the room was dark. I was too young to know how to count, but I took some careful note of the many headlights which passed diagonally from the road through the windows and skipped across the perpendicular planes of the walls, like rubber balls, again and again. One of these lights, I knew, would announce my mother, but I had to wait—I felt—an eternity. To me, this recollection is still rife with heartache and is my reference point for the birth of my consciousness, i.e., my existential suffering.

This is the first time I have written about it, because until now I was too lazy to describe it. Brooke, however, writes from the point of view of infant Giles with a patient, tireless, and freakish genius. There were times where I felt she had made a chiropractic adjustment in my brain, revising what I understood to be the logic of an infant, and not in the way I expected:

> Pain and humiliation. Not so much the soiled nappies pressed over his mouth and nose, as the brisk, impersonal unpinning and flipping from back to front, and wiping. Is she wiping shit off the Prince's bottom or off the table? Impossible to tell from her expression or her voice. Does that sensation belong to me? wonders the Prince. Does that expression belong to me?

Again, "Where am I? Who am I?" If you can't answer these questions, you may be suffering from a concussion.

This isn't the only freakish thing about the book. For example, I would argue that Giles, the main character, is not really a character in any usual sense. He lacks the lowest level of agency and self-definition, although to describe him as passive would be incorrect. More like a human being who has been mostly lobotomized. And yet I feel I understand him, and know him. He is familiar. Simultaneously, I have no anxiety about his well-being. But I do cringe as I read of the cruel abuses by his nurse and parents. I don't really care what tragedies he suffers during the war, but I like to imagine them. I have no skin in the game at all, in the end, when his fate is up for review. Am I a monster? Or has the book taught me to opt out of the usual mind games that a novel plays with a reader? Worry usually provides suspense. But you have to care in order to have worries. I didn't care, and I didn't worry, but I was suspended, consistently and dramatically, in the mirage of the novel, a world that baffled me and yet made perfect sense.

Another disorientation: the perspective attaches onto characters whose tangential narratives are immaterial, the point of view skipping around souls, as though picking people out in a crowd and following them for a minute, and then skipping again. It is jarring to a wonderful effect, mimicking the movement of the protagonist's depersonalized adventures.

The first publisher of *Lord Jim at Home* presented it as a novel about the upper middle class in England, as if it were an anthropological study or a work of classic Naturalism, which it most certainly is not. Glancing at the initial criticisms of the novel, I see some advantages to living in this modern age. Even in a favorable review in the *Times Literary Supplement*, back in 1974, it was clear that the critic Stuart McGregor, a man of good taste, maybe, completely misunderstood the book. In describing the last stretch of the novel, after Giles comes home from war to a mother who greets him politely and then goes back to her game of bridge, he writes, "His postwar story, with its long succession of failures mounting to a sad but long-foreseen climax, is a monstrous parody of the way nice, well-brought-up people think and behave."

I don't think so. I think it is an accurate portrayal of how fucked-up people behave, artfully conveyed in a way that nice people are too polite to admit they understand. I'm grateful it's back in print. I think the world may be readier than it was.

Ottessa Moshfegh
Pasadena, 2023

LORD JIM AT HOME

ONE

The house on the cliffs is furnished with an *eau de nil* carpet and a rosewood desk. In the garden are rhododendrons and tamarisk. In the dining room is an oval mahogany table polished so that it reflects, like a *camera obscura*, the blue of the sky and muted green of the lawn. A soft, blurred pyramid of light in the dark room, smelling of meat.

At the rosewood desk the Queen is writing letters. She has a round face, pink and gentle. Her hair is thick, light brown, with soft waves. Her ankles are also thick. She is small, but a cloak trimmed with ermine suits her, and a crown or tiara sits easily upon her head. She has written many letters at this desk. One is to that famous newspaper the *Times,* asking them to find for her the very best nurse for her expected child. Only the very best will be good enough for this infant, wrapped in inherited lace, to be christened in the church where his forefathers have been christened.

A nurse with red hair like flame, and azure blue eyes and a stone face, travels down from another kingdom in the North, where the princes and princesses have grown old enough to be sent away. She joins the cook, the maid and the gardener as a servant of the household. The only slave is the infant Prince. He is the necessary foundation of the structure, but he doesn't know it. And the foundation is at the bottom.

He is kept under control by two weapons; just enough of his desires are satisfied to prevent open rebellion, and fear.

He is regularly fed, washed and powdered. 'Can't abide a child who smells,' says the nurse to the maid. At one month, his sagging body, hairless, toothless, clad only in a smocked angel top, is precariously balanced after each feed on a tiny enamel pot. At seven months, gasping, half blinded, mouth and nose full of shit and the stench of ammonia from his own nappies, he is clean and sometimes dry during the day.

All day he lies in his cot, arms tucked down, and stares at the white ceiling of the nursery, or in his pram and stares at the dark rhododendron leaves against the sky. At night he lies alone in the deep velvet blackness, no living body beside or around him, no thudding heart, breath, movement or voice, strapped flat on his back so that he cannot turn and smother himself in the lacy pillow.

Once a day, in the *eau de nil* drawing room, among the guests and teacups, he is transferred from the starched arms of his nurse to his mother's soft bosom and powdery smell, and fed, when the nurse has gone, with kisses and licks of sugar. 'Oh dear, nurse would be cross, but he is such a darling.' Then comes the exquisite pain, torn away from this tender sweetness, fingers clutching, body arched, screams of despair. Even a rat would have learned that a broken string of pearls and knocked over teacup meant that next day there would be no love, no sugar. The Prince learns in the end, but a rat would have learned sooner.

The Queen has no real understanding of discipline. She professes to agree that her child should not be allowed downstairs unless he can behave himself properly, but during the day she sometimes creeps up the back stairs when the nurse is busy elsewhere, to coo at and caress the infant as he lies in his cot. The door opens. The Queen's pink face and brown hair become a blur as she moves away. Her soft voice turns into a guilty whine. Her presence fades through the dark cavern of the open door. The nurse's skin holds the light like marble. She is the strong arm of the establishment. It is her duty to ensure the propagation of its self-righteousness. Her position is that of a servant, but her authority is second only to that of the King himself. She is the éminence grise, and conscious of her power.

Fear as a weapon of control. Fear of deprivation is useful. Deprivation of food shows, but deprivation of the affection and presence of the mother does not. It also has the advantage of letting everyone at court see where the power lies. Fear of pain is of little value until the infant's nervous system is sufficiently developed to understand what pain is and where it is coming from. Fear of the dark, and of solitude, on the other hand, can be used almost from birth.

The Queen, returning from a banquet, listens anxiously to the choked and exhausted sobs, screams, hiccups from the nursery. She creeps up the stairs, holding her long skirt round her. Her hand is on the door. Nurse appears in a white flannel nightgown. 'Oh dear, nurse, I'm sorry, I just thought I might . . .'

'There's nothing wrong with him, Madam. If you go in now you will only upset him.'

'But . . .'

'He's got to learn.'

'But surely isn't four hours . . . ?'

'You must do as you think fit, Madam.'

The door closes behind her turned back. The Queen stands outside the door of the nursery wringing her hands. The breathy screams and cries continue. Long strings of saliva tremble, sticky, no longer wet. 'I'm here darling. It's mummy. Don't cry, mummy's here.' A soothing whisper on the other side of the door. After some time the choked screams die down. The child is sleeping. The Queen, cold and stiff, creeps downstairs.

'Where the hell have you been?' asks the King, humped half asleep in the turquoise and white bedroom.

'I'm worried about the baby. He cries so much.'

The smooth, soft skin of her forehead creases with anxiety. She is making her own small rebellion.

'He's got to learn who's master,' says the King, pulling the satin covered eiderdown up round his shoulders and tucking it under his chin. The infant Prince is his enemy, gathering strength to put his eyes out, chop his balls off, take his kingdom. I am bigger than you, and I am stronger than you, thinks the King, and I will win.

'Don't blame me, darling, it's not my fault, I'm only trying to do what's best for you.' The Queen still wrings her hands, kneeling before the awful figure of her son. She steps out of her crepe de chine cami-knickers and lays them over the back of a chair. 'She's been trained, you see. She knows how to deal with children. I'm such a silly old thing, darling, I never know what to do.' She pauses before putting on her nightdress, and smiles at herself in the mirror.

In the morning she is astonished to see how small he is. His pink, creased face, unfocused eyes, and jerky, wavering movements do not after all express revengeful and accusing rage. It is perfectly all right. Everything is normal again. Hugged and kissed, in smock and sausage curls, he is only mummy's darling baby boy—and being so good today.

Later the floor of the nursery becomes the Prince's territory. Increasing movement has given him the freedom of a cage. He sits on a tartan woolen rug behind his wooden bars, and waits to see what the world will offer him. The rug is fringed at either end, and he spends one morning chewing part of the fringe into wet strings with his gums. The next day both fringed ends have been neatly sewn down. Turn your attention, Prince, to a teddy bear and a jointed wooden doll. Far away, across the large expanse of mottled green linoleum, in front of the fireplace, lies a rag rug; a forest, a jungle—black and beige and pink and maroon.

This becomes the centre of his attention. Who wants to shake a rattle when by a process of inherited sensual knowledge he knows that some at least of those crushed and flattened pieces of rag, the beige ones certainly, the pink perhaps—and the maroon? don't know, to be determined by experiment—if pulled will stretch themselves out softly, changing their nature, becoming thin and tall instead of short and fat, and then, let go, will fall back with a sudden sharp movement into their original softness. The infant Prince groans and squeals and humps himself up onto his knees and rubs his head from side to side. Softness and elasticity and shape that changes as you pull and press it, pink and beige. In the tiny cushions of his fingers and his lips the sensations exist.

Once, when his nurse is out of the room, the Prince by cunning manipulation of his heels and bottom manages to slide the rug across the linoleum and push the playpen after it until he almost, stretched hand through the bars, one finger touching, clutching, ouch! oh! oh yes, pain has become a useful method of control.

Pain and humiliation. Not so much the soiled nappies pressed over his mouth and nose, as the brisk, impersonal unpinning and flipping from back to front, and wiping. Is she wiping shit off the Prince's bottom or off the table? Impossible to tell from her expression or her voice. Does that sensation belong to me? wonders the Prince. Does that expression belong to me?

The hair at her temple is orange, and pulled back tightly under her cap. If it was released it would spring into a curve, round and full. Flattened, it retains the fossilised impression of a curl. It cannot be straight. It twists back on itself.

She is very competent. The child is always clean. His white boots are neatly laced up, without a mark on them. His white socks, showing just above the top of the boots, bite softly into the shiny flesh. His dimpled knees are bent double, as if they were made of plasticine. Carried, in a rush of air, on a bony arm, along corridors covered with linoleum and down wooden stairs to wider stairs covered with green carpet. Sudden silence of the clumping footsteps. The crackling of starched cotton becomes loud. The light upstairs is white and cold, the stairs dark. The carpeted corridors and rooms muted, pale and green. The air becomes warmer and more voluptuous as they descend. The smells are different. So are the sounds. Doors open and shut. Voices murmur and rise musically. Sharp, stifled, bell-like notes of silver on china. The teacups are translucent. Light lies in them dark amber or pale gold. Today Father is there as well, the King himself, not properly contained either in his clothes or his body. Squeeze him a little, prick him with a pin, and blood will gush forth. His shoulders burst out of his dark grey suit, his neck bursts out of his shirt collar. It is as wide as his face. There is no difference between his neck and his face. The blood pulses, thick and dark purple, behind his skin. His brown eyes shine hotly, squeezed outwards by remorseless pressure. The resonance of his voice makes the teacup tremble faintly against the saucer. His hair is dark and thin and neatly brushed. He wears no crown. He does not approach the Prince too closely. He remains at the other end of the room, talking to other large, grey men. But his voice makes the Prince's throat ache, and gives the sugar a strange taste, in spite of the cooing circle of ladies-in-waiting, with their soft hands and pale skirts and swaying waves of hair.

It is pleasant to be back in these surroundings. Passivity becomes, after all, pleasure instead of shame. The Queen's bosom is soft and full under her pale green blouse. Her neck is soft. He can feel her skin tremble as the blood pulses beneath it. A touch as delicate as a butterfly's wing. She raises her hand to brush away a strand of hair. The

Prince's eyes stare, pale blue, unfocused, towards the ceiling. They stare out and see inside himself sensations woven together, black, flecked with grey and red. He sucks on his tongue. His hand flutters downwards. Impossible that any human touch could be so soft. The Queen shakes her head impatiently, but does not take her eyes from her friend, whose lips are different shades of red inside and out, and whose cup is stained with an imprint of the skin texture of her lower lip.

'Geoffrey goes before the selection board on Friday.' She speaks and drinks with her upper lip flaring backwards. The Prince's hand finds a different texture at the base of his mother's neck. Rougher and cooler, but still soft—crepe. A raised seam round the neck, and others leading downwards, little raised patterns covering his mother's body. The Prince's hand follows a path downwards; gently, slowly, aimlessly, with the tip of one finger. The Queen says,

'Geoffrey's just the sort of man we need.' The Prince's hand comes to rest over his mother's nipple, and an expression of faint anxiety on his face is noticeable in retrospect as he relaxes. A gush of milk, which has never before flowed for her child, rises from the springs of the Queen's bosom and stains her dress.

'Oh Lord, darling,' cries her friend, 'the little beast has wet you.'

The Queen springs to her feet with a scream of shame and astonishment. The Prince is banished to arm's length. No one wants to take him from her. On the Queen's breasts are two round stains of deeper green. The resonant voices are silent. The grey men turn to look at the Queen.

'Nurse! Nurse!' But there is still half an hour before the nurse is due to collect the Prince. Someone rings the bell. The Queen presses the Prince to her bosom to hide her shame. 'I must go and change.'

He is privileged. Because of his wickedness and the Queen's shame he is privileged to fly upstairs in her arms and lie on the ice cold shiny satin counterpane while she pulls off her clothes, sobbing.

'Beastly, horrible little boy.' Her lips are trembling, they turn down at the corners like a child's. She sniffs. Her voice trembles.

'Oh I can't bear it, I can't bear it.' There are little buttons and buttonholes at the back of her blouse. She cannot undo them. Her friend has followed her upstairs. She helps undo the buttons.

'They're such filthy little pigs. One really ought not to have anything to do with them until they're at least two.' Light is reflected from the shiny satin counterpane and the white walls. The triple mirror on the dressing table under the window is dark except for the white faces of the two women. Tears are running down the Queen's face. She takes off her blouse and throws it on the floor with a shudder. She looks down at herself and says in a thin, frightened voice, 'It's come right through.' The coffee coloured lace is sticky. To take off her camiknicks she first has to take off her skirt. Now she knows the taste of humiliation. The nurse taps on the door.

'Shall I take him away, Madam?'

'Yes. Take him away.'

Away from the cool white light of his mother's bedroom, from the powders and scarves and lace. From the dumpy woman in her stockings and girdle sitting on the stool in front of the dressing table, with her friend starting to undo her brassiere, and tears on her cheeks.

The more the Prince's desire for his mother increases the more he is deprived of her. The long emptiness of nursery days turns bitter. He holds himself in suspension, waiting for her. He no longer releases gifts of himself into the cold tin potty or the marble hands of his nurse. He takes food into his mouth but does not swallow, or swallows but does not digest, and vomits it up again, later, unchanged. 'I shall not breathe, or grow, or live until I am in the arms of my mother.' He is not doing the right thing, so Mother is not allowed into the nursery, and he is not allowed downstairs for tea. Sometimes his mother comes upstairs and stands in the doorway of the nursery looking at him. But however much he screams and struggles she does not take him in her arms. She looks at him, anxious, troubled, but wary now, of his power.

'He's got to learn, Madam.' She goes away, relieved.

The nurse is a fighter. She has strength, courage, skill. She is not to be beaten. She revels in the sound and smell of battle. The harsh crack of her hands on desperately flailing limbs, the webbing straps that bind the child to his mattress pulled tighter every night. She glories in it. She glories in an adversary worthy of her strength. The savage must be controlled, he must be tamed. He must learn how to be a child. He cannot know, poor ignorant, screaming wretch, what a child should be. But she, the nurse, has been taught, over many years, by the expectations of those who employ her. A child should be quiet and malleable. He should have no desires. He should have no will. Willfulness is the devil. He should eat and sleep, eat and sleep again. Occasionally, clean and neatly dressed, he should gurgle and coo at selected relatives. Of the dark battles of the nursery nothing should be seen. This child is a worthy adversary in the strength of his desires and the violence of his struggle, but he has no cunning. He can find no other means to achieve what he wants. She feels a certain amount of pity for him, and contempt. In a harsher society he would never have survived. There is no bounce, no spring to his character. He cannot swallow a defeat and then attack from a new angle. He continually proclaims his misery and his despair. The nurse, bored and disgusted, shuts him in the toy cupboard when she can stand his screaming no longer.

There at least he has plenty to occupy him. But he can't concentrate. Locked into the uneasy blackness he is possessed by fear. He lacks light, warmth, comfort. There is no soothing voice to answer his cries, no arms to hold and rock him.

Stupid child, do you not see that if you do what I desire, if you eat and excrete, and are silent, and grow fat, then you shall have your heart's desire? Then you will be held in loving arms for one hour every day unless the Queen goes out? Do you not understand? Why are you so ignorant, stupid and uncouth? If I shut the door of the toy cupboard, and the door of the nursery, and the door of my own room, and sit quietly sewing or knitting there, I can hardly hear your screams. I am not aware of the unnatural extravagance of your feelings. When I take you out, after several hours, you will be limp and quiet. You will eat, between hiccups, and quite probably sleep as well. You and I are engaged in a private battle. It has nothing to do with that damp and ineffectual lady the Queen. I am on your father's side. I understand him better. He is the King. He knows the meaning of authority. He can take decisions and bear responsibility. He is not afraid to hold lives in the palm of his hand. There is a flame of understanding between us. I am a strong woman, and not afraid of my strength. I submit to no one. I owe my allegiance only to the King.

The Prince does not know where he can find support. He sees the Queen, but she will not hold out her arms to him. The nurse is an iron hand, pressing down upon his head. Her red hair, the crackling of her apron, and her cold, hard hands are a barrier that keep the softness of the world away from him. It is true that he is ignorant and stupid, and does not know how to adjust himself. The hysterical passion of his crying prevents him from seeing how life could be made easy. He learns too slowly. In any other experiment he would have been abandoned.

One day the Prince is taken to visit the old Judge, his grandfather. They have a lot in common. They both dribble and are incontinent. The old Judge, in his wheelchair, wrapped in rugs, leers at his grandson with contempt. His eyes sparkle. He hides a secret knowledge to himself in the sun porch. His secret knowledge is his age. Ha ha ha, he says to the child, you have to wait till you get to be my age. You'll never get to be my age, miserable, puny thing. I am ninety-one years old and I can shit in my pants and nobody rubs my nose in it. After dinner I sit in my panelled dining room, alone, with a servant standing behind my chair, a docile audience if I have no other, and I suck on my cigar and roll the port around my tongue for as long as I like. I am respected. I wear a velvet smoking jacket. I am a judge. I have worn the black cap and sentenced men to death. That is why women wipe my bum with creams and lotions, and turn me over in my bed with care.

The Prince lies in his mother's lap. He is good. The sun is balmy on his face. The fears of the dark cupboard have shrunk to the size of an old man wrapped in a dark fringed rug. His mother will protect him. She is tickling his face with a feather and making him laugh to show his dimples. From his position lolling back comfortably in her arms he can see blue sky striped with white wooden bars which enclose the window panes. Under the sky is a curve of green, and in the far distance, on the outer corners of his vision, one on each side, a tiny dark tree. He cannot see the dark old man unless he turns his head uncomfortably sideways and backwards. He practises the movement while keeping his eyes fixed on the sky. His mother's face looms over him like a brown and pink cloud.

'Don't wriggle darling, you'll fall.' She taps his face with the feather, playful punishment. The air in the sun porch is warm and still. It smells of cigar smoke, freesias and liniment. The smell of the freesias is painfully fresh and sweet.

'Isn't it lovely to feel the spring sunshine?' The old man raises his eyebrows and clashes his gums. The door opens and Miss Henrietta, the Judge's sister, comes in. The Queen is glad to see her. She is only eighty-three, and was once a great beauty and engaged to a Lord. She wears her hair in a soft roll, with a bun on top, and a velvet ribbon round her throat, as she has done since she was a girl.

'Our civilisation is dying,' she says. 'It is no longer possible to buy silk knickers with a draw string waist.' She removes a cushion and sits down on a straight-backed bamboo chair. 'I have written to Harrod's and Gorringe's and the Army and Navy Stores.' The sun porch has a brick floor with Persian carpets on it, and a table with magazines. 'A civilisation must be judged by the minor comforts it can provide.' The Queen nods and the old Judge does not bother to say the things that come into his mind. 'No woman of real sensibility can stand elastic round her waist.' Miss Henrietta ignores the Prince. He is of no interest to her.

In the nurse's sitting room the two nurses drink tea delicately, sucking the moisture from their lips after each sip, and placing the cups back exactly in the centre of the saucer. The nurse with red hair is wearing a navy cap and gabardine coat for this outing. 'You've got a better room here than mine,' she says. 'But I couldn't abide looking after an old man. He must be worse than a child for mess.'

'It's the washing I can't stand. I made it quite clear before I came. There's got to be a woman to do the washing.'

The old man's nurse has thick eyelids and thick wings to her nostrils. The lips of her cunt are thick. The texture of her flesh is dense. Each hair grows sturdily outwards; the space between them is visible.

'Let's just lift you up a bit, your Lordship, while I slip this under you. There, that's better, isn't it?'

'Kiddies are too noisy for me.'

'You can train a child. You can't train an old man.'

'He's not too bad. Sometimes gives me a glass of port.'

Later on the child is sent home with the nurse, alone, at her mercy, while the King and Queen remain to have dinner with the old man. He likes to go through his ritual in public once a week. After tea he has a little nap in his wheelchair in the sun porch while the Prince, also having a little nap, is packed into the moses basket and the back of the car. Much whispering and shuffling so as not to wake the Judge. A remarkable number of bonnets, shawls and blankets are necessary to protect the precious child from draughts. The Judge's chauffeur in charcoal grey uniform, the peak of his cap like an extra-long, sharp nose, drives the black Humber at funeral pace so as not to jog the infant Prince. The nurse sits right angular in the back, one hand possessively on the moses basket. The Prince sleeps.

The glass partition between the front and back of the car is closed. The chauffeur knows the roads well. He keeps his eyes fixed on the rear view mirror. He can see one cheek, one ear, one flattened curl of red hair and part of a navy gabardine hat. He puts his mouth to the speaking tube. 'Lovely hair you've got, Miss.'

The nurse ignores him. In her mind she is connected only with her social superiors. She does not know quite where to place the chauffeur. He is servile to his masters. He is her servant now, conveying her where she wants to go. Yet on the other hand he is in control of this smooth and powerful black machine. He is also a Cornishman, with thick black eyebrows and a voluptuous Mediterranean profile. Her bony knees press closer together and she compresses her lips. Her dark uniform excites the chauffeur more than the Queen's soft contours and inviting silks. He is already the lover of the old man's nurse. He knows the thick rubberiness of her body. Her skin and flesh are all one, solid, difficult to tell where the bones are. This woman's skin is thin and white. You could pick it up between finger and thumb. Her flesh must be soft and loose. No cushion of fat. You could surely feel every bone, trace the route of her intestines. He imagines her twat. Pale orange hair curling softly, lying back flat on the pads of flesh, and the purple, crushed split of her clitoris in the middle. There is a dull thud under the car.

'What was that?' Her voice is shrill, though he cannot hear it because she does not know where her end of the speaking tube is. But his eyes are on her face as it jerks across the mirror, and he sees her lips move.

'It must have been a cat or a rabbit.' They are driving through a small wood. He swings the car up a steep rutted track under the trees. He is a sentimental and straightforward man. He has his own cat, in the flat above the Judge's garage, but his mind can only be absorbed by one idea at a time. He gets out and shuts his door with a hollow thump. He opens the back door for the nurse to get out.

'Come and see.'

The car is hidden from the road. It is very early spring. There are no leaves on the trees. The ground is still covered with dead leaves, the top layer intact, rotten underneath. He takes the nurse by the hand and leads her down to the road. The road is empty and dark under a tunnel of trees. Its surface is slightly damp. Blueish grey. A cat is lying in the middle with its neck twisted and its stomach spilling out. The yellow eyes are staring upwards. It is dead. The chauffeur picks it up gently and carries it to the side of the road. There is no one about. He leads the nurse back again to the car. He opens the back door and the partition, and lifts the moses basket into the front seat. He motions the nurse in and shuts the door behind her. He kisses her mouth and neck and hair, but she will not open her mouth nor let him take off her cap which is secured by steel hairpins. He takes off his cap. His hair is thick and black, long on top and short at the back and sides. It falls over his forehead, which is now flushed. He can barely feel her breasts under her thick coat. He tries to undo her skirt, but she fights him, violently and silently. He lifts it up, and the skirts of her coat, so that they cover her face, and she lies still. He removes a pair of blue serge knee-length knickers, and a pair of white flannel ones. She is wearing dark grey lisle stockings attached by black suspenders, and thick, heavy black walking shoes. Her twat is just as he had imagined it. It winks up at him, neatly curled, pale red hair, and a purple split. The skin on either side of her suspenders is ribbed milky and blueish white, untouched, like sour milk left standing for days. He licks it then edges his tongue zigzagging up her cleft. A sigh from underneath the heavy serge skirts. She has to have one face hidden. His business is with the little gaping one down here. Her buttocks are so thin they sag away from her pelvis and fill his hands neatly, one each. He follows with his tongue each curl of hair. They lie there neat and flat, as if she has just been to a pubic hairdresser. Underneath her blanket of skirts the nurse thinks of her tidy bedroom and white flannel nightdresses. What goes on in the back of the Judge's car is none of her business.

The old man wakes from his nap and is wheeled upstairs. A lift has been installed to take him to his bedroom. The sides are open like a cage, and he can see odd angles of the house as he is conveyed upwards. There is not much room in the lift. The nurse's thigh bulges round the side of the chair and presses against his shoulder.

The walls of the Judge's bedroom are covered with dark red brocade; there is a red turkey carpet; the bed has four carved posts and a wooden canopy. During the day the windows are hung with fine white curtains, almost obscuring the view of the sea.

The nurse is also the old man's valet. She dresses and undresses him. She is lazy, and often does not bother with his trousers. While he lies on the bed the commode is detached from the underside of the wheelchair, emptied, rinsed and reattached. His buttocks are wiped and massaged with cream, and he sits again. The flaps of his long-johns are not done up in case of accidents. His dangling ivory feet are stripped of their red leather slippers and brown woolen socks. They wait patiently, ribs and knobs of bone, veins aimlessly wandering, purple rivers, nails?—yellow outcroppings, extravagantly shaped, to be covered with black silk socks and black patent leather evening slippers with Petersham bows. The nurse has replaced all the Judge's shirts with dickeys and made-up ties. Miss Henrietta has not yet noticed. The nurse stands back to admire her handiwork. He too surveys himself in the mirror; a little dog balanced precariously on his hind legs with a ruff around his neck. His hair is poodle hair, fluffy like a white wire brush. Only a few wavering stalks remain on the top of his head, but it grows thickly down the back of his neck and out of his ears and nostrils. The nurse has trimmed this bushy growth, and scraped a few hairs (soft and brittle like the bones of tinned sardines) off his cheeks and chin this morning.

Now for the trappings of dignity; the maroon velvet smoking jacket shrugged round his shoulders and buttoned. Eagerly the Judge leans forward, bending back one chicken wing at a time to fit into the sleeves. The tartan rug is smoothed over his skeletal white knees, tucked in from waist to ankles. He would have preferred to be wearing his robes and wig, but they are shut away in the wardrobe. He has not entirely abandoned the idea of wearing them again one day. However, he is pleased with his image in the mirror. He does not have to wear his robes and wig to make his authority felt, nor to strike fear into the hearts of those who sit at his dinner table.

The black Humber, with the chauffeur satisfied at the wheel, has made several journeys between the King's palace and the Judge's house, two of them with the Queen sitting on the warm back seat. The journey is a short one. The Judge likes his guests to change for dinner. The Queen returns with the late afternoon sun still high and white above the sea. The Judge likes to dine early. She is wearing a peach coloured velvet dress with a blue Chinese dragon embroidered across the stomach, and a fox fur stole. When she sits down the dragon's body is lost among the folds of her belly, and his scaly tail curls around her left hip.

In the drawing room the Queen, the Judge and Miss Henrietta sit sipping sherry and listening to a radio programme. Usually they listen to the radio programme as they drink their soup, but tonight the King is late. The parlour maid pops her head around the door anxiously, and Miss Henrietta motions for her to go away again. They have not yet put on the electric light. The furniture is dark and heavy, and begins to lose shape among its own shadows. In a green leather frame a photograph of Miss Henrietta when she was young catches the light. It is on a small table made from an elephant's foot that the Judge once brought back from Africa. The photograph is pale, in sepia and cream. Miss Henrietta stands beside her fiancé. He is in uniform. A few days later he will go to India and die, doing his duty. His pale eyes stare out steadily above his rich moustache. Miss Henrietta rings the bell for the maid.

'You may turn on the lights Wilkins.' She does not suggest another glass of sherry. The comedian's raucous voice and laugh become quieter as the lights go on. They have been dancing and crackling like glow-worms in the dark air. The Judge shuts his eyes, momentarily irritated by the change, and misses a joke. He says in a sharp voice:

'I should like another glass of sherry if we are to continue waiting for my ill-mannered second son.' Miss Henrietta compresses her lips, disapproving, but rings the bell. Wilkins has just closed the drawing room door behind her and crossed the hall. She hears the bell from the top of the kitchen stairs and scuttles back again. As she reaches the drawing room the front door bell rings. She is caught between two jangling summonses. She stands paralysed, and both ring again. The Queen saves her. She hurries out of the drawing room, one hand anxiously clutching her bead purse against her stomach.

'You attend to the Judge, Wilkins; I'll open the door.' She bustles past, a scented matron hoping to be able to work some magic so that when she opens the door her husband will be neither late nor drunk.

Wilkins' hand trembles as she pours out the sherry. Luckily she has taken the Judge's glass from him so it only spills on the silver tray on top of the piano. Miss Henrietta has refused a second glass. From the expression on her brother's face she realises that they will have to wait at least another half hour for their dinner, and the beef will be overcooked, and the Yorkshire pudding flat. Cook goes off promptly at eight on Sundays, so Wilkins, a woman much affected by emotional temperature, will have to serve the meal. Miss Henrietta would like to sack Wilkins. She would also like to sack the nurse.

Outside in the hall the muffled whispers of the King and Queen have drawn closer. Now they enter. The King looks smaller, and the power of his body appears more loosely organised than it does at home. He and his wife, standing protectively beside him in the doorway with her hand on his arm, are both short and stocky. They will never look perfectly tidy. The Queen's tiara will always be slightly askew, her ermine robe falls awkwardly off one shoulder. The King's crown, however firmly it is set on his head, will always make a certain lock of hair stick up, peering drunkenly over a ruby.

'You may pour my son a glass of sherry, Wilkins,' says the Judge.

'No, no thanks Pater, I'm ready to go straight in to dinner. Sorry to have kept you waiting.'

'I'm quite aware of the fact that you are drunk. You will now, however, sit and drink a glass of sherry with me.'

Why the bloody hell doesn't he die, thinks the King, sitting on the edge of a chair. Is he going to live forever? There is a line of brown scum round the corners of his mouth, and ash on his waistcoat. He takes a packet of cigarettes out of his pocket.

'Please, Austin, I'd prefer you not to smoke in here.'

'Sorry Aunt Henrietta.'

Power is in my hands now, thinks the King. I have just been drinking with the man who is going to be our next Member of Parliament. I'm a partner in one of the biggest firms of solicitors in the county. I'm respected by everybody, except this old weasel here.

'I had an interesting proposition to discuss with you this evening, Austin,' says the old man. 'But I doubt if you will be able to appreciate its significance at the moment.'

Why the hell couldn't he have mentioned it at lunch? We must stop this bloody awful habit of spending the whole day here on Sunday. The King swallows his sherry in two gulps, and gives an involuntary shudder of disgust. He has been drinking gin all afternoon.

For the second time in one day they troop into the panelled dining room and eat soup, and leathery beef, and hard pudding. Glass decanters in silver trellis baskets glint on the sideboard. The Judge's eyes are small and black, like currants. Miss Henrietta and the Judge eat as if they are performing a ritual unconnected with food. The Queen thinks anxiously of her bowels. She finds it difficult to digest two heavy meals in one day. Out of nervousness she accepts a second helping. The King thinks, breathing heavily and eating so that gravy spills onto his tie, why is it I who am here and not my brothers? When Gerald comes down, once or twice a year, my father speaks to him as if they were equals. Walter he despises somewhat, as he despises me, but Walter does not live here. Walter found himself a job in London, in the family firm of an old school friend. Walter is the slave of someone else's father.

'You are weak, Austin, and you are stupid,' says the Judge. 'Nearly as stupid as your friend Geoffrey Thorpe Bates. But he at least has had the wit, or the luck, to get himself into a position of power and independence. Now I had intended to suggest to my friend Sir Ashleigh Gibson, who you know is appointed Sheriff of the county this year, that he should nominate you as Vice-Sheriff. You are also, perhaps, aware of the fact that although the office of Sheriff is a yearly appointment, the Vice-Sheriff is usually appointed a number of years in succession, and the office often descends from father to son, or within a single firm.'

Robin Hood, in lincoln green, twirling a lasso, gallops across the sideboard. The Queen blinks.

'Neville Marriott, who has been reappointed Vice-Sheriff under seventeen successive Sheriffs of the county, died last month as you know. There is no one in his office who is willing or capable of carrying on, so I have suggested that the post be offered to you.' The Judge pauses, licking his lips and savouring the construction of his sentences. Miss Henrietta delicately touches the corner of her lips with her napkin. She too is constructing sentences, to Gorringe's, on the subject of elastic round the waist.

'With my help,' continues the Judge, 'you should be able to fulfil the functions of the office adequately, and it will give you a position of power in the county which I fear you would be unable to achieve alone.'

The King's face is dark. Blood pulses behind his eyes. He turns his head from side to side like a bull who doesn't know where the next sharp pain is going to come from.

'Oh how divine,' says the Queen, 'thank you, Father.'

The Judge rearranges his false teeth and takes a sip of wine.

'The duties of a Vice-Sheriff are not onerous; he must be able to advise the Sheriff on points of protocol and etiquette in connection with the conduct of the Assize Courts, be responsible for the entertainment of the Judge, and stand in for the Sheriff at functions, like executions, where the Sheriff himself is unable to be present. With my help,' says the old man, 'you may be able to carry out these duties competently enough.'

The Judge is satisfied. He continues to smile. Within himself he is infinitely light, infinitely agile. He flies and dances round the room like Puck, like Tinkerbell. He has the power to come, to go, to be young, to be old. His power over this purple, lumbering animal is absolute. His mind is so clear that nothing can cloud it, whereas he can see like the bloom on a grape a blur or curtain in front of the bloodshot eyes of his son. I am a matador, I run, I dance, I flick my cloak, the crowd roars approval. I can tease this creature to a frenzy because he is tied to the ground by his stupidity.

His own strength only serves to entrap him further. He is pinioned, hypnotised, helpless, by my will, my wit.

'Wilkins you may bring in the cheese and port,' says Miss Henrietta. The Judge is conscious of danger. Darkness presses in from the sides of the room making his hands, his maroon velvet sleeves, his plate, his knife, the silver ornamental pheasant in the middle of the table shine with an unctuous and unnatural glow, as if they were part of a seventeenth-century Dutch still life. There is also a slight feeling of disappointment, because in order to attain the purest sensation of his own power, he needs an audience. However as the Queen and Miss Henrietta rise from their seats, leaving their napkins crumpled on the table in aristocratic abandon, the King collapses over the table sending the dregs of his glass of wine flying and breaking a plate with the impact of his jaw. The three women and the old man remain in arrested motion like children playing a game of statues, while the wine courses slowly across the polished table and forms a pool round the feet of the pheasant. They are all suddenly aware of their physical limitations, as they stare at the dark, heavy, inert figure of the King. The Judge feels in his skinny white biceps the frustration of trying to lift that dead weight. The women are accustomed to frustration. Their reactions are ready-made and instinctive. Wilkins drops the cheese board. Miss Henrietta sits down and rings the electric bell, hidden under the carpet and operated by the foot, with which she summons the next course at meals. The Queen pats her husband's body with her hands. Hands as ineffective as a kitten's paws with the claws drawn in. She is an oriental lady, shuffling hither and thither on bound feet, agitating a fan and uttering birdlike cries.

The nurse in her sitting room cannot hear the cacophony of bells and voices. She is fetched by Wilkins who hopes that the spoiled cheeses will be forgotten in the hubbub. The nurse surveys the scene like a general, and despatches Wilkins to find the chauffeur.

'I'll wheel you into the drawing room, sir, and you and Miss Henrietta can listen to the wireless and have your Horlicks while we get Mister Austin home.' The Judge's currant eyes are hooded. He swallows his anger, puts it by to be polished carefully for use on a future occasion.

The chauffeur has just come back from the pub, and is in his shirt sleeves, crooning a love song to his reflection in the mirror. Wilkins pants up the stairs.

'Oh will you come quick please, 'e's passed out, Mister Austin, 'e's got to be taken home.'

The chauffeur covers a burp with the back of his hand and wrenches his mind away from a froth of Guinness and fags and laughter and bubbles of red hair. He pulls on his cap and jacket and thrusts ten Craven A into his pocket.

Above the garage roof the moon is almost full. The lonely square of his window looks very yellow as he glances back. Wilkins' white cap and the bow of her apron shine as she picks her way across the gravel drive. The chauffeur imagines striding the wheel of the car as it sails silently down the drive and out into the road, to the little wood half way between the Judge's house and the King's, and thump in among the dark trees with a soft crackling of bracken, or over and over, graceful wide turns in the air between the cliff edge and the sea, a black bird, scarcely visible. Disaster should always be silent and black, a rush of whirring wings, discovered in the morning small, distant and already finished. Debris to be cleared away, or left to rust and rot.

Could the hands and arms of the old man's nurse be made of the same stuff as those of the Queen? She has lifted the King's heavy body upright on his chair, slapped his face, undone his collar, peered under his eyelids. Now he sits, mouth half open, a rim of white between his lids, precariously balanced, King Kong, about to sway blindly this way or that. Has he won a victory by abandoning the fight without striking a blow in his own defence? The Queen is concerned only with the immediate, 'poor Austin is not well,' and the apparent, 'his father has found him a wonderful job.'

The car draws up outside the front door. The nurse and chauffeur each place a shoulder under the King's armpits. His legs drag behind him like the tail of a mermaid bumping helplessly over the dry rocks. Wilkins, when she has finished scraping cheese off the carpet, will make Horlicks for the Judge and Miss Henrietta. The Judge's anger grows as his routine is interrupted by this idiot son who can't hold his liquor.

The chauffeur thinks of the red-haired nurse hidden under her white flannel nightgown. She will probably not be called downstairs. Physically she is not a strong woman.

TWO

The Prince grows, but he is never very satisfactory. He cuts no teeth till he is over a year old, does not walk until he is two. He is pale and skinny. He has no charm. At three, instead of babbling happily of Mama and Papa and bow-wows and pussy cats he hangs his head and shuts his lips tight. He would suck his thumb if it had not been covered with bitter aloes. At night his arms are still strapped to his bed. When he comes downstairs to have tea with his mother he will not move from her side, and clutches a piece of her skirt so tightly that it is damp and crumpled when it is time for him to say goodnight, and she has to change her dress. She allows him this. She tells no one. It is their secret.

Whenever a visitor approaches to give him a kiss he cringes away, panting with fear. The King is disgusted with him. 'He's not normal,' he says. He can hardly bear to look at him. The Queen is worried that perhaps the nurse is too strict with him. She confides her fears to the family doctor.

'Once I saw him in his bath, and there were funny blueish marks on his shoulders, poor little lamb. She told me he had fallen down, but I did wonder if perhaps . . .'

The doctor is a worthy man. He knows right from wrong. He takes the Queen's soft hand between his own and strokes it gently. 'If you are worried, my dear, you must get rid of the nurse. After all, this is your child.' But no, this is too much responsibility for the Queen to bear. 'After all,' she says, 'she did have the very best references.'

The King does not like her to perform menial tasks. On the nurse's day off the kitchen maid bathes the child and puts him to bed. In her heart the Queen vows secretly that when she has another child she will hold his naked body in her arms at least once a week. She looks at the nurse defiantly, astonished by the boldness of her own decision.

'Darling, you really ought to get rid of that nurse,' says her friend, the MP's wife. 'She really is the most godawful bitch.' 'But she manages him so well,' says the Queen. 'You're going to have trouble with that child, you mark my words.' The Queen sighs with worry and bites the inside of her left index finger. She feels strength growing inside her, but it grows very slowly. She makes another vow, to the pale and miserable Prince. I will protect you, my darling, I will look after you. Her anxiety is allayed somewhat by her own secret vows and the advice of her friends. Now her defiance is tinged with guilt as she looks at the nurse. We are working against you, she warns silently, her heart fluttering.

One day, on the nurse's afternoon off, the Queen sends the kitchen maid out as well and calls the doctor.

'I'm a little worried about his cough,' she says. It is November. A fire has been lit in the drawing room. They are alone in the house. After lunch the Queen and the Prince sit together on the sofa and read Struwwelpeter. As her son leans against her, cuddling his cheek against her arm and pointing to the pictures, the Queen's heart swells with the pride of her achievement. With a few small gestures she has made everything normal. The Prince is not only contented, he is playful. He drums his heels on the side of the sofa and hums a little song. She needs no help. She is all powerful. She begins to regret having summoned the doctor.

The bell rings. Tinny electric reverberations die away slowly. The silence is hollow. There is no one else in the house. Never before has the Queen been alone in her own house. The logs in the fireplace crack and split with a sigh, and the flames dance over their bodies. The Queen clutches her son's hand firmly in her own and they go to open the door.

The doctor is a portly and responsible man. He wears a morning suit, which inspires confidence. He sits on the very edge of his chair, his hat and bag on the floor beside him. He leans his elbows on his knees and folds his hands together. 'I'm very glad you asked me to come round. I've been worried about this little fellow for some time now. He's not developing the way he should. You naughty boy, you're not developing the way you should. What would your father say?'

'I've heard it said that your nurse beats him and shuts him in a cupboard as a punishment. Is that true?' The Queen's eyes open wide. Her hands flutter. Her expression becomes sulky and resentful. Everything had been lovely before the doctor arrived.

'Oh I'm sure she wouldn't do anything like that, she's so well trained.'

The doctor turns to the Prince, who, wisely ignored, has now begun to peep out from behind the sofa. 'Does nurse ever shut you in the cupboard when she's cross?' The Prince looks from his mother to the doctor. He does not know what is required of him. He raises his head in a half nod, then sees the beginnings of a reaction on the doctor's face and moves his head slightly to one side. The doctor is annoyed. The Prince is relieved. He feels he has averted a catastrophe. If the doctor, or his mother, dared to attack his nurse she would kill them. The doctor thinks, what's the matter with the little bastard? Can't he see that I'm his only champion, trying to save him from that woman?

The Queen undresses him in front of the fire, and the doctor takes out his stethoscope. He puts the ear pieces in the Prince's ears and the other end against his watch. The Prince stares at him with round eyes, then smiles with delight. 'Tick tock, tick tock,' he says. The Queen hugs him. 'He's getting to know you. Doesn't he have a lovely smile?'

He is so thin, the naughty boy, he will not get fat. 'Nurse says she has such trouble getting him to eat.' On his narrow shoulders and tight little bottom there are pale marks of old bruises.

'Yes, it does look as if he's been beaten.' The Queen tries to rub the bruises away. 'Sometimes she has to give him a smack to get him to eat up his lunch. Austin says it's all right.' 'Hmm, hmm.' Now the stethoscope is in the doctor's ears, and the cold end pressed to the Prince's chest. He wriggles his shoulders, but stands still like a good little boy. His tummy is kept warm by the fire, and Mummy's hand is on his back.

The doctor says, 'There's a very nice girl in the village, only fifteen, but she's got three young brothers and is used to looking after children. A very pleasant, reliable girl. Now that he's no longer a baby you don't really need a trained nurse any more, do you?'

'Oh but I couldn't ask her to go. What would I say?'

The Prince smells danger. If his nurse goes who will look after him? The giants and monsters who lie in wait for him in the dark, or tear his limbs off when he wets his bed? He puts his thumb in his mouth for comfort.

The door flew open, in he ran,
The great long legged scissor man.

'No, no, no.' The Prince cowers against his mother, ribs going in and out like a bellows. The stethoscope winks in the doctor's hands. Snip! Snap! Snip! The Prince's eyes have rolled up into his head so that only the whites show, and he screams like a railway engine. Is he having some sort of a fit? Perhaps he's epileptic? The doctor thrusts a wooden spatula between his teeth and slaps his cheeks. His body is rigid. The Queen tries to pull her knees away but he clings on like a leech.

Ah said Mamma, I knew he'd come
To naughty little suck-a-thumb!

'Oh dear,' says the Queen, 'I don't know what to do with him. I couldn't cope with this on my own. I've got to have someone who's been trained.'

The doctor gives him an injection to quieten him down, and after a few minutes the Prince stops crying, and falls asleep. The Queen dresses him again. There are tears in her eyes. She puts her hand on the doctor's arm as she says goodbye. 'I don't know what I'd have done if you hadn't been here.' Her head doesn't even come up to his shoulder. He allows himself to stroke her hair.

'In any case I would advise you to think over what I've said, my dear.'

'I will.' But when the door has closed and she is alone in the hall she sighs and shakes her head. Her burden is too heavy.

Food looms large in the Prince's life. He eats out of a china plate with a high rim and a picture of the cow jumping over the moon on the bottom. He has a silver pusher and a silver spoon, flattened at the end. He drinks out of a silver christening mug. Sometimes the kitchen maid cleans it carelessly and his milk tastes of polish.

He and the nurse eat at the same table, but not the same food. They eat in the nursery, at a wooden table near the door. At mealtimes a white tablecloth is spread over it. If he spills anything on the tablecloth he gets a smack. Mealtimes are silent. The nurse is not a talkative woman. The Prince sits in a high chair, so that his plate is on a level with his chest. He stares at scrambled egg, congealed like vomit, and bitter spinach. He craves for sweetness. On the far side of the table sits a bowl of tapioca pudding with a spoonful of jam in the middle. He has ceased to desire the jam. The pudding no longer clothes its frogspawn globules in warm, sweet custard. It has become cold and hard. Scrambled egg, spinach and tapioca pudding form a barrier, an insuperable mountain that he must climb before he can continue to live. He has sunk so low in his chair that his chin is leaning on the table. The nurse has lost her patience. Twice the kitchen maid has climbed the stairs to take away the dirty plates and twice she has been sent back again.

A marble hand jerks the Prince upright.

'Don't you want to grow up a big strong boy?' He shakes his head. He shouldn't have bothered. The question was rhetorical. He gets a cuff on the ear.

'Don't you cheek me. You're going to eat that lunch or I'll kill you.' She picks him up by the scruff of the neck and shakes him. How dare he pit his puny, miserable little will against mine? He will do as I say. He *will* do as I say. The sash window is half open. It is spring again. There is a sweet scent of narcissus. The nurse pushes the window as wide as it will go and hangs the little boy out of it.

'Do you want me to drop you? Will you eat your spinach?' The friendly green lawn swings dizzily below him. There is a bush with yellow flowers growing against the house. It would be nice to dig in the flower bed. Perhaps find a snail or a worm. His legs and arms make tiny kicks in the air. A brightly speckled thrush swoops past him and picks a snail out of the flower bed and dashes it against a stone. The flesh gleams watery, silky. The air and earth rush round again and he is standing on the nursery floor. The mountain of spinach, scrambled egg and tapioca has shrunk back into proportion. The Prince meekly swallows spoonful after spoonful as it is thrust into his mouth, then vomits it all up onto the white tablecloth.

•

He and the nurse have a dull life together. They don't communicate much. Sometimes in the afternoons he is taken to play with other children, but it takes him all afternoon to get used to them. They think him a wet, stupid little boy. He trails along, holding his nurse's marble hand, or stands by himself, watching. The nurse is ashamed of him. He does not reflect credit on her. She hates him for it. When he falls down and hurts his hand or his knee he always cries louder than the other children. It's quite possible that once his blood starts coming out it might never stop.

The nursery is cold, bare, empty and silent. Also tidy, clean and regular. There are dark corners in it: the toy cupboard, for instance; and there is a cloud, maroon and grey, a three dimensional transparent cellular structure which blots out the wooden table between meals. Outside the door, too, it is dark, with a breath of clammy air coming up from the kitchen, and the cross cook, and the kitchen maid with aching legs. Three times a day the white tablecloth forms itself into a rectangle of doom.

The only comfort in the night nursery the Prince brings there himself, in his own body. Lying healthily flat on his back with his arms strapped down he has to find for himself subtle and unusual forms of pleasure. He has developed a technique for sucking on his tongue, or as an alternative his two front teeth. Pleasure can be achieved by crossing his legs and varying the pressure of his thighs. He has the sensations of Viyella pyjamas, flannelette sheets, and sometimes the roughness of a woolen blanket against his chin to consider; also the goings on inside his body.

The soothing pressure of a full stomach, or bladder, or bowel. The rumblings and gurglings of wind. The taste of toothpaste or vomit. In winter the darkness is absolute when he is put to bed. The curtains are drawn, the door shut, and like a rubber duck held down at the bottom of the bath and suddenly released he shoots up to float bouncing gently, turning and twisting dizzily between the floor and the ceiling. Swooning in space with the darkness velvet under his hands his body takes on strange shapes, huge, liquid, swelling head and knees, hands like a giant's, fingers grasping from corner to corner of the room, then suddenly shrinking, wizened, like the inside of his mouth when he has managed to put a thumb painted with bitter aloes into it.

The nurse is bored. This kingdom is too small, too out of the way. She likes to feel the action and hubbub of power-ful men around her. The Queen is slowly, secretly plotting against her, and the nurse too is plotting against the Queen. She writes letters to her friends. She scans the columns of the *Times*. Once or twice a week she sees the chauffeur. Her half day is on Thursday, and she has one Sunday a month. She seldom bothers to change out of her uniform, because the chauffeur prefers her in it. She has thought of marrying him, but her ambition would not be satisfied. She would rather serve the rich than be her own master.

The old Judge's nurse, too, has thought of marrying the chauffeur. She has looked after the Judge for seven years now, and by rights he should die, leaving her a substantial legacy, enough to get married and settle down on.

He doesn't take any notice of her hints. Doesn't seem to understand what she is trying to say. One evening, in the summer, while the sky is still full of light, she has put him to bed, propped up against his pillows, with his pyjama jacket rucked up behind his shoulders as always, and glasses poised on his nose so that he can have a last look at the obituary column of the *Times*. She tries again.

'I might have to leave you soon, sir.' She is standing by the window, gazing out over the series of headlands grabbing out into the sea. Even her bulky body in its white overall has a certain female wistfulness, silhouetted against the twilit sky. In the chauffeur's flat over the garage the light goes out, and after a few moments he appears downstairs. White shirt sleeves, hands in pockets, whistling, he walks jauntily down the drive.

'It's like this, sir. I'm not so young as I used to be, and if I want to get married I shall have to do so quick.' She turns to look at the Judge. A lovely woman like you, of course you should get married. Here's a cheque for a thousand pounds. He says nothing. The sheets and heaped pillows look yellow in the light from the reading lamp, against the cool, blue grey shadows of the rest of the room. The bedhead is reddish wood, inlaid with a pattern of flowers. The bedside table and base of the reading light are made of the same heavy wood, and inlaid with flowers to match. The Judge ordered them when he was married, together with a wardrobe, a chest of drawers, and a dressing table.

'I've been saving up, sir, for my bottom drawer ever since I was a girl. But it's not easy.' She pauses. The old man says nothing.

'If I knew that I had expectations sir, if you see what I mean, I might find it easier to bring him up to the mark.'

'Come here.' The Judge peers at her over the top of his glasses. He waits till she is standing by the bed. He pushes the newspaper to one side.

'Closer.' He tries to pull and wriggle himself into a more upright position. She leans over to help, lifting him up and rearranging the pillows. He puts a hand under her skirt.

'Whatever are you doing, sir?' Her thighs are so fat that he can scarcely push his hand up between them. He gestures impatiently for her to stand with her legs further apart.

'Well,' she says, 'I never thought . . .' But she moves her legs apart, and even presses closer up against the bed. The Judge's fingers have reached the impenetrable barrier of her knickers. He purses his lips and moves his eyebrows up and down. His fingers poke and press, delicately. Is that her clitoris or a fold of rayon? What a bush! The upper and inner sides of her thighs are covered in hair. He can feel it between her knickers and stocking tops. She is built on a grand scale. I could drive up there in my wheelchair, thinks the Judge. He tweaks at her underclothing.

'In future, in my presence, you will no longer wear these garments.'

She is flabbergasted. 'What, you mean walk around without any knickers on?'

'Exactly.'

'But I'll catch my death!'

The Judge removes his hand like a snake, and seizes the *Times*. His eyes flash. He has been unable to prevent a string of saliva from escaping down his chin. He sucks some of it back and wipes the rest of with his hand. Cold and clipped, he says,

'It is possible, if you give satisfaction, that I may write a small legacy into my will. However,' he points a bony and accusing finger at her, 'do not forget that it is easy to alter a will at any time, and that I demand absolute obedience.'

'Oh yes, sir, oh thank you very much, oh a legacy, oh thank you, sir!' A legacy of five hundred pounds seems to her like more than a thousand pound notes.

The next day in the sun porch, as Miss Henrietta nods off after lunch, the Judge beckons the nurse close to him, to see if his instructions have been complied with. He has said nothing all morning, made no move, in spite of the unusual mauvish pink which has tinged her face and neck, and the number of occasions on which she has pressed herself against him, clearing her throat. But now, as she bends to tidy the magazines on the coffee table, he pushes his hand up, past the mountains of her thighs, through the dark forest, and plunges the bony and accusing fore-finger into the warm wet darkness of her hole. She can hardly restrain herself from crying out loud, because she had had her back to him, and also her body responds to any caress like a whale leaping to a harpoon. The Judge giggles silently, and digs his nails sharply into her damp and slippery inner parts, as she tries to turn round to face him. He experiments with various methods of control; a sharp twist, a jab at the clitoris, or a yank at the pubic hair at the very top of the inner part of the thigh proving most effective. After twenty minutes the nurse has produced so much vaginal fluid that she has made a little puddle on the floor. The Judge suddenly realises how tired his arm is. He lays his head back, shuts his eyes, and drops his hand.

'I want to go for a walk.'

Miss Henrietta opens her eyes.

'A very good idea, Charles. It's much too hot in here. Look at that woman's face, it's bright purple.'

The Judge's sexual energy declines after that first long exploration. In fact for several days he has to use the other hand. However he does like to thrust a finger up his woman several times a day, usually in the lift, in the sun porch after lunch, and when she is getting him ready for bed at night. When she is menstruating it seems to him that she wears pads and belts for longer than is necessary, and he still refuses to allow her to wear knickers. Occasionally he will not touch her for several days, but enjoys the thought of her naked buttocks jostling against each other under her crisp white uniform, and her anxious face with its cream cheese skin and thick, hairy upper lip, looking towards him, fearful for her legacy.

Since she has delivered herself in this way into his power he begins to indulge himself in other fantasies. Sundays with the King and Queen become almost peaceful. The old man has lost interest in baiting his son.

After a few weeks he decides to explore further areas of his conquered territory. Bedtime is usually chosen for these occasions.

'Would you be so good as to undo those buttons?'

'What? My uniform?'

'Certainly, your uniform.'

'But . . . whatever will I do if someone comes in?'

'You may bolt the door and draw the window curtains.'

She walks slowly to the door, looking at him over her shoulder. He does not relent. She pushes the bolt into the socket. Looks at him again. Goes over to the window. Draws the curtains.

'You are a one,' she says. 'I'm that embarrassed.'

'Now the buttons.'

Slowly she undoes them. A white petticoat is revealed.

'Come on, come on . . .'

'I'll have to take it right off.' She is flustered. Awkwardly she pulls her arms out of the sleeves of her starched white uniform, and pushes the petticoat down around her waist. Her gross tits strain against the bra and bulge over the top. She looks at him pleadingly. His black button eyes are fixed on her like knives, and saliva dribbles out of both corners of his mouth. She undoes her bra, and the breasts cascade out like waterfalls, sagging down below her waist. The purplish blush has spread over her face and neck and the whole of the top of her chest now. Her nipples are huge flat brown moons that cover an area the size of a small plate. Around the edge of each one sprouts a ring of black hairs.

The Judge starts to giggle out loud. He laughs like a horse whinnying. For a moment it seems as if he might have a fit of hysterics and choke on his own laughter, but he controls himself. The nurse has been standing in front of him, her breasts swaying gently, her flush getting deeper and deeper.

'Go over to the dressing table.' She turns her back with relief. 'Bring me the silver hairbrush.' She brings it over to the bed.

'Bend over.' She takes a step backwards.

'How do you mean?' He wipes his chin with a corner of the sheet and leans towards her.

'Do you think he will marry you if you don't have any money?' She looks at him with dull annoyance, and shrugs her shoulders; then turns round and starts to pull her skirt up above her buttocks.

'No, not today. The other way.' She peers up at him through a jungle of sleeves and petticoat straps and strands of hair, shrugs her shoulders again, and shifts her feet round without standing up. Her breasts hang down below the edge of the bed. More than a foot of shimmering female flesh. He pats one with the hairbrush and it swings to and fro. The old Judge turns the hair brush round and starts to brush them gently, with special attention to the nipples. Down and round. The nurse groans and thrusts her chin forward. He concentrates on the hairy circles round the edge of her nipples, turns the hairbrush round again and starts smacking them with all his strength.

'No, no.' Red marks appear on her dangling white flesh. It's like shooting a pistol into jelly, thinks the old Judge. After a few seconds he is exhausted and puts the brush down, panting from the exertion. He has plan. He may be over ninety, but Abraham was over one hundred. He doesn't want to wear himself out.

'That's enough for today.' His face is putty coloured. The nurse gives him a drink of water and settles him down for the night. Her breasts, still with the red marks on them, flop against his face, but he has lost interest for the moment.

She shakes her head as she lifts them back into the bra. 'You are a funny old cuss. After all these years. I'd never have believed it.'

Sunday. Walking round the lawn after luncheon. The Queen has an announcement to make. For a number of minutes she blushes and laughs little bell-like trills, and starts sentences she is unable to finish, 'I think the maid will have to . . .' 'I don't know how we shall manage . . .' Finally the King interrupts.

'Pater, we're going to have another boy. At least I hope he'll be more of a boy than this one.' He glances at his eldest son, who is quietly poking his finger into a hole in the lawn.

'Humph.' The Judge is annoyed. He does not like to be reminded of his son's virility. They have reached a charming retreat at the top of the cliff where Miss Henrietta has had two wooden benches arranged under a pine tree to command the best view across the bay. On summer afternoons they often have tea here. Miss Henrietta nods her head in approval. Families exist to be perpetuated.

'Don't go too near the edge, will you, dear,' the Queen calls to the Prince.

'Don't fuss. You'll make him into more of a namby-pamby little milksop than he is already.'

The cliff does not fall away steeply at first. There is a gentle slope, and then a hollow full of rhododendrons. 'We used to play down there all the time when we were children.'

They breathe in the smell of pine needles and the sea.

The King has been Under-Sheriff of the county for some years. He enjoys the ritual of which he is a part. He enjoys sitting at the right hand of the Judge, in court. He enjoys walking in procession through the town, preceded by a band, wearing velvet knee breeches and buckled shoes. At the Imperial Hotel there is always a crowd around his corner of the bar at lunchtime. He hobnobs with the great, and has tales to tell.

'Austin, I would be obliged if you could arrange my chair so that it is level. I hope you will show yourself more competent with a perambulator.' A little push and the wheelchair will go sailing into the rhododendron bushes down below; bounce, twist, and with luck go on over the cliff, a small black object, the old man still in control, busily turning the wheels with his hands, across the few feet of vertical azure sea and over the horizon. But then, trust him, he'd be round the world in a flash and on them from the rear, laughing like a maniac, his round aluminum legs whizzing.

The King does not need his father any more. Sometimes he says to the Queen, 'I think he's going to hold on till the Second Coming.' The Queen always replies, 'He is a wonderful old man though, isn't he?'

The Judge has been a lot of things in his life, and now he's a wonderful old man. The nurse knows it, better than anyone else.

'Here,' he beckons to her, and grasps her hand tightly. 'In the back of the wardrobe are my robes, and on the shelf there's a Fortnum and Mason carrier bag with my wig in it. Get them out.'

It is eight or nine years since the wig and robes have been put away, stuffed with mothballs, and the paper bag has become soft, and tears as the nurse lifts it. For the first few years of his retirement the Judge had taken the wig out and put it on again several times a month to admire his familiar reflection in the looking glass. He had never intended to retire so early. For a long time it had been his secret ambition to be the first centenarian judge. But after his stroke he had been eased out. He resented that. The keenness of his mind was quite unaffected. It was only his legs that were paralysed, and what does a judge need legs for? He felt that he was still in the full flower of his capacities at eighty-three. In the courtroom he could play with a jury or a witness like a skillful angler playing a fish. He was a man who needed time to perfect himself in any area of life. He had barely experimented with sex until his marriage at the age of fifty. He had been able, if he so desired, with unimpeachable subtlety to turn the skills and rhetoric of any counsel against his own client. He knew how to appeal to the most vulgar instincts of the crowd. He knew how to be high minded. He knew how tender is the conscience of rightminded people. He had been a man at the top, the very pinnacle of his profession. Age was an irritating and unexpected hazard.

The nurse lays on his bed the black carrier bag with its row of tiny coloured flowers, and the scarlet robe. She smooths the cloth, running her hands over it with respect. The old Judge seizes the bag and opens it, his hands trembling with excitement. He tears off layers of tissue paper, shakes out mothballs, until he has revealed the empty skull of justice. Tenderly he holds her up, and turns her round.

For twenty years his brains sweated into these rows of horsehair sausage curls. What cerebration went on beneath them. What rapier sharp witticisms, what cunningly conceived epigrams astonished the innocent, the guilty and the representatives of the law alike from that blank space. In his memory the many thousand times he has presided over a court have amalgamated into one long drawn out rustle and shuffling of feet as the whole court rises for his entrance. The booming voice of the usher, the respectful bowings of heads, the trusting sigh of the ignorant in front of the learned, those who are about to be judged in front of the one who is to judge them.

'Bring the mirror.' Slowly, carefully, he sets the wig upon his head. It seems heavier than it used to, and comes lower down on his forehead. Can his head have shrunk? He twitches his nose and eyebrows, and shakes his head gently. He had forgotten how hot and prickly horsehair is. The nurse brings the mirror and holds it in front of him. It has a silver back, matching the hairbrush. A comb and clothes brush, all with his initials on, complete the set. A gift from his late dear wife.

'Hold it straight, woman.' He shifts his position until there stares back at him the face of a man in his prime. He admires himself for a long time, black eyes narrowed.

'Now the robe.' The nurse places it round his shoulders and folds it double over the pillows. She does up the gold chain and hook at the neck.

'My, it is heavy. Lovely stuff, though.'

'Yes.' He lies back on his pillows. Now I am at my most potent.

'Take off your clothes.'

She obeys him without a murmur now. In fact she rather enjoys the erotic role she has been forced into. After all she's safe with him. Nothing can go wrong, and it adds a bit of spice to life. She'd give a lot to see Miss Henrietta's face if she could have a look at them now. She takes off her uniform and folds it neatly over a chair. When she turns the Judge has managed to pull his old cock out of his pyjamas all by himself. It gives her a shock to see it drooping there, greyish brown, with purple veins on the scrotum. Not that she hasn't seen it a thousand times before, washed it, wiped it—she knows it as well as she knows her own hands; but it gives her a funny feeling to see it when the Judge is wearing his wig, and her with no clothes on.

'Whatever do you want now?'

The Judge's mind is full of Abraham and Sarah; and the God that peers down at Abraham out of the clouds is wearing a long grey horsehair wig.

'You may remove my pyjama trousers, and then kiss it.' He motions towards his cock.

The nurse is disgusted. 'Well I never heard of such a thing!' How disgusting! She knows he is clean because she washed him just half an hour ago, and he doesn't seem to have piddled himself since. But all the same, that's the sort of thing dirty foreigners do! She purses her lips. She likes her food, but is careful of what she eats. Plain English cooking is good enough for her. Who would have thought the old Judge had such dirty ideas? Does he think he's going to get it up then? Poor old cuss, he has another think coming. She starts to pull off his pyjamas.

She's more at ease with her own body now. A fat woman, with very white skin except for her forearms.

The skin on the back of her upper arms is rough and covered with tiny purple spots. Has been ever since she was a girl. She has no waist, but plenty of everything else. She hangs the pyjama trousers over the foot of the bed. There are no muscles at all on the old Judge's legs, just folds of skin. He has always been very proud of the fact that his legs are not hairy. Sometimes, in the privacy of his family, he used to pull up his trouser legs and show off his smooth white skin.

'Look, feel, smooth as a girl's.'

The nurse wrinkles up her nose with distaste, but the Judge has his eyes shut and does not notice.

'Come on, I'm waiting.'

She peers at the limp object waiting for her caress. Picks it up with one hand. Brushes off some talcum powder. Hope he doesn't piddle down my throat. Puts it in her mouth. Rolls it around between her tongue and teeth. Doesn't taste of anything much except that dratted talc. Quite a smell, though. So soft that if she squashes it up she could get it all in at once. His poor old nuts hang down almost as far. The skin's so brown and wrinkled they look like walnuts left over from last Christmas. The Judge feels a faint warmth and stirring.

'Now your breasts.'

What? she tries to say with her mouth full, half chokes, and comes up coughing.

'Quickly, quickly, do it with your breasts.' He wriggles his shoulders, doesn't open his eyes. The nurse looks round, seized with the urgency of the moment, 'oh yes,' she sees what he means, and picking up a breast in each hand starts to roll his cock between them. 'Ah, yes . . .' The nurse is balanced very awkwardly on one elbow, leaning over the bed. 'Ah,' he says, 'Ah . . .' She can feel faint autonomous stiffenings and twitchings. He remembers long, long ago when he was a thin, dark haired small boy with a pale face and thin lips, lavatories where the walls were painted green and the lights shone yellow, water trickled endlessly down the walls, and pleasure was always mixed with power and fear and haste.

'Get on the bed,' he says. 'Carefully now, kneel with one leg on either side of me—carefully, carefully.' She clambers up. She is a heavy woman, and an awkward one. The mattress is very soft. He is panting with urgency. So is she. At last she is there.

'Now rub it up and down, up and down, up and down.' She seizes his cock in one hand, corrects her balance with the other. It fills her hand now. She rubs it around in her large, hairy bush, brings it in to the centre, she is thinking of her own pleasure now, the Judge's eyes are wide open, blazing with triumph. She lunges at him with her big bottom, slips, and falls heavily on top of him. There is a thin cracking sound, like someone breaking a biscuit. The Judge's eyes change colour very slowly until they are like grey pebbles. He has penetrated the woman. He is inside her. For a moment the nurse does not understand what has happened. She flounders like a whale on the beach trying to get onto her knees again. As she manages it the Judge's cock slips out of her.

'Are you all right?' He doesn't answer. The lids slowly sink down over his eyes.

'You didn't half give me a surprise. I never thought you could do it.' He is still and silent. She climbs off the bed. His body looks flatter than before. One leg lies at an awkward angle. She remembers the cracking noise and begins to feel frightened.

'Oh lor, oh God, what have I done?'

She shakes his shoulder, and pats his cheek gently.

'Are you all right, sir?' She feels his pulse. He's not dead. I must have broken his pelvis when I fell on top of him.

'Oh Lord-a-mercy, I didn't mean to do that. I'd never have hurt you.' He'll not survive a break like that at his age. Feeling herself become a nurse again she realises that she has got no clothes on. The patient looks a little odd as well, with a judge's wig and robe over his shoulders, and nothing on his lower half except bedsocks. He could do with another wash, too. She is so accustomed to the sharp voice of impatient authority from the old man lying in the bed that without it she dithers between her clothes and her patient uncertain where to start. He should have his pyjama trousers on. With a broken pelvis he shouldn't be moved. He should have a wash. He must have his wig and robe off at least. The light from the bedside lamp still shines yellow on the pillows. The turkey carpet is still red and warm underfoot. The door to the wardrobe still gapes, half open. The chintzy curtains with their gross red roses are still drawn. Nobody has seen what happened. There is nobody to talk to.

The Judge's sharp face is almost the same colour as his grey wig. The nurse gently takes hold of it, a hand on each side, and pulls it off. His head falls back onto the pillows. He looks less forbidding now. More like a patient. She puts it down on the chair. Then slips an arm under his shoulders, unfastens the hook, and pulls off his robe. It almost knocks the lamp off the bedside table as she drags it free. Things are almost back to normal now. He's just an old man lying in bed with a broken pelvis. If a doctor doesn't get to him soon he'll die. But she can't let a doctor see him in this state. She goes over to the basin in the corner, brings back an enamel bowl, sponge and towel, and wipes him clean.

'Open your eyes. Come on. Be a dirty old man again. Tell me to put on your robe and wig and dance around with my boobs hanging out.' She pats him dry, shakes on some talc. 'You'd enjoy that, wouldn't you? Eh?'

He doesn't move.

'Oh lor, what am I to do now?' She wipes herself and gets dressed quickly. She puts the wig back into its tissue paper and torn Fortnum's carrier bag on top of the cupboard, and hangs up the robe. Very, very carefully she lifts his matchstick legs and inches his pyjama trousers on. 'I know I shouldn't have moved him doctor, but I couldn't let you see him like that.'

'Could you tell me, nurse, how the accident happened?'

'Well, er, doctor, you see something fell on him.'

'While he was in bed? What fell on him?'

'It was, it was, um, me, doctor.'

'Aha, so you're the murderer. Constable, come and arrest this woman.'

'No. No, no, of course I didn't fall on him. He fell out of bed.'

'Well, why is he in bed now?'

'I lifted him up and put him back.'

'You, a nurse, don't know any better than to move a man with a broken pelvis? You'll never work again. You deserve to go to prison.'

'Of course I wouldn't have moved him doctor. I know better than that.'

Very, very carefully, concentrating all the support under his hips, trying to keep his right leg in line with his body in spite of its tendency to dangle down towards the floor, his head and arms trailing like pieces of seaweed out of a shrimping net, she picks the old Judge up in her arms, and kneels awkwardly, mouth half open, knees and ankles creaking. He's not heavy, but it's awkward to keep his frail old body steady. She can feel the two disconnected pieces of bone rubbing against each other.

'Hmm,' says the doctor. 'It looks to me as if this break was caused by a heavy object falling on the patient, rather than by the patient falling out of bed.'

'Yes, well it was like this, sir, he must have pulled the bedside lamp on top of him. With the sheet, you see.'

She pulls the top sheet half off the bed, across the bed-side table, and places the heavy wooden lamp across the Judge's hips.

'Oh yes,' says the doctor. 'I can see how it happened. We were too late to save him. The shock, you know, in a man of that age. Sad case. Wonderful old chap, the Judge.'

Some five years after the nurse had come to work for the Judge he had added a codicil to his will, leaving her a legacy of three hundred pounds. He had left the same amount to his chauffeur, and had seen no reason to change either bequest. After the funeral the nurse and the chauffeur decided to pool their luck, get married, and open a greengrocer's shop in a small town about fifteen miles away.

The Prince's nurse, although she has no desire to marry him herself, deeply resents her lover marrying anyone else. She gives in her notice.

'No, Madam, I cannot cope with a new baby. I came here to look after the one child, and Master Giles is quite enough trouble by himself, I assure you. I shall be leaving at the end of the month.'

The Queen is in hysterics. She is six months' pregnant. 'Why couldn't she have told me before? Why did she have to wait till now? However am I going to find anyone else in time? What shall I do?' She clasps the Prince to her swollen belly and sheds tears on his curly golden hair.

'I look after my mummy,' he says sturdily, and she smiles through her tears and lays her cheek against his. She has quite forgotten her plans to be brave and decisive and get rid of the nurse herself. The doctor arrives and gives her a sedative, and makes her promise to rest in bed, and promises in return to find her a very good girl from the village.

THREE

Now the scene changes. The idyllic period of the Prince's life begins. His chains are loosened. All is softness, warmth and light. He and his mother walk hand in hand along the cliff top, or down to the beach to watch the little waves shushing onto the grey-brown sand. The summer visitors have all gone. No other little boys dig sandcastles or collect shells. Only one woman lies in a deckchair, eyes closed, a hand on each side of her belly. The small curved bay is like a room, or the warm hollow of a bed. The sky is veiled with cloud, the sea milky. The small boy, wearing shorts and a warm jumper, feet bare, potters between the moat of his castle and the sea, one arm stretched out to balance his bucket full of water, careful not to spill a drop.

On top of the cliff the house is bigger. The rooms all fit together. When you go in through the front door the drawing room is on the left and the dining room on the right. In front of you are the stairs, and Mummy's bedroom is above the drawing room. Then at the end of the passage are the wooden stairs that go up to the nursery. The nursery is a different colour; pink and yellow instead of cold greyish white. When you go in through the door the fire is on your left, behind the door, with Nursie's rocking chair in front of it and the rag rug on the floor. The table is straight ahead of you, in the corner. The toy cupboard is opposite the fire, and the window is in the wall between them. Nursie has a wireless, and she is always singing as she plays with the Prince or tidies the room. She is smaller than his old nurse, and moves more quickly, and her hands are soft and warm. Sometimes at lunchtime she sits the Prince on her lap and feeds him—one for Mummy, one for Daddy, one for Nursie. They both know lots of nursery rhymes, and can sing them together.

The night nursery is still a bit dangerous. The straps have been taken off his cot and he can sleep curled up in a ball to stop them getting at his tummy and his little willie, but he has to be careful. When Nursie has tucked him up and kissed him goodnight and turned out the light she leaves the door open a crack so that he can see the light outside, but nearly every night they manage to get in somehow and he has to scream at them to go away. Sometimes he has to scream without stopping for half an hour because if he stops they come right back again. Nursie is there to look after him when they have finally gone, washing his face and giving him a nice warm drink and singing to him while he goes back to sleep again, but it's hard work, and very tiring.

The King is angry and sarcastic because his eldest son is still so small and pale and thin. The baby is fat and rosy. At first he sleeps in a cot in Nursie's room, but when he gets bigger and doesn't need a bottle in the middle of the night any more he moves into the night nursery, and the Prince has a new bed and chest of drawers in the day nursery, in the corner where the table used to be, and the table is moved underneath the window. All day Teddy lies on the counterpane winking at them with his boot button eyes that have been sewn on by Nursie to replace the old ones which fell out.

When Nursie sits in the rocking chair, her legs crossed, rocking gently backwards and forwards, giving the baby his bottle, the Prince likes to stand beside her. He puts his hand on the arm of the chair, moving with their movement, and stares at the fat pink cheeks of the baby and the level of milk in the bottle gradually sinking. The baby is so round, so fat, so soft. The prince puts out a finger and touches his cheek. Sometimes his mummy comes upstairs to give the baby his bath, and the Prince is allowed in to watch as Mummy and Nursie soap and rinse the baby in the warm, steamy bathroom, and pat dry his round pink bottom and creased, waving legs. If he's very good he's even allowed to shake on some talcum powder before Nursie gives the baby's bottom a little pat and a kiss and pins on his nappy.

But best of all is when the baby is asleep, and his mummy comes upstairs to have tea with him alone. His own darling mummy in his own warm little room. He becomes almost hysterical with excitement when he knows she is going to come, and jumps up and down screaming like a little express train. If Daddy could hear him he would shout, 'Will you stop that filthy row,' and his mummy wouldn't be allowed to come, so the Prince tries to press the screams back into his mouth with his hands. He jumps up and down and pants so quickly that he looks like a dog when someone has thrown a ball and he is not allowed to go and fetch it. He stares at Nursie with round eyes and smacks his own mouth so hard that it is all red and sore.

He puts a special cushion for his own little mummy in the rocking chair and stands by her side with his head on her shoulder and his thumb in his mouth while she reads him a story. She reads about giants and witches and goblins and lions that eat people, to keep them away. His mummy is very clever. She knows how to keep giants and goblins away. The firelight is orange, and her skirt is blueish green. She is wearing a soft blue jersey, and a curl of her hair tickles his forehead. Her voice is rather high, and she doesn't speak in a funny way for the witches and giants and take a deep breath before she turns over the page like Nursie does. Nursie is toasting crumpets in front of the fire, and when they are all done she will spread them with butter. The baby can't have any because he doesn't have any teeth.

Nursie says that if he eats up all his meals he will grow up to be as big and strong as Daddy. Daddy is very dark, like the edge of the cliffs and he is not allowed to go near them. If he goes near Daddy, Daddy's voice gets very loud and the vibrations of it make the creases in his trousers quiver. Daddy's knees move backward and forwards inside his dark grey trousers like caged lions walking to and fro. Sometimes the King tries to teach his son how to write his name, or catch a ball. The Prince makes marks on the paper, just as his daddy has done, but they are not the proper magic ones, and the King's face grows purple and his voice makes the ashtrays tremble on the table. The lions are not there when he is sitting down, but they roar in his voice. The Prince knows that if he waits patiently a nice old lady, (so long as he doesn't make a mistake and she turns out to be a witch), will tell him the secret. He manages better at catching a ball, out in the sunshine, at a safe distance from his daddy, with Mummy and Nursie standing by clapping, with his hands cupped like a boat in front of him and knees together.

Sometimes in the summer his cousins come down from London for a holiday, and when all the children play cricket the Prince plays best of all. He can hit the ball right over the garden wall and into the road. Daddy says, 'Not bad,' and his eyes don't flash like they do when the Prince cannot understand his sums or his letters.

Sundays they go to have lunch with Great Aunt Henrietta. The King sits in the old Judge's place at the head of the table, and continues the tradition of the household by keeping the women folk informed of the goings on in the big wide world, and baiting his son. As a great treat and privilege the Prince is allowed to have lunch with the grownups on Sundays, while the baby stays at home with Nursie. He is dressed up in his new sailor suit and his shoes are polished and his hair combed with water to try to make it lie down. The golden curls of his babyhood have become light brown and busy. Nothing can make them lie neatly. During lunch he is not allowed to speak unless he is first spoken to by one of the grownups, and he has to eat everything on his plate. The King tests his obedience by giving him lumps of fat and gristle. But the Prince soon perfects a technique of storing nasty pieces of meat between the outside of his teeth and the inside of his cheek, and spitting them out later in the garden or the lavatory. Since a piece of gristle had been discovered hidden in his handkerchief he is no longer allowed to bring a handkerchief in to meals. This creates problems when he has a cold, because he is not allowed to sniff either. Watching a rivulet of snot creep down his upper lip one day Miss Henrietta says, 'If this child was properly dressed in long woolen leggings and not allowed to go around in all weathers in those absurd short trousers he would not catch cold.' The Prince cannot move. He is hypnotised by the snake of his own phlegm. So is the Queen. Neither of them has emptied their plates. The Queen looks desperately from her implacable husband to her son.

'Eat up your food,' snaps the King. He shovels in another forkful of beef and cabbage, and pours himself another whisky. The Prince can neither shake his head nor open his mouth. The snot has reached his lips, and if he opens them it will creep in.

'Oh Austin, please,' gasps the Queen; she is nervously opening and shutting the clasp of her handbag. The King leans towards his son and bellows.

'Eat your food or you'll get a beating.' The Queen's hand darts out with a handkerchief clasped in it and wipes the Prince's nose. The King ignores her and the crisis passes.

Another day the King discovers the Prince's food store.

'What have you got in your mouth?' The Prince shakes his head. His mouth is too full for him to answer.

'Open your mouth.' Eyes wide with terror the Prince makes a strangled gulping sound. His lips remain tightly closed. The King pushes his chair back. He marches round the table. He puts his hot, thick hand on the Prince's neck.

'Spit it out.'

The Prince spits onto his plate some large pieces of warm fat, with several veins peeping through. He retches and almost brings up the rest of his lunch, but manages to control himself.

'You will sit here until you have chewed and swallowed that food.'

Pudding is brought in, but the Prince's plate is left in front of him. The King swallows his glass of whisky and soda and makes a grimace. It does not taste good with treacle sponge. The Queen does not dare to look at her eldest son. She rehearses helpful speeches, 'Come on darling, just cut it up into little pieces and swallow each bit down with a sip of water,' but does not dare to say them. When she and Miss Henrietta, dawdling, have scraped up the last spoonful of treacle, they go to have their coffee in the sun porch, leaving the Prince alone in the dining room, sitting palely over his congealing plate. His chin is sinking closer and closer to the table, and his feet dangle listlessly several inches from the floor. The sun shines outside on the grass and the sea, but the dining room is dark and still and empty. Wilkins clears the table round him and pours him a glass of water, but she dare not express her sympathy more openly.

After a while the Prince becomes quite used to the gloomy dining room. He is an adaptable child. He looks round with interest, kicking his heels rhythmically against his chair. The silver pheasant lives on the sideboard now, and the port decanters have been put away. On Sundays, when the King comes to lunch, a decanter of whisky takes their place, but he has taken that with him into the sun porch. The walls are panelled in wood all the way up to the ceiling, and there is a thick, maroon coloured carpet. On the walls are little electric light bulbs made to look like candle flames, with plaster candles. They were turned on during lunch because very little daylight comes in through the gothic dining room windows, but Wilkins turns them off when she has finished clearing away the plates. The room is dark, with a cold blueish light outlining the heavy furniture, and the picture frames, and the small boy in his sailor suit. Miss Henrietta is having a nap, and the King and Queen have gone for a walk. When Wilkins has finished the washing up everything is absolutely silent. Before she goes off for the afternoon she pops her head round the door. The little boy is still sitting there, the lumps of fat untouched. Wilkins pauses, listens, then scuttles over and picks up his plate. She hisses, 'I'll tell him you ate it, love.' The Prince watches as she disappears through the swing door into the kitchen. He doesn't feel any particular relief. Nor does he move. It seems to him that his entire life has been spent on this chair. He is used to it.

An hour later the King and Queen come back from their walk and look into the dining room. When the Queen sees that his plate is gone she cries,

'Oh good boy, you ate it,' and holds her arms out to embrace her son. The King stands in the doorway. He is intolerably bored by clifftop walks and the company of his wife. The presence of his sleeping aunt and his dead father weigh on him heavily.

'Did you eat it?' he says, 'or did you throw it away? Sly little bastard, I wouldn't put it past you.' The Prince says nothing. There is a noise from the kitchen. Wilkins, instead of going off to her room, is hovering anxiously. The King strides over and opens the door.

'Wilkins, did you take away Master Giles's plate?'

'Yes, sir.' She wipes her hands backwards and forwards on her skirt, forgetting that she has taken off her apron.

'I thought he'd finished, sir.' Triumphantly she nods her head. She is not telling a lie, and she is not betraying the child.

'And had he finished?' roars the King, thrusting his head forward so that the line of his jaw is visible instead of being lost in the thick muscles of his neck. Wilkins' mind is not agile enough to evade this new challenge; she stares back dumbly. The King turns to his son.

'Did you eat what was on your plate?' The Prince knows what his father wants of him. He wants him to say no. He shakes his head. The King turns round again to face Wilkins, power building up in him. He makes the room hum like an electric generator.

'Where is that food?'

Wilkins is still defiant.

'I threw it away, sir.' There, that'll teach you. Expecting the poor little boy to eat those nasty scraps. Not fit for a dog.

'Where?'

'In the dustbin.' Not strictly accurate. She had first scraped the bits into the bucket under the sink and then emptied the bucket into the dustbin outside the back door.

The King strides across the dark, stone flagged kitchen, through the scullery, and opens the back door. There is a paved area, some steps, water gurgling in a complicated arrangement of black drainpipes, and two large, battered dustbins. He lifts the lid off one. It is full of cinders from the Aga. He replaces it with a clatter, and a cloud of pink-ish dust rises up. He lifts the lid of the other dustbin. It is half full of old newspapers, potato peelings, tea leaves and scraps of food.

'Get it out.' He thrusts the dustbin lid at Wilkins like a discus thrower. She straightens her shoulders and smooths down her skirt. She is not his servant. She says,

'If you want it you can get it out yourself. I think it's downright cruelty to children.' She sniffs, turns on her heel and marches off to her own room.

The Queen is standing in the doorway. She shakes her head and wrings her hands.

'Oh no, Austin, no.'

The Prince hasn't moved from his chair. He sits on his hands swinging his legs so that the toes of his sandals brush against each other. He stares at the wall not thinking of anything much. He knows that the battle is over. Outside the back door a sharp little wind blows the cindery dust into the faces of the King and Queen. Water gurgles in the pipes and is vomited out, in protest, down the drain. Inside the house Wilkins slams the bathroom door. The King plunges his free hand into the rubbish. His face is nearly the same colour as the dining room carpet. He feels as though he is going to get a cold. That blasted Wilkins has used newspaper to wipe out the roasting tin, and now his hand and sleeve are covered with cold dripping. A scatter-ing of tea leaves clings to the dripping. The smell is awful. He pushes aside the potato peelings and some outside cab-bage leaves, also wrapped in a ball of sodden newspaper. Aha, he can recognise the curve of every piece of fat. The cross section of a vein winks at him like an old friend.

'Go and fetch a plate, Margaret.'

'What? Oh Austin!'

The Queen has been thinking, Henrietta should really have that fir tree cut down, it would let so much more light into the kitchen.

'I said go and get a plate.' He holds up his trophy between finger and thumb, like the winner of the consolation prize in an angling competition. The Queen gives a sigh and click of the tongue which are intended to express to the world in general, really this is too absurd, how can Austin behave like this?—but she dutifully trots off to fetch the plate.

The idea enters the King's head of grasping his son by the bush of unruly hair, forcing his head back, and stuffing the whole contents of the dustbin down his throat, congealed dripping, damp tea leaves, newspapers, rotten cabbage stalks and all.

The Queen comes back with a white kitchen plate, chipped on one side, with a pattern of blue flowers round the edge. This seems like an act of defiance to the King, who has expected the same plate that had sat in front of his son throughout the meal, with the same pattern of cold gravy on it. However, he controls himself. He says nothing, but lays the piece of fat carefully along the middle of the plate. The Queen is about to carry it in again.

'Wait, there was more than that.' He puts the dustbin lid down with a hollow clang on the ground where it rolls backwards and forwards, scraping along the stone.

'Oh do hurry up, Austin, there's a nasty wind.'

But the King is stubborn. He has his nose down like a ferret, and digs among the trash with both hands. He throws handfuls of newspaper, cabbage leaves, potato peelings onto the ground where they blow about shifting and turning over jerkily, giving no purchase to the wind. He places several more pieces of fat onto the plate. One has a rim of mildew round the edge, and looks as if it had been chewed and abandoned some time ago by a dog. The Queen wrinkles up her nose.

'Now really, Austin, you cannot expect the child to eat that. You'll make him ill.' She flicks it off the plate back into the dustbin. 'Come along now, that's quite enough.' The King looks round the squalor he has created in his father's back yard, and grinds his teeth. He follows his wife inside and slams the door. He washes his hands in the sink. The whole kitchen smells of soda and grease.

In the dining room his wife has placed the plate of cold fat, now decorated with a few tea leaves and portions of Saturday's dog track results from the *News of the World,* in front of her child. She goes to fetch a clean knife and fork and cuts it up into small pieces, bending over him solicitously.

'Daddy wants you to eat it all up like a good boy, like you should have done before.' She sits sideways on the chair beside him and feeds him first with a lump of fat, then with a sip of water to help it down. The King watches for a few moments from the doorway, frowning and breathing heavily. Then he walks out of the room, no longer interested. The Prince abstracts himself from the situation. He chews nothing, he tastes nothing. He gazes at the wall and swallows automatically. He is not even sick. When he has finished the Queen gives him a big kiss on the top of his head.

'That's a good boy.' She is light hearted and girlish now. She takes the dirty plate out into the kitchen. She pulls Giles' arm through her own, hugging it close to her as they leave the dining room. She sighs with relief; she and the Prince together have managed to do what they ought to do, and please Daddy.

Daddy is waiting in the hall, with his coat on.

'Come on, we're going home.'

'But what about Aunt Henrietta?'

'I've said goodbye.'

They bustle into their coats and into the car. The Queen, as usual, sits in the front seat with her eyebrows raised, eyes half-closed, and a faint, sweet, smile on her face. She is praying.

To the Prince the weekends are like black telegraph poles seen from a train, regularly waiting to stun him. During the week he can relax a little, playing with his Nursie and his little brother down on the beach or in the garden. The Queen usually goes out in the afternoons, in a pretty flowered hat, or a straw hat and a pair of gloves. Sometimes her friends come over to their house, and they put up the card tables and play bridge in the drawing room, and Clara the maid brings them tea. Nursie sometimes says to Clara when they are having their supper in the kitchen, the door to the back stairs open so that they can hear when Master Giles has one of his nightmares, 'How can they stand it shut up playing cards every day when it's so lovely out? And they've most of them got little children. You'd think they'd want to play with them, wouldn't you?'

Nursie and Giles and Robert are happy in the garden, or going for a walk, or playing on the beach. Sometimes they take the pushchair for Robert and go to the woods to pick primroses, or along the lanes in the autumn, gathering blackberries.

'Not the ones right on the bottom,' says Nursie, 'they get the dust from the cars, and a dog might have made a mess on them.' It is difficult for Robert to reach anything much higher than a dog's hind legs, but Giles stretches as tall as he can, and bravely puts his hands in under the leaves to find the hidden juiciest ones. He doesn't cry out when the brambles scratch his wrists, but carefully pulls off the berries, not squashing them, and piling them in his small wicker basket. When she sees how many he has picked Nursie cries out.

'Ooh, look at all those lovely berries, Cook will be pleased.' The Prince's hands are so stained with juice that she doesn't notice the scratches until they get home and he is in his bath. He squeaks with pain as the water touches his wrists, and Nursie washes off the blackberry juice as carefully as she can, with soap, till she can see the tiny drops of blood like rows of brown coral beads on his soft wrists. She sits him on her lap and dries him in a big white towel, and puts on his winceyette pyjamas and felt bedroom slippers with Mickey Mouse faces on them, and red Jaeger dressing gown. Then she rolls back his sleeve and dabs iodine on the scratches, very gently.

'It'll sting, lovey, hold your breath.' He holds his breath and shuts his eyes tight, and it does sting, but he doesn't cry.

'There's my brave boy.' Nursie hugs him tight and rocks him on her knees. 'Now we'll go down and say goodnight to Mummy and Daddy and tell them what a brave boy you are.'

Golden light streams into the hall through the windows on either side of the front door. The black and white tiles on the floor shine. The roses on the window sill are drowned in light; it flows through and over and into them until they have no shape at all, but only incandescence. The umbrella stand and clock and barometer are touched with the fingers of God. Walking down the green carpeted stairs Nursie and Giles feel the warmth touch their feet and knees and climb up their bodies; they throw their heads back like converts descending into the holy river for baptism. When the light touches their faces they give a shout of joy.

The King has just come in. He walks back into the hall, thinking he hears his wife. She has not yet come back from playing bridge.

'We picked ever so many blackberries this afternoon, sir,' says Nursie. 'And look at poor Master Giles' arms, all over scratches.' The Prince steps forward into the slice of shadow, holding out his arm and blinking in the sudden darkness.

'Humph,' says the King. 'Lot of fuss about nothing. Little crybaby.' He turns back into the drawing room. Behind him the carpet glows like grass.

'But he didn't cry, sir,' calls Nursie triumphantly. 'Not even when I put on the iodine!'

He is making up for lost time now, though, standing between the two shafts of light with his arm held out for Daddy's approval, a six-year-old orphan abandoned in the storm in his brave red dressing gown. He is so silent and still that Nursie doesn't realise he is crying at first, until she kneels down to look at his face and finds tears running down his cheeks so fast they make one continuous stream, and his poor little mouth fixed in a rigid rectangular grimace. When she picks him up his little body is as stiff as a plaster saint in a church procession, and she manages to run all the way upstairs with him, his face slowly turning purple, before he can take enough breath to make even one scream.

It takes her over an hour to calm him down, upstairs in the nursery. He doesn't even hear when she talks to him, safe on her lap in the rocking chair, with the blackbird singing outside the window.

'Nursie knows you're a brave boy. Cook's making a lovely blackberry and apple pie out of the berries you picked, for Mummy and Daddy's dinner.' The child doesn't cry like other children. He either makes his express train noise or a sort of continuous groaning, like the sound he is making now. His eyes are wide open, full of tears, though they've stopped running down his cheeks. But he doesn't seem to see anything, or even know where he is. Nursie rocks him and strokes him and sponges his face and hands, and eventually he stops crying and falls asleep, exhausted, on her lap. She tucks him into bed and leaves all the doors wide open when she goes down for her supper.

'Poor little mite, it can't be natural for a child to cry like that.'

When Cook offers her some apple and blackberry pie she pushes it aside. 'I don't fancy it, somehow.'

•

Twice a year, at the opening of the local Assizes, the King has to walk round the town in procession with the Judge. For a long time the Prince thinks that this is his grandfather come back to life. He was, after all, buried in a church, and it seems perfectly natural that he should rise twice a year like a phoenix in his scarlet robes to the blaring of trumpets, and vanish again into the courthouse.

The Queen, with her hat, gloves and smile, and silk doubly folded over her bosom, vanishes into the church to watch the ceremony of blessing and dedication, but Nursie and the children, in their matching blue tweed coats with velvet collars and blue tweed caps, line the streets with the common people. The people standing on the pavement make room for them in front. There is never much of a crowd, but Nursie has no shame in saying, 'They want to see their daddy,' and smiling at everyone around her as she pushes the children forward. The excitement of pressing against these unknown thighs and shopping baskets, toes continually slipping over the edge of the pavement, stumbling into the gutter, pulled back by kindly hands, is intoxicating for the Prince. 'Look, look,' he cries, 'there's my daddy!'

There are people standing on either side of the church steps. They murmur and shuffle as the organ music comes to an end and the church doors are pulled open from the inside. It is a sunny day, with a sharp wind and grey clouds in the sky. The nineteenth century gothic church porch is outlined with curved ribs of stone, neatly shadowed black and white. It is February, and the stones and roads of the town still shine with the damp greyness of winter. The sun glints on the brass and silver instruments of the band as they come out of the church, one by one, and form up in the street. They take a step backward, a step forward until they are in twos, a deep breath, a pause, heads nodding in time, then *pam pam be dam pam pam pam* and off they start. Meanwhile the Judge himself in his scarlet robes, and the court officials and the Mayor with his chain, and most splendid of all in his pale blue velvet knee breeches and buckled shoes, blue coat and white ruffled cravat, the King, have all come out of the church and are following the band in stately procession. From the church porch it is possible to see the courthouse, which is just fifty yards up West Hill, but to make the procession last longer they usually turn right and go round by the High Street.

Running, dodging past feet and legs, with only an occasional glimpse of the procession, but with the sound of the band ringing in their ears, the Prince follows them, puffed up with self importance. His little pale face is solemn and portentous as he struggles to keep in step, his head turned towards the street for flashes of red and blue. It is he, and not these other people lining the street, who touched the soft velvet of the King's thigh this morning; who was allowed by Clara to rub the buckles of his shoes last night. The responsibility for the procession rests on him alone. Puffing, panting, clutching Nursie's hand, he stands at the corner to make sure things are all right as they cross West Hill, and then the open space in front of the courthouse, and climb up the steps, vanishing inside as if their heads had been chopped off. The band stops, its long rectangle bunching into a compact square, and finishes the tune it has been playing with a flourish. The Prince shuts his eyes tightly and prays that they will start another, but when he opens them again all the young sailors (this year it is the band from the Naval Cadet School) are wiping their mouths and adjusting their caps behind their pink ears and packing up their instruments.

Nursie kneels down beside the Prince and wipes his face with her hankie and puts his hat straight and tries to unlock his clenched fists.

'What a lucky boy, with such a handsome Daddy!'

Even though his cheeks are dirty and his collar crooked, Robert's face is round and pink, so Nursie does not have to spend much time making him look nice as she does with Giles. They are going to meet the Queen in a cafe to have an ice-cream as a treat, before driving home for lunch.

Sunday lunch at home. Great Aunt Henrietta is dead. The King considers moving back into his father's house, but the Queen objects. It is so damp, she says, and inconvenient. All the lunches that she has eaten there, subservient, as a young bride, rise up in her throat and make her gag. In her home now she has a certain amount of power. The doctor is her ally. He comes round late at night when the King is drunk, and takes off his shoes and trousers, and while the Queen holds back the satin covered eiderdown, pushes and heaves him into bed. He gives the King injections. He prescribes rest. He prescribes change. He kisses the Queen's hand and presses her against his bosom to give her strength. When the scandals of the King's behaviour in Court become too loud he diagnoses pneumonia, and commits him to a rest home for a cure. The Queen, under the satin covered eiderdown, thanks him for his kindness, his thoughtfulness, his loving care. 'I don't know what I would have done without you, Thomas,' she murmurs, her brown curls lying on his shoulder.

On Sundays now the doctor often comes to have lunch with them, and while the King is away, rules are relaxed. The Queen smiles indulgently while Robert, unasked, tells her about a dead fish they found on the beach this morning. She pats their hands and allows them to get down from the table when they have finished eating.

When their cousins and Uncle and Auntie from London are staying as well, it is quite a merry family party, and the children laugh and talk and even blow bubbles in their glasses of water, and make bread pellets at one end of the table, while the grownups talk, unselfconscious and undisturbed at the other. The London cousins have a freer life than Giles and Robert, even though they do not live on a cliff top, over the sparkling sea. They do not have the same responsibilities. They are allowed to play with the other boys in their street. Giles and Robert, when they go out, unless it is just down the cliff path to the beach, have to wear their tweed coats, or sailor suits in the summer, and have their socks pulled up. They are not allowed to play with the village children. When Giles is eight years old the servants have to call him Master Giles, even Nursie. He can no longer be petted like a baby. The life of a Prince is a hard one.

While the cousins are there, however, and the King is in his rest home, the Prince revels in jokes and games. Deep, deep among the rhododendrons they show each other their bottoms, and the little boys show the girl cousins their willies, and persuade her to let them see her funny bald wee wee. In the nursery they send themselves into gales of hysterical laughter by whispering 'potty' and 'big business' until Nursie gets quite cross.

'Now Master Giles you're much the oldest, and you've got to show the others how to behave. Silly things.' Giles is proud to be the oldest, but worried about not knowing any jokes.

When the King comes back from his rest home he is thinner, and pale, and his eyes look large. His collars no longer cut into his neck; the purple blood no longer pumps through his cheeks and suffuses the whites of his eyes. When he sits at the dining room table his clothes droop on his body and his body droops on the chair. The Prince is frightened by this shrinking of the solid bulwark of his father. It is he himself who is meant to be pale, thin, cringing, miserable.

The Prince has no judgement. On the first Sunday after the King comes home, when the cousins have gone, but the doctor has joined them as usual, the Prince tells a joke. It's the one about the father who will not allow his children to speak at table, and the caterpillar in the cabbage. The Prince borrows the intonation and manner of his uncle, of the King himself, of other men in dark grey suits he has heard telling jokes. He pauses before the punch line and takes a sip from his glass of water. The Queen looks anxiously from her son to her husband, who is staring morosely down at his plate. The room is shadowy. Light comes in from French windows opening onto the garden, and is reflected in glasses of water, white plates and table napkins, silver dishes on the sideboard. Robert has his table napkin pressed over his mouth. Giles continues.

'And the father says, "All right my boy, you can speak now. What have you got to say?" And the boy says, "Oh it's too late now, Daddy. There was a caterpillar on your mouthful of cabbage but you swallowed it."'

Silence, broken by Robert bursting into hysterical giggles which he tries to stifle in his napkin.

The King looks up, straightens his body wearily; blood slowly darkens his face.

'Of all the cheeky . . .' he pauses, leans forward and bellows,

'Get out of my sight. Get out. Out!' The children slip down from their chairs and flee the dining room. Giles is not quite certain whether his joke has been a success.

FOUR

Now it is time to go out into the world. At nine years old young men of royal birth leave the milky softness of their mother's side and are sent away into the care of a country gentleman to be tutored in the arts of government.

[Ladies and gentlemen of the jury, you see before you a privileged young man.]

It is one of the best schools in the country. The King himself was educated there. A photograph is taken of Master Giles in his new long grey uniform trousers, standing in the garden of his home. He is a young man to be proud of with his curly hair and wide smile. Still a bit skinny, but the long trousers make him look ever so grown up. 'He'll be all right,' says Nursie to herself as she slowly packs his trunk, piles of neat grey and white clothes, on all of which she has sewn Cash's name tapes. Then she packs her own, because the Queen is going to economise and manage with Clara. The nursery looks bare already, and much tidier than usual. He'd better not have any more nightmares because there won't be anyone at school to hold him tight, nor at home either, when I'm gone.

The Prince is proud of his long grey flannel trousers. In them he is a man like his father. When you are a man you no longer have to worry about the horrors of childhood. Life has risen to the level of the knees. Square, small boy knees. Dirty, grazed, scrubbed, enquiring, cheeky, brave, pathetic. Now covered by trousers. You dare to be dirty, grazed, scrubbed, enquiring, cheeky, brave or pathetic! You dare, you loathsome lump of gristle, and you'll soon see where that gets you.

The Queen in a feathered hat accompanies the Prince to school. For the occasion they borrow the Judge's erstwhile chauffeur from his potatoes and cauliflowers. On the way they stop for lunch at a roadside inn. 'You'd better have a good meal dear,' says the Queen, smiling fondly at her child. 'It's the last you'll get.' The Prince, in long trousers, wonders if he should order a whisky and soda, like his father. He ploughs through a large fried plaice overlapping the edge of the plate, with a serrated wedge of lemon on top, and a heap of chips. He is not quite sure if he is hungry or not.

'Is it nice darling?'

'Mm. Super.'

The Queen picks at smoked salmon and roast beef, and they finish with solid yellow trifle. In the public bar the chauffeur is drinking Guinness and eating cheese sandwiches and pickled onions. He enjoys a bit of a trip now and then.

The school is square and dark grey. There is a long drive of dark grey asphalt in front of it. The Prince's knees and thighs ache as he climbs the giant steps up to the front door. In the hall, boards creak under their feet. There is a smell of polish. Blueish light filters in across empty rooms, through open doors. The Queen tells the Headmaster what she feels he should know about her son.

'His father is Vice-Sheriff of the county now, you see, and wasn't able to get away.' The feathers of her hat caress the Prince's cheek. They are shaded from pink to red, and when they have gone there is no more colour.

The Prince finds himself in a dormitory. There is mottled grey linoleum on the floor, and iron bedsteads painted white, with round black castors like curved toes. The beds have no coverlets, but thick brown blankets, a strip of sheet at one end, and a pillow not much thicker than the blankets. A starched white matron walks briskly across the linoleum floor. Her stockings make a rasping sound, rubbing together on the inside of her thighs. She unpacks the Prince's clothes and puts them in drawers. The room is high and full of white light. Other little boys come and go. They have purpose. Groups of them in their grey trousers, or shorts for every day, huddle beside radiators, intent and whispering, scuffle down corridors, straggle into dusty classrooms where the wooden floors and desks give you splinters. The Prince soon learns to become part of their movement. He is lost in a mass of grey flannel boys. Sometimes, however, he is called upon by name.

'Trenchard, what does the date 1381 mean to you?'

Giles stares back with anonymous eyes. Do not separate me from the flock.

'Anyone else?' Hands bob up.

'You will write out one hundred times, Thirteen Eighty-One, The Peasant's Revolt begun.'

I cannot understand any directive that is issued to me alone. I am one of a group. While picking at my desk I got a long splinter under my nail. I cannot remove it with the point of my compass.

'Well, Trenchard, did I not set you some lines to do yesterday?' All right, I can quite understand being told to stay at my desk after school, and having a piece of paper and a pen, and the words I am supposed to copy placed in front of me. That way I can see there is no mistake.

'This boy is incapable of concentration. He doesn't seem to understand what is said to him.'

It is difficult to draw the line between private and public acts. Pulling your socks up, for instance, starts as a private act, but soon becomes subsumed into the mass. Among a group of small boys, running, one will stop, fall on one knee, and with fumbling, quick fingers retie the knot of his shoelace, not looking down, but staring after his friends, then, as he gets up, in the movement of running, wrench his socks up over his earnest, bright, winking calf muscles.

'A wonderful animal, the human boy.'

Farting in the bath is a private act. Lying once a week in six inches of warm water, with light filtering in in fan-shaped patterns through the frosted glass, each globule of light containing its own shadow, not listening to the hearty splashing through the green painted wooden partitions on either side, or the intermittent banging on the door and cries of, 'Buck up, you beastly sprog!'

Your willie floats on the water. By cupping your hand and smacking it gently down on the water you can imprison an air bubble and watch as it gollups to the surface. A big one leaving a vertical wake behind it, followed by little ones, full of light, darting from side to side. You can produce more and bigger bubbles with a fart, though, sometimes a lovely tunnel or tube of air comes bursting through making mountains and rings of water. You bend down to catch a whiff of the warm, comforting, savoury smell of your own cabbage and bacon, and a faint tinge of oil spreads out over the surface of the bath a transparent, broken cobweb of rainbow colours. His body relaxed, following with tense concentration the bubble of air through the large intestine, now stopping frustrated, now butting its way gently forward, a clockwork toy moving over a wrinkled rug, Giles turns his mind inward, like a punter listening to the four o'clock race on the radio. There is danger in this indulgence. Always the possibility that control may slip, the instinct be uncertain, the sphincter close a moment too late and a turd float up to the surface. Round and hard and black, or yellow, disintegrating like the butt of a cigarette. Terror is a cold chill at the bottom of every sensation, as cold as the enamel bottom of the bath, which the water never has time to warm.

After five or ten minutes the footsteps and the voice of authority are heard, and Giles leaps out, unwashed, onto the wet, crumbling cork mat.

'What do you think you are, a ruddy bathing beauty?' He dashes past, head down, six inches of striped towel wrapped coyly round his middle.

An act that should be private is peeing, and it should be more private still when performed in the dark, all the world asleep. Giles's dreams mislead him. Sometimes he dreams that he has woken up in the dark dormitory, sat up in bed, paused to look round at the motionless beds, each boy silently humped into his own sleep, and crept across dusty, creaking boards and cold linoleum and even colder stone to the bog. Pushed open the door, turned on the yellow light that swallows up the blue night light, and added his shredded arc to the constant trickle of water. In these dreams he becomes conscious in the moment that the stream leaves the safety of his body. It is impossible that his pyjamas and sheets should be sopping wet and the stream still gushing forth. He is bathed in heat that in a moment becomes icy cold. The private act has become public. Matron, crisp, starched and perfect, stands bellowing at the foot of the bed. Her chin is six inches long, her jaw like a steam shovel, her teeth great masticating Stonehenges waiting for their sacrifice. She stands, Colossus, at the foot of the bed, one red hand pointing to the door, the other grasping acres of protective blanket and miserable sopping sheet.

'You filthy little boy!' Sounds of disgust, groans, vomiting, echo from the walls.

'Go and report yourself to the Headmaster,' she roars like a lion. Great capital letters march around the room sharply flexing their arms and knees. Beat kick punch kill. Giles wonders who can have wet the bed. It certainly is a filthy and disgusting thing to do. The Headmaster is quite right to beat him. He is made to undo his belt and take down his trousers and lean over the arm of a chair covered in blue grosgrain. What would happen if a boy should piss all over it while he was being beaten? The stain, a soft rounded cone, would grow astonishingly dark and deep. It would be beautiful. The chair would be marked. The boy would stand up, whimpering and pulling up his trousers, still hiding the telltale whiff of steam, the smell of urine, Mount Fuji, indigo against a blue sky. In the very sanctuary of righteousness he has left his filthy stain. No beating can be punishment enough for that. He is nailed by the offending member to the ceiling of the Assembly Hall, for all the world to see and wonder at.

Matron also finds holes in Giles's sheets. He sits on the bed, kicking his heels and looking out of the windows. This is the hour when the dormitory is accustomed to settle down to emptiness and silence. Matron is going to bring the Head himself, after morning hymns and the intoning of the Bible, to look at the sheets. The holes are not very large. Small, round, ragged and damp, with sharp creases radiating outwards. A rat has been lying in bed with Giles all night, chewing away busily with his sharp little nose and buck teeth.

'We can't have this sort of thing, you know,' says the Head, shaking his head and moving his upper lip gently so that his moustache caresses his nostrils.

'Destruction of school property.' His mind is not properly in gear this morning. Usually the destruction of school property, such as the stabbing of innocent desk lids with compass points, can rouse him to frenzies of indignation. But he has no rhetoric prepared for the chewing of holes in sheets. This child is so anonymous that he cannot remember having noticed him before. He has probably had occasion to beat him once or twice. He is not prepossessing; so pale, dirty and unkempt he looks as if he spends his life underground, buried under a heap of other little boys. 'He seems content to lead the life of a mole.' 'To be a sort of

Ishmael.' The Head composes phrases for the end of term report. ['This is the act of an utterly wicked man,' says the Judge.]

'Trenchard, did you bite these holes in your sheets?' Matron stands by with arms akimbo.

'No, sir,' says Giles, sitting on the next bed and swinging his legs.

'Aha.' He could, of course have been beaten for biting holes in his sheets, but it does not form part of the tradition of the school, and the Head likes a bit of precedent. However to be beaten for lying is perfectly acceptable.

Altogether Giles is proving even less satisfactory at school than he has been at home. There are other little boys whose nails are dirty and bitten, fingers swollen with permanent chilblains, shoes untied, socks falling down, knees, neck and teeth covered with a patina of grime, but they all manage, after a while at least, to learn enough of the rules of living in this particular establishment to know when to expect punishment and when to expect praise. Giles never learns. He seems not to care. He is impervious to beatings.

At home he boasts to Robert.

'Next term I won't be a new bug.' He tells his mother, 'It's ripping.'

Things have changed at home. He has been away for fourteen weeks. The pattern of the house has reformed and closed behind him. The nursery is cold and grey again. Before he went to school he picked a bunch of primroses for his Nursie and sent them to her 'with lots of love from Giles.' Now he doesn't think about her. The Queen and Robert have formed an alliance. They walk down to the beach, hand in hand. There is another hand for Giles, but young gentlemen in long grey trousers do not hold hands with their mother. Giles cannot remember where his mother's bedroom is. Clara looks like a stranger to him. But he is not surprised. There is a slight frown between his eyebrows. He tries very hard to be what a young gentleman of rank should be.

The edges of his vision are enclosed by straight lines forming a grey square. They grey square encloses him, and through the aperture he can see another grey square. This is the entrance to the school, the front of the school house.

Matron is commonly known as the Hag. Winter is mud-coloured, blurred with acrid fog; unnaturally long. At the beginning of the day it is impossible to imagine the end of it. At the end to remember the beginning. The day is designed like a mountain, the week and the term like a range of mountains. Up, up, scramble the little boys, knees grazed and bleeding, feet numb with cold, fingers desperately scrabbling, blackened with frostbite, behind them the howl of the wind and the crack of the overseer's whip.

'Come on there, Trenchard, stop dawdling little slacker, up you go. Always shirking, can't concentrate for two minutes together.' Day-dreaming is the enemy. Day-dreaming and idleness. The devil prowls night and day on the lookout for boys who pause in their struggle. Oh, the devil can thrust such evil thoughts into their heads, such evil acts into their chubby and frostbitten hands, if he should catch a boy with a glazed, far off dreaming look in his eye.

Of course you can rest when you've reached the top of the mountain. That's what the battle is all about. When you have reached the top of the mountain you can lie back and rest till the end of your days. Every night you struggle and heave yourself up over the top of the highest ledge, to attain which you have been striving all day, and lie on your stomach panting in the darkness, your own breath tearing through your aching lungs, the only hot and living thing, filling your ears with noise. The noise subsides. Slowly you raise your head, and in the faint glimmer of morning light another ledge of black, shaly, crumbling rock stretches above you, blotting out the sky. Behind you the crack of the whip and the voice of the overseer unchanged. You have achieved nothing. Ledge after ledge, summit after summit stretch upwards. There is no end.

To be allowed to pause in the struggle is rare and precious. Giles achieves it on those days when he awakens to the familiar damp sheets. Then, after breakfast he waits in line with other sinners at the bottom of the stairs in the front hall, on the crocodile boards outside the study door. Lumpy porridge stirs uneasily in his stomach, but he is safe. Nothing is expected of him. There is nothing he can forget or be late for. He just has to concentrate on not blubbing. For a few moments he can relax, if he can just manage to keep the actual swishing out of his mind, which is quite easy with a little practice. But once back in the classroom they are there waiting to trap him, the facts he cannot remember, the rules that open under his feet like holes in the ground. The square on the hypotenuse equals the sum of the squares on the other two sides. There is football this afternoon, and Giles will be trampled into the mud because he is still the smallest boy in the school, though not the youngest. Q.E.D. What happened in 1066? The history beak has a squint. Hands bob up. Giles's hand bobs up too.

'Trenchard?' Better not to mention the squint. The arm wavers. 'Well?' Silence.

['Are you trying to tell me,' asks the Judge, 'that this man did not know exactly what he was doing?'] What would Nursie say if she could see him now? 'Is that what they send boys away to school for, so their poor little bottoms end up looking like a railway junction, crisscrossed all over with scars? Look at him! He's so thin and pale, and he's got great big circles under his eyes. He should be sitting on my lap in the rocking chair in front of the nursery window, he's still not too big.'

'Trenchard, if you don't know the answer will you kindly refrain from raising your hand?'

'But sir, all the other boys did.'

'Has the possibility occurred to you, that perhaps all the other boys know the answer?' He knits his eyebrows and thinks. He would like to say, 'Please, sir, if all the other boys know the answer why don't I?' but his guardian angel, never again to appear when needed, taps him on the shoulder and suggests it would be unwise. Why indeed does he not know the answer? [He says to the Judge, 'I made a mistake, I promise I won't do it again.' The Judge says, 'His father gave him everything. Are you suggesting that such an education, and with such a background, he did not know the difference between right and wrong?']

Only half way through the morning, and already it feels as if the day has been going on for a hundred years. Two more hours of imprisonment, shifting from buttock to buttock on the splintery bench; running ink carefully into the indentations of the grain of the wood, rivulets, tributaries, waterfalls, oh please, please come, I'm waiting,

I've waited for so long, I've waited for so long. The awful, heavy, black intoxication of sleep, red with black scallops round the edges, like the wings of a butterfly. Rich smell of wood and ink. Ink tastes like blood when sucked from the pointed spoon of a relief nib. Careful not to prick your tongue. The air is thick with dust and heat and the droning of voices. There is no escape, no escape, no escape.

'Come on, buck up. Who can tell me how to form the future tense of a regular verb of the third conjugation?'

Oh the silence. Oh the waiting. Oh the sluggish minds and sore bottoms. The bell rings. Oh thank God. The triumph and relief. Freedom. But there are still forty minutes before lunch. Those forty minutes too, pass. They creep dully by with no great increase in human knowledge.

It is between things that the life of the school goes on. At least that is how it appears to Giles. Between lunch and games, games and tea, supper and bed. In the locker room, among the smell of sweaty boots and mackintoshes Giles can play Tag or It or hurl boots at some wretched new bug cowering in a corner until the approach of authority instantly converts the mass of hysterical demons into an orderly pattern of quietness. Giles has no intimate friends, but he is not an outsider. He has a great capacity for blending. He rounds out a group.

'There was nothing very noticeable about him,' writes the young engineer, rubbing the end of his biro against the tip of his nose in the wooden bungalow in the green and sweaty jungle. 'But I do remember that he would often wake up in the night screaming, or cower into a corner of the room screaming, "Don't hit me, don't hit me," when no one had threatened him at all.' The young engineer stares down the dusty, brownish red road towards the river. He is shocked by the news from home, as any honest, humane and public spirited person would be. He thinks of his schooldays, and how lucky he has been to make, by chance, a series of small decisions which now allow him to make his living in distant parts of the world.

Giles has never made any decisions about his life, though he knows well the thoughtful expression and clear enunciation that such a mental act requires. He also knows how to cling on, how to endure. Like a barnacle clinging to the bottom of a ship who unwittingly travels round the world, he clings on, eyes closed, to the life of a small boy, and grows. He would perhaps have done better to drop off somewhere in mid-Atlantic and sink down through the blue and slate grey and black water until he was crushed into a jelly by the increasing pressure. Lapped into nothingness by the dark swell of hidden waves. But he knows of no precedent for such a letting go.

There are golden afternoons. The grass shines green and figures of small boys, white flannel instead of grey, pause, and run, and stand rock steady.

'Head still, bat straight, turn your shoulders.'

Above the sight screen the distant line of hills dips blue and soft instead of khaki. The turning red ball magnetises Giles. It follows the straight path to his eyes and causes his muscles to raise the bat and bring it forwards with a clean, smooth motion. These are the only occasions on which he achieves approval, and the only ones on which he doesn't need it. The ball hits the bat with a solid *thunk* and curves towards the trees. The scent of grass is sweet in Giles' nostrils as he runs. Daisies at his feet are no temptation to him in the outfield. 'A good eye.' 'A fine straight bat.' 'A good innings for his House.' After each ball the elements shift slightly and adjust their relationship to one another like the multicoloured image in a kaleidoscope nudged by an involuntary movement of the arm. The bowler turns his back on the game and walks slowly towards the hills, head bowed, turning the ball in his hands, lightly, delicately transmitting life into the unctuous leather skin and the snake like, kipper-back-boned curving seam. By the time he turns round, impassive, the ritual sacrifice has been performed, the mystery fulfilled, and the bowler as a priestly vessel, is about to interpret to the congregation. The instrument is passed from hand to hand. He adopts a crouching posture and begins to run with lethargic strides. There is a tightening of attention among the outfield, a slow swivelling of heads. The bat twitches in the batsman's hands. His feet press into the ground. The idea of weight shifts from one to the other. The bowler's speed increases. His heavy feet draw strength from the ground. The earth rejects them. Power travels up his body until with a huge convulsion he expels the ball. The bat darts out, snakelike, licking with a red tongue. The white figures tremble, and far in the outfield one starts to run for his life. The bowler's magic has gone. He stands with bowed shoulders and empty hands. The batsmen run. In the distance a small figure makes a small movement and the result is grand. The red ball flies back to the centre, growing huge and demonic. It is caught with the slap of leather on flesh and then on wood. The batsman lies spread-eagled on the grass. He is not out. Everything has grown larger, lighter, more colourful. Smiles and the panting of breath; a muddy groove in the fresh green grass; voices raised, 'Howzat!' The sound of falling bails and bails and wicket reassembled. 'Jolly well run.' 'Gosh I'm puffed.' The wood is gold and shiny with slight indentations, pads powdery with blanco, streaked with grass stains. Flannel trousers soft and coarsely woven. Ribs rising and falling, slight ache in the diaphragm. Laughter and exhalation, and then abruptly life is drained away as the bowler turns and walks slowly, with lowered head, towards the hills. At the end of the over, mysterious and beautiful as a minuet, each white figure moves; briskly at the centre, with slight shifts of meaning and intention towards the periphery. The kaleidoscope is shaken and the pattern reforms.

If you were to count up Giles' possessions you could start with a straight bat. His grip is good, hands close together and near the top of the handle, and he has a fine, smooth, stylish forward stroke. There his housemaster stops, tapping his pen on the blank page. The boy comes from a good family. A fine family. Grandfather a judge. But you can't very well put that on a report sheet. He is not recognisably stupid. Stupidity looks different. You can see the lumbering mind and pursed lips of a stupid boy pursue a fact as far as his energy will take him and then give up. But Giles' eyes are clear and candid. The housemaster has had a man to man talk with him.

'Anything troubling you, Trenchard?'

'Oh no, sir.'

'Happy here are you?'

'Yes, sir.'

'What about home? Everything all right there?'

'Oh yes, sir.'

You never can tell. Sensitive little buggers, some of these boys. Something goes wrong at home and their work suffers. Some people don't take that sort of thing into account, especially at a school like this, but it's my opinion that the mind and body are pretty closely connected. No, nothing wrong at home.

'Your work hasn't improved much this term, Trenchard.'

In fact it's been so bloody awful it can hardly be said to exist at all.

'I know, sir. I'm sorry, sir. I don't quite seem to have got the hang of it yet, sir.'

I wonder what the hell he does in class all day, he doesn't seem to read comics or draw dirty pictures.

'You know, Trenchard, if it doesn't improve soon I shall have to suggest to your parents that you might be better off somewhere else.'

'Oh no, sir, I couldn't possibly go anywhere else. My father was at school here.'

Yes. Well.

'Well then, you'll have to try a bit harder, Trenchard, won't you?'

'Oh yes, sir, I will. Thank you very much, sir.' His eyebrows crease together in a frown of deep sincerity. Likeable little chap, but we really can't keep him. He's upsetting the others in the dormitory.

If Giles himself were asked about his possessions he'd certainly start with a straight bat, but he'd include other things too. Thighs, for instance. Flexed ready to run under his white flannel trousers, the top muscle round and full like the shape of a softened milk bottle, the thin end drawn together, threads in the hand of a weaver, pouring down into the joint of the knee. He has toes too. Each separately capable of movement and crowned with a nail. In the shower sometimes, with the water drumming down faint and tinny on the wet, grey-black, shiny, gritty concrete floor he sees toes with no nails. The steam rises up in the yellow light and the high sweet voices and raucous laughter and good fellowship and giggles, and he has to fight to keep his eyes away from those blind toes. Skin stretched over rounded lumps of bone. In the night they come towards him, scraping over the concrete floor, birds with no beak or eyes.

He has arms, too, and hands. Boys are all limbs at that age. No fingers. The thumb is important for a good grip but the fingers take on a communal identity with the hand. It's not the same for bowling of course, but he was never much of a bowler. It's funny, he doesn't mind so much about fingernails. His toenails are long and smooth, and never cut until the Hag gets into a bate about the holes in his socks. His fingernails are never cut either, but that's because he manages to bite them down to the cuticle. What else does he own? Ribs? Not yet, later. Calves perhaps, mouthing little slogans as he runs, 'Oh rattling, ripping, jolly dee.' Bit of a swizz really, all that flesh and bone he can't really count his own.

The Pater is pretty shirty when he hears. He has to go down to see the Housemaster himself one Sunday, missing a whole morning's drinking. Giles is a failure. There's no use shutting your eyes to facts. He's a miserable little failure. The family doctor is never short on advice. Send the little beast to a trick cyclist. A what? Nobody in the Imperial Hotel Bar has ever heard of one outside the Bumper Joke Book. You mean there are some of them practising their nasty little tricks (ha! ha!) not a hundred miles from here? Red faced and healthy they clash glasses and pour more liquor into their throbbing veins. Pater sees them popping up in Court sometimes, talking through their hats. He knows how to deal with them, though.

'You expect me and this jury of reasonable men—and lady (he bows to a simpering crone who has got in by mistake; laughter) to believe that because this lout (pause) saw something nasty in the woodshed at the age of three (pause) he is allowed, nay, expected, to tie up a harmless publican, soak him in paraffin, and out of frustrated greed and a vicious desire for revenge set fire to him?' Piercing and triumphant stare round the courtroom. The audience gazes back, eager for more. Oh. No, of course it's not all right. None of us is safe in our beds with people like that roaming round the streets. We lick our lips, under our Sunday hats and bald heads. We know what is right and what is wrong. Austin has after all inherited some of his father's skill in manipulating a jury.

If it had been up to Giles he would certainly never have left. He didn't want to let the side down, tarnish the family name. He can't really see what was wrong, himself. However the other school is all right too. The countryside round it is soft. The trees are full and velvety, like cushions. Even in winter the hills are still green, and the trees still soft, though brown. Twice a week he goes to see a lady in a town nearby. She seems a very pleasant sort of person, though they don't have much to say to one another. He goes because that's one of the places he's meant to be. To himself Giles is stocky and powerfully built, with honest, trustworthy eyes, wavy hair smoothed back from an open brow, and a legal turn of phrase. To the lady he is small, more like twelve than fifteen pale, silent, with a bush of uncombed hair and swollen inky hands. He never says much to her beyond 'hullo,' and, 'how are you,' and, 'all right thanks,' and, 'jolly good really,' but he gets quite used to seeing her.

Somebody has started a war. In the night bombers thunder over the school. They start with a distant rumble and then open up to a full-throated roar. The boys in the cellar raise their heads from straw pillows covered with black and white striped mattress ticking. With shining eyes and half open mouths they give themselves up to the noise of the Lancasters. The vibrations are loose and heavy, and continue for a long time after you would expect them to be finished. In two or three years they themselves will be old enough for the adventures and the explosions. As a matter of fact the explosions are already an intimate part of their lives. Almost every night the lost howl of an air raid siren sends them jostling and shivering down the narrow stairs to the basement, where they sleep cosily in rows on slatted bunks made by the woodwork department, and lumpy mattresses. Each boy has one immensely thick hairy army blanket, soft purplish brown with large red stitching round the edges, to wrap himself in. The air in the cellar has none of the components of ordinary air. There are no smells of grass or earth or food or floor polish, the air is dry and distilled, with faint invisible tornadoes of dust and coke fumes from the boiler. But gradually the ticking mattresses, the army blankets gently impregnated with sweat, the new wood of the bunks, blend together in a more human element. Soft cones of blue light shine always above their heads, making sudden midnight excursions the normal, the expected. Sometimes it is possible, by climbing onto the top bunks and peering through the high windows along one wall, to see the wavering spears of search-lights, and hear the sharp rattle of the ack ack, and sometimes, like a gift, a star slowly turning, a plane shot down is contained within the frame of the window.

When Giles goes to see the lady he wanders through a grey and desolate countryside. Sometimes the siren howls while he is in the train or the town, but he very rarely goes to a shelter. The whine of the siren brings pressure to the front of his head. He walks in a perfectly ordinary way, but would very much like to see bombs falling in front of him, and houses tumbling down. When he sees small piles of rubble, still smoking, with pieces of staircase and bookshelves and lavatories held up in the air by a floral wallpaper, and smug houses with four walls on either side, he is terribly excited and horribly disappointed. He would like to have seen it happen. He is never in time to see the destruction and hear the terrible screams. All that is left are knots of onlookers, and some wardens or ambulance men in uniform.

'Poor old lady.'

'Stubborn though, never would go to the shelter.'

'If it's time to go, she said, it's time to go. Only yesterday. Queueing for fish we were. Wonder what she did with that bit of cod.'

'She never knew what hit her,' says a warden with a sweet red face and peaked cap too large for him. 'Move along there please.'

Giles scrapes the toes of his shoes along the road. He wishes she had known what hit her. He doesn't go to see the lady at all, but wanders round the town looking for more satisfactory disasters.

['Consider your verdict,' the King said to the Jury.

'Not yet, not yet,' the Rabbit hastily interrupted, 'there's a great deal to come before that.']

The war does not stop, as some of the boys have been afraid it might. They continue to grow, quietly, with their eyes fixed upon a point in the future when they will become men, and heroes. Their dreams are full of tumult and violence, but so is the world outside. The quietness of their life at school in the green bosom of the earth is like a held breath. Invisibly the string is tightened, they rise towards the light. Others leave before them, creating no change, and names are added to a new, shining, gingery coloured board in the Assembly Hall. Numbers which form a date are painted onto the board in Roman letters, with glue, and then gold leaf is laid across it. The sign painter works alone, on a stepladder, in blue dungarees. The art master watches. He is annoyed. He could have painted the names himself, and the signpainter could have taken football practice.

Finally the moment arrives, Giles has said goodbye to the lady. He has taken his exams and passed, contrary to expectation. He has uncles in the army and the navy. Only the vibrating world of bombers is closed to him.

On the second day of the holiday he goes into the naval recruiting office at Plymouth and volunteers. He is going to save his country and be a young hero. His family, however, fails to greet the news with the currently acceptable vocabulary of clasped hands, eyes gazing meltingly into eyes (he is at last an inch or so taller than his mother), and a hearty paternal slap on the back. Instead they sigh sharply, roll their eyes, whisper urgently in corners. It appears there is some difference in serving your country as an officer and as a rating. It is decided in the end, though, to make the best of things as they are.

'He wants to work his way up through the ranks,' says his mother at a bridge party, and the formula proves surprisingly acceptable.

The young hero is left alone for his last few weeks of freedom to play cricket with schoolboy cronies on the local cricket ground which lies like a jewel above the town, with wooded hills coming close on one side, and the sea, flat calm, a powdery, purplish blue, beyond the harbour. Ships are always visible, coming to or sailing from Plymouth. A destroyer balances neatly on the otherwise invisible blue line of the horizon. Grey frigates busily chug back and forth, with the occasional puff of smoke and distant dull thud of guns. Little trawlers turned mine-sweepers, coastal patrol boats painted in camouflage stripes of grey and white and green. Several times already this summer, as the Atlantic convoy routes became safer and more escort vessels, even including a cruiser, had been based in Plymouth to harry the German E-boats and coastal traffic on the other side of the channel, it has been possible to have a grandstand view of the war at sea. Between overs and at tea the cricketers gaze out from the protected green bowl of land and watch ships actually engaged, tiny, slowly maneuvering dots, in the business of life and death. They can identify most of the ships, and recite their histories.

Giles is not the only hero, there are others, home on leave. But he is going to be one of them. They chaff him in a friendly way. One twenty-year-old sub-lieutenant, who has served in corvettes on Atlantic escort duty for the last two years, lends Giles his binoculars. He is dressed in uniform, so dark a blue it is almost black, smooth and tight over his chest, with a sheen on the cloth from a hot iron, and heavy gold buttons. His trousers and the indentation of his waist at the back are marked with soft folds. Over his buttocks and shoulders the serge is wrapped tight. On his sleeve there is a gold stripe. Through the binoculars Giles can see a round portion of a frigate leap closer towards him. The colours become darker. The dazzle goes. He can see figures in rating's uniform coiling ropes and passing ammunition from one heap to another.

The sub-lieutenant says, 'It's all over now. They can't take it anymore. Jerry lost 45 U-boats in one month, and he decided he's had enough.'

The sub-lieutenant takes his binoculars back.

'Luxury cruising,' he says, 'that's all that's left.'

FIVE

Life as a sprog is not much different from life at school. Bell bottoms instead of trousers. Buttons at the sides. Shiny seam under the crotch instead of white petersham at the waist pulled into sweaty grey horizontal ridges. No bother about keeping your shirt tucked in. New areas of freedom at the back and sides of fresh young necks rising out of square collars.

You start off in a stone frigate, sort of Butlin's holiday camp, but you still walk on deck, and have to ask permission to go ashore. Later, instead of rows of white beds in the pale, chilly light of a dormitory, hammocks slung curled in on themselves like black slugs on the stalks of a thistle or overgrown cabbage, pale green, strung with dewdrops in the early morning mist. But these hammocks are themselves pale, gently moving shapes, free from all rigidity and harshness, soft cocoons in the dark clanging iron belly of the ship. The air is thick and warm, there is never too much light. The iron sides of the ship, running with moisture, cold to the touch, ringing out with a hollow icy clank at the touch of any metal, are a barrier against the deep water. They shriek and creak against the pressure of the sea. They curve protectively round the young men. When they are breached the jagged splinters curve inwards, lips pursed, lacking the will and the malleability of flesh.

Giles feels at home in a crowd. He enjoys singing 'Jealousy,' in harmony, with soupy quavers, with his mates as they hose and scrub down the decks in the grey dawn. He enjoys the permanent running battle with Petty Officers on the subject of hats.

'Try to remember you're in the Royal Navy and not in the chorus line of a bleeding musical comedy!' He starts low, PO Jervis, but finishes with enough of a blast to knock the offending cap to the back of your head. Giles can't play this game too well because unless he wears his cap jammed down low on his forehead in pusser fashion his springy bush of hair pushes it up until it teeters an uneasy two inches above his scalp and falls off. He would like to push his cap to the back of his head and widen the legs of his Number Ones with a cocky disregard for authority, like Riley, because he enjoys being bellowed at by the officers.

Oh how good it is to be an underdog! To be incorrigibly, unmentionably stupid. Too stupid to get up in the morning without a kick up the arse, too stupid to think, too stupid to understand. Too stupid to be responsible for your own life or death.

'Go fetch, Fido, go fetch! Good dog. Die for your country.' A new pattern of reactions can speedily be engraved on the brain by a system of physical deprivation and repetitive demands, bolstered by the giving or withholding of reward (tots of rum, leave), and punishment (mulct of leave or pay, extra duties or D.Q.s). The rating learns to react appropriately to certain stimuli: the voice of an officer, or the Action Station buzzer. Praise and approval, sparingly used, also play their part.

He's a fine fellow, the British seaman. He truly is the lifeline of our country. Without his cheery courage and self-sacrifice, often unsung, Britain would have been starved into surrender, bending her proud neck beneath Jerry's jackboot. They are willing to die, these boys, which is just as well, because die they do. They die in the icy green water of the Bering Straits, and they die in the grey Atlantic. They die brave and perky with a joke on their lips and never a complaint as they freeze solid or burn up like the wick of a candle; as their guts hang out or their limbs fly off from bleeding stumps with a life of their own. They die in a sea of innocence. Their hearts lift as they go into battle. The greyhound of the seas streaks towards the enemy. Oh it is glorious, glorious as the guns start to crash and thunder. They stagger on decks made slippery with the blood of their chums. Is that Charlie, that bloody tuft of hair on the side of the gun turret? We'd both been courting the same girl, and the best man had won. I think of you now, Mary, as I ram home the shells into the red hot breech of the gun. We dance like dervishes, Mary, in the blinding flashes of light, ears deafened by the gush and hiss of steam, faces glowing red, blackened with soot, pulpy red as a shell splinter smashes into it, carrying away a nose and half a forehead, leaving the neat white billiard ball of an eye to shine for a moment in the darkness before he puts his hands up to hide it. Oh they treat us so warm and tender in the sickbay. Like nursemaids, they are to us.

'Come on lad, keep your pecker up.' This one's lost his. Here's another with no flesh left on him at all.

'What can we do for you, mate? Swimming around in the oil, were you?'

If you're swimming in the sea, I'm told, and there is an underwater explosion, the force of it shoves the water up your arse hole, the biggest enema you ever had, buggered by the great big ocean.

Yes, we saw your ship go up, lovely sight it was. You could feel the explosion in your guts, even from where we were, half a mile away. You felt the rush of air pushing the breath out of you and then hear it, not a sharp noise like a crack of thunder, but a long drawn out KER-WHUMP, and a great billow of flame shooting a mile up into the sky, clouds of sparks and a fiery glow reaching to the stars. Round the edges the flames are red and orange, and devour the ship with avid tongues. Tiny figures, black against the pure white center of the fire, balance on the ship's rail with jerky movements of the arms and legs and dive into the oily black sea, swiftly followed by the flames. You're a brave man, matie, I can see all your ribs. You could too, if you looked down. There's a chap over there been screaming for ten minutes. He looks all right from the front, then the ship lurches, his head falls forward sharply and you can see that he doesn't have any flesh on the back of his head or neck. The screaming has stopped now. There's a rich smell of roasting meat, but it doesn't come from the galley. Doesn't make you feel very peckish either.

•

Giles too is prepared to die. He must be, or he wouldn't be here. He is obedient. He goes where he is told with great relief. 'Aye aye, sir,' and a smart salute. His mind is full of death and violence. The stories of his shipmates are disappointing. They are reticent. They are girlishly modest about death. He stays close to men who have already sailed in other famous, brave or unlucky ships. To men who have been torpedoed, bombed, rescued. Survivors. Men who have felt the darkness of the sea close over their heads. Who have abandoned ship, their home and their protector. Men who have been lost in an orgy of violence. Whose bodies might have been spattered among the debris with their mates. Also modest and ashamed he asks them no questions, but manages to be next to them while dhobying or polishing the brightwork.

The sea looks different when you are on it. The horizon is circular. The sun rises up on your left hand and goes down on your right. The stars surround you in the middle watch, poised above the waves. The colours are the same, but your relationship with them is different. You are the darkness at the heart of the misty pearl or the translucent emerald. The sun, round, self-contained and orange, is your neighbour. The stars are your signposts. The weather is your landscape, the condition of your life. The damp mist surrounds you more closely than any room. Your eyes stare blankly, unfocussed like a child's. Your face is smooth and empty of expression, until out of the whiteness another figure constitutes itself, and two sailors look at each other.

You notice the sea more when the weather is fair. When it gets rough, waves knotting together like cramps in the stomach, the sea becomes personal. It becomes its effect on your body and your ship. To every matelot it is malicious, arbitrary, violent, like a drunken mother. A sailor sits on the locker, feet in his heavy seaboots and several pairs of thick stockings numb with cold. Round them slops six inches of black salt water with a scum of vomit on top. His locker has burst open and his Number Ones and once clean underclothes lap against the dirty water. His duffel coat is stiff with salt. Frost melts off his eyebrows and cheeks. Slowly, with pursed lips, after a four-hour watch, he raises a rusty tin half full of hot sweet tea to his mouth. His stiff muscles are adjusted to the ship rising and smacking down head on into the troughs of the waves, but not to the cross swell which rolls her over forty, fifty degrees and sends him staggering like a tightrope walker on a diagonal plane to the opposite side of the mess deck, and neatly swirls the tea out of his improvised mug to join the cess-pool at his feet. His face creases like a child's at the awful disappointment of it.

The ship is their home. Home, street, garden, school-yard. The local town with the cinema and shop on the corner. More of a village really, this small destroyer built just after the First World War. The cinema a rickety screen and old whirring projector set up in the church hall. The ship could pass for a slum anywhere on shore if you consider the amount of space available, and the amount of living that has to be done in it. Twenty men in the front parlour, lockers to stow all their gear, tables to cook and eat on. Rails or hooks to sling their hammocks. They overflow into the companionways. In the dim light at night, scuttles battened down, they sway gently like cocoons, noses buried in the raw, vegetable smell of rope canvas, and a folded sweater for a pillow. There are no women to wash and clean and prepare the food. They are self-sufficient. They do not need women. They are free. They are friends. Naked in the shower room they scrub their hammocks and elbow their way to the wash basins. Rattler Morgan has a light hand with the duff. Every morning the cooks of the day peel the spuds and chop the cabbage and the meat for dinner, and stagger up iron ladders with unwieldy pails of food to the galley. Every day they try to bribe Rattler Morgan with sips of rum to make the duff. He usually allows himself to be persuaded.

'I don't know how you lads can make such a muck of it,' he says, standing in front of the long table, feet apart, swaying gently with the movement of the ship. His hands are white, powdered smooth with flour. He has been an Able Seaman for thirteen years, and knows how to make himself comfortable. He smiles automatically as he slaps and kneads the duff, and raises the shiny, semicircular patches of skin where his eyebrows would have grown if he had had any.

Every meal spreads a new layer of warm smells over the mess deck. The air is thick with smells. Diesel oil, paint, soap, damp wool, food, bodies. Sweat and bodies.

Each smell is a strand in the pattern of their lives. The quality of their lives envelopes them as they climb down the hatch out of the searing freshness of the North Sea, felt rather than smelt after the chill around the nostrils and at the back of the throat. It's a little like life in a boarding school or an unknown cheap hotel. There are two ways of going about it: either a certain physical diffidence about committing yourself, or else you can take possession immediately of your allotted space. Looked at from the outside their life is bare and grim. There is no room for physical comfort. There does not seem to be much room for emotional comfort either, but it's there. Easier for some to find than on shore, in a house, with the land outside spreading messily away in all directions.

They have to look after themselves. In the intimate patterns of daily life they themselves are mother, father, housewife, child. They scrub and clean, they wash and mend, they cook. There is a place for everyone. You haven't pushed in where you're not wanted. Someone else put you there; chose you by name and drafted you to that ship. If you're too dumb to do anything else you can scrub or paint, and if you're too dumb or lazy to do that you can still be a number on the casualty lists.

The war has very little to do with it. They are not there to fight, they are there to live together in the ship. They sail North through the icy, grey, heaving seas to Iceland. In and out of fiords. Bare rock with a rim of brown vegetation coming down to the water; close, with a shock of intimacy. They rarely know where they are going next. Rumours are brought back from the Heads, where some lucky sailor, indulging in a luxurious crap, has heard the Captain's Steward talking about Gibraltar. Reflected images of sunshine dance through the ship. A black rock like the blunted horn of an old rhinoceros rears up out of the flat blue sparkling sea. It is decorated with monkeys and girls with Spanish eyes and English voices. Colourful cotton skirts, long thin rectangles of red and green and black on a white ground sway round their calves. There are cigarettes and nylons and beer. The matelots, pallid, hairy bodies no longer clothed in layers of wool impregnated with salt and damp, but fresh in white duck, arm in arm, stroll through the town.

There is nothing to do in Iceland. The town is tiny and the roads unpaved. There is one shop and a canteen. Fine, strong looking girls stride around in boots and take no notice of the sailors. The harbour fills up with merchant shipping. The *Patusan* goes out on patrol; chases, but does not find a submarine, accompanies a cruiser on exercises. The sailors do not really believe in the submarine. They think of home. The pub on Saturday night seems like heaven. It is inconceivable that they could ever have been bored or chokker. They don't demand very much from life. No one takes it badly if you find a quiet corner for a fag when you're out of sight of the Buffer or the PO. The discipline of the ship depends on the officers, right? They've got the responsibility, let them shout and worry, I'll work when I have to. But it's a different story on the mess deck. There it's their mates that suffer if someone doesn't do his share, and no one's going to stand for that. Just as well that their standards of comfort aren't very high. It's funny. Give them their tea, and their tot, and their meat and duff and a few fags, and they don't even care much where they're going. They'd rather have a trip to Gib than a trip to Russia, but a few of the blokes who've been on runs South sound as if they'd pinched a ride on the *Mauretania*. 'Lovely. You'd have a pay a guinea a day in peacetime.' You can tell from their faces they don't think it's right.

•

They nickname Giles 'the Lord,' because of his posh accent. He told someone his Grandpa was a judge and he'd been to a fancy public school. The blokes were a bit wary of him at first, but he was a decent lad. A good chum. Never put on any side. Never even made C.W. Stayed on the lower deck all through the time he was in the navy. At least he certainly did the three years we were together in the old *Palusan*, in the North Sea, and out East, as I told them when I wrote to the papers when he had his trouble. We got to be quite chummy. He was a little bloke, and got quite pissed off if someone teased him about it. What would he be? Five feet five? Five six? Something like that. He had a fresh, open, reliable look about him. When you first met him you thought, 'Oh he's not going to be an Ordinary Seaman for long,' but when you got to know him better he was—well, he was a bit dozy. He'd gaze at you with that honest sort of stare as if he was listening, and all the time he was miles away. He was sloppy too. Not lazy, sloppy. He wouldn't stop work to have a fag, or a natter, he'd just stop for no reason. He wouldn't even squeeze out his cloth or throw away his bit of cotton waste. The Buffer was always after him.

'Mister Trenchard,' he'd say, ever so sarcastic, 'I think this must be yours,' holding up some horrible piece of oily rag. And there he'd be, the poor old Lord, on the next make and mend day, scrubbing the deck again.

Giles' head is full of blood. In capillaries it chugs busily up and down the hills and valleys of his brain. In his imagination it streams down from the sky and moves in the water. He scratches a scab on his wrist and flakes off layer after layer of skin until the blood pours out. Pieces of metal whine out of the blue sky towards him and smash into his body, scooping out his intestines. His bowels trail along the deck. Yellow globules of shit, their journey through the colon interrupted, huddle together inside the slit open pipes. The eyes of his friends are continually attacked. They appear and disappear. Each part of the ship is a weapon. The clews of his hammock can strangle, the guard rails buckle and toss him overboard; the lifeboats fall and crush him. Price and Morgan and Halliwell stand huddled in the lee of a whaler, duffel coats over their overalls, fingers clumsy and red with cold, touching but not feeling each other as they cup a match from mouth to mouth. A film of light, harsh and brilliant and pure as steel, stands over the sea and sky. Giles, looking up, feels the shafts of his eyes penetrate deep, deep, past the light and into the blackness of space. The sky is the palest, purest blue; the sea glimmers slatily; the breath of Price and Morgan and Halliwell pours from their mouths and nostrils like fire from the mouths of dragons. Death stalks them. If a shell should smash the davits, the whole weight of a boat, whose intentions are good, whose purpose is to save their lives, would turn enemy and crush Price and Morgan and Halliwell. Able Seaman Trenchard, failing to warn them, is an accomplice in their death. The horrors of his imagination are real. This is war. This is the purpose of war. To give shape to the menacing blackness of space behind the blue sky, the silver death in the water, the streams of blood behind the smooth forehead. This pale forehead, grey brown hair crusted with salt, frizzing more than ever in the fresh, damp air, these straight eyebrows, delicate veil of lids, jumping eyeballs, hide many patterns and possibilities of death. Those he has been trained for. Those he has seen, heard or imagined. Those he fears. Death lurking in the pure blue sky is not new to him and now he can put a name to it. Junker 88, Fokke Wolff, Heinkel U-boat. Tin fish, torpedo, shell, splinter, oil, fire, steam, water, ice. They have to come out into the open. Sometimes they happen to other people and you are still alive. Sometimes you make them happen to your enemy and you are still alive. Sometimes they happen to you and you are dead. Or you are still alive, having lost a lump of flesh, a yard of skin, a pint of blood. Picking over what is left a doctor can make something of it. A catalogue at least. If you can know, or name what is left, nothing so dreadful has been lost.

They are going North. Day by day they sail further into the white daylight. It is summer. Late summer. The middle watch, huddled into the gunshield, can still see the shape of the ship as the sun dips in a shallow curve under the horizon. The light is cold and grey. The slapping and hissing of the charcoal coloured waves holds a note of contempt. The ships of the convoy are all grey. The only human warmth is in the vibration of their engines. The orange sun swings round the rim of the horizon like a ball on a string swung by a child. Round and round he goes, dizzy, staggering, intoxicated, the weight of the ball in his outstretched arm pulling him along, he leans back in the green leaves and sweet smells of the orchard, supported by his own momentum.

When the port watch come back on deck after four hours in their hammocks they are in a new world. They have reached the end of the water. They have come to the ice. The white brightness is like flame flung into their eyes. A hundred miles to the North, across this glittering jumble, this Billy Bunter fantasy of shattered birthday cakes, lies the North Pole. They have edged upwards, as far as ships can go, with their backs to the wall. The wall is miraculous. Out of a cobalt blue sea and into a cobalt blue sky rises the ice. There is no glitter on the surface of the sea. All the light is sucked into the ice. The surface of the ice does not glitter either, not when you are close. It is only in the distance that the spears of light glitter with unbearable triumph. The surface of the towering ice wall within arm's length of the ship has a filmy sheen. In the centre and core of the prism light is separated into colour. Purple, green, indigo. The shadow of their own mass suddenly deepens the colours, blotting out their milky whiteness. Their depth is infinite. Like the Snow Queen they invite you into their icy embrace. The sailors stare and grumble, moving stiff legged in their many layers of clothing. They chip endlessly at the film of ice that covers the ship. Frozen spray clings in icicles to the superstructure. In this cold a ship can be in danger of foundering from the sheer weight of ice on her superstructure. The blue of the sea, where the ice slides down into it, is so pure, so violent, that it gives off an illusion of heat. Surely, if you put out in a small boat from the lee of that purple and indigo shore, and leaning over the side trailed your hand in the water, you could lie back, eyes closed, head raised to the sun and dream. Strange how the senses can deceive each other. That dream would be your last. One touch of that exquisite cobalt fire can stop the blood in its tracks, turn limbs white then black, and freeze the smile on your face forever.

There is tension on the ship, and lethargy, from waiting and lack of sleep. They have already been in action once. The convoy was spotted by German reconnaissance planes when they passed Jan Meyen island, and since then it's been shadowed continuously, with one attack. It is generally considered that the waiting is the worst thing, and that once you bring a gun to bear on the enemy and press the trigger you forget all about your fear and tiredness and boredom. You're caught up in it, as row after row of Heinkels stream out of the snow clouds towards you, laden with bombs, guns blazing, and all the ships in the convoy blaze right back, red tracer zipping through the sky like firework night, and the boys are working like clockwork loading, firing, ramming home, each lad concentrating his whole heart and mind on his own job but at the same time, so sharpened are his senses, keeping up with what is happening to his chummy ships in the convoy.

It's astonishing with all that lead in the air and all that high explosive in the sea that more damage isn't done. Most of the torpedoes streak busily through the water, giving the other sort of fishes a fright, until they die of exhaustion and sink with languid slowness through the miles of strange lives and the glowing white eyes or wing tips of self-illuminating deep sea animals to the black and oozy bottom. What happens too, to the shells, big as a baby, a man needs both arms to carry them, two hundred men on fifty ships, their arms full of weight and blast, hundreds more maneuvering these dangerous infants into the air, and yet still the Heinkels come on. One falls here, one there, jolted out of line, staggering sideways, falling black and red, sizzling, into the sea, but fifty more release their eggs, rise up wearily, full of effort, riddled with holes, and are sucked back into the white bosom of the snow clouds. How can the air absorb all this metal, and the fragments of men and ships when a bomb finds its target? Snow starts to fall heavily, obscuring the battered ships from each other. The guns are still so hot that they turn the snow to water. So would the men's flesh, heated by excitement, but they are well covered with balaclavas and flash helmets and flash gloves over their action rig, and the snow searching for entrance can find none, and lays its white crystals on them for a moment.

It's a relief when the port watch is piped to tea, and the Heinkels have vanished to their borrowed Fatherland in Norway for another day, and the buzz of chat down the ladders and companionways and in the mess deck is like the sound of the crowd streaming out after a good match between Arsenal and Wolverhampton Wanderers. It's not as bad as they expected. It's not as bad as the ruddy Blitz when you might get the whole house falling on top of you.

Giles goes along with the general feeling. But at the same time he could be a bit disappointed. The horrors are still in his imagination. Not that he'll admit it. The part of himself that he knows about is concerned with not dying and not being afraid and doing his job right and the convoy getting through. But lying at the bottom of his mind is the blood and that stupendous explosion that makes all the others look like nothing beside it. Any explosion that he can survive is nothing. How can it be if he's survived it? On the other hand if he doesn't survive then it's nothing too, because he's dead and doesn't know about it. A couple of bombs falling on an ammunition ship obliterating five hundred tons of ship and one hundred men in an instant is nothing much. Just a sudden gap in the line. It's not that he can't take in such a huge tragedy. It's not enough. The sort of explosion that he is hoping for is one that will smash the world in an instant, one glorious stew of icebergs, water, ships, men, houses, mothers, fathers, nurses, schools, all bursting upwards, screaming, knowing what it is that destroys them, never reaching the cold emptiness of space where the planets spin round, but bursting upwards over and over again, endlessly, in screaming, roaring, bloody pain. And what is it that destroys them? Surely not a young seaman, well-educated, a gent, always trying to please though not always succeeding. Surely not a little boy with bitten nails, or a mute infant? No, come on now, that's nonsense. We know guns can destroy and that's perfectly all right. And it's perfectly all right that this same young seaman should play his part loading shells into this great lovely metal phallus lifting itself upwards, making a perfect gesture of its whole being towards the target. He can cause explosions, oh sure. He, or other chaps like him, can drop bombs, or release torpedoes, or fire depth charges, just so long as it's not really him that's doing it. Just so long as he's only a loader or a button pusher.

Giles wants something better. He wants to do the job himself.

Dear mother, thank you for the socks and cigarettes. It's ripping to have a parcel when we come back into port. One chap in our mess gets more mail than all the rest of us put together. His wife writes every day. I hope things aren't too bad at home. I'm saving up some chocolate (it's called nutty in the Navy) for my next leave, Love Giles.

It doesn't worry him that he's not allowed to describe the beauties of the distant green ice mountains, the thirteen ships out of thirty-four that have been lost on the convoy, the weeks of steaming grey heat and the vicious mosquitoes when they finally arrive in Russia. It seems quite natural, too, not to mention the one direct hit which the *Patusan* had sustained on Y turret, which had killed the entire crew with the exception of Giles who had been blasted straight through an open hatchway onto A mess deck, missing an iron stanchion by a quarter of an inch and suffering nothing worse than a few bruises.

What do you do with an incident like that? Thank God? Weep? In fact any of them that were alive owed their lives to some such mixture of luck and chance. When you've been dodging bombs for two, three hours at a time, wave after wave of Heinkels zooming down out of the clouds or the clear sky with nothing on their minds but to land those eggs where they'll hurt most, when you've been play-ing the game so long, and you're winning, because you're still alive, it almost seems like time to give the other fellow a chance. OK Jerry, your turn now, I won't bother to dodge this one. *Wham! Splat!* Ah. Bullseye. Does the Captain have to struggle against thoughts like these? Can he really be so concerned, hour after hour, day after day, for weeks on end, with the life of his ship? When, straining their eyes in the cold grey twilight counting and recounting, they find one ship less in the convoy than there had been the previous night, no trick of the eyes, but a physical shock, a blow, when they understand that there is no solid object between the sea and the sky, there where they expected to find it, does that not make him pause and think, what the hell, why make any more efforts? It might have been us. None of my skill could have avoided that silent streak in the dark sea. Suddenly in the quietness of the night we would have lurched over with a sickening shock. The sounds of confusion, the clatter of feet, voices, cries, the acrid smell of smoke swallowed up by water busily gurgling into every corner of this toy boat, until with a deep sucking noise it slides under leaving a momentary signature of swirls and bubbles and a few bobbing heads on the surface. The Captain remains awake, in a state of tense concentration, ready at any instant for the button to press and the little wheels in his brain to start turning and clicking to move them out of the path of approaching death already in the air or sea, twenty hours out of twenty-four. This ceaseless, grinding effort is so that they will remain alive, and yet he has taken his ship and his men out into this suicidal sea. Sometimes in the middle watch Halliwell says to Price, 'We're fucking stupid. If we didn't want to get blasted we should have stayed at 'ome.'

'Get blasted in our fucking beds instead.'

•

Another rumour from the Heads. There must be a bit of truth in this one. There's a ruddy great hole in the deck where Y gun turret used to be. They patched it up a bit during the long four weeks in Archangel, but they didn't have much equipment there. They didn't have much of anything there. No beer, no girls, at least none that would swap a few jokes with the matelots. No shoes, no chocolate, no food. And flat. Oh to be in good old Blighty where you can at least get a pint of bitter and a good laugh. They're decent blokes, Uncle Joe's Ruskies. Good fighters. And Natasha's a lovely girl, or she would be if she was allowed to be a bit friendly. It's a long weekend in the Urals for her if she's caught fraternising. You're bored, but at least you're not being bombed out of the water. And after four weeks it's over, and you're off again thank God, setting out on the long trip home, when you won't be so bored, though you might be bombed out of the water. In spite of the patching up they'll be due for a boiler clean and some serious repairs by the time they get back, let's all hope for a good bit of leave. It's too much to hope for that they'll be ordered to Guz for their boiler clean, and Giles can show his family round the ship. But it happens.

At least it happens that they peel off from the convoy in the North Sea, leaving them to be escorted back to Iceland by another flotilla of destroyers, and make their way down the East Coast and into the good old English Channel now just about clear of enemy shipping, and back to Guz.

Guz, Guz, glorious Guz! This is Giles' country, and they've got two weeks' leave. What does he care if his father and mother don't even come to have a look at the ship? The Navy's your father and mother, brother and sister, wife and child. The Navy needs you. The Navy'll look after you.

His chest has filled out. He stands straight, swaggering in his Number Ones. Like most of the other lads he's had a zipper put down the front (unofficially, it's against regulations) for a smarter fit. His collar is smooth, not a crease, kept in place round the waist with tapes. He swings along the road, whistling to himself. A couple of pretty girls nudge each other and giggle.

'Oh I do like a sailor boy.'

'Isn't he luvly!'

'Hullo Margaret.'

'Master Giles! I didn't recognise you.' She blushes. She looks as if she is going to cry.

'Are my parents home?'

'Your mum is. I mean Mrs—I'm ever so sorry, I didn't . . .' He gives a wink and a cheery wave, just like any of the lads would have done, and carries on down the hill with his rolling sailor's walk.

Margaret and her friend look after him. They look at each other. They don't know what to say. Is their afternoon spoilt? They burst into embarrassed giggles, they start shrieking helplessly, falling into each other's arms, holding each other up. 'I do like a sailor boy!' 'Isn't he luvly!'

Giles carries on through the gate and up the gravel path, cutting across a corner of the lawn, which always drives his father mad. His hands are rough and calloused on the brass doorknob. There are fine lines at the corners of his eyes, and his fair skin has been reddened by the freezing winds of the North.

'Who is it?' his mother calls, as he comes into the hall. She is having a bridge party, only three people. Close friends.

'It's me, mater.' He stands in the doorway, smiling. A bulwark of the sea.

'Darling, how lovely.' She had not forgotten he was coming. She dithers, clutching her cards, and looking from the table to her son.

'I'll play your hand,' says her partner, who is dummy. She lays her cards down with a sweet smile of thanks, and runs to greet this brave son of hers.

'Oh darling,' she says again, clasping her hands in front of her and having to stand just a little on tiptoe to kiss his cheek. She looks him up and down. He doesn't look quite how she'd expected. What was it that was different from Lady Philpott's son?

'You've changed.'

'I was blown through a hatchway. All the rest of the lads on Y Gun were killed. I was bloody lucky to escape. They were all blown to smithereens.'

It is absurd, but the people at the bridge table pause and gasp at the word bloody. They do not want to think about young men being blasted to smithereens. Giles' mother has realised what it is that looks different from Peter Philpott. Giles doesn't have any medals on his chest, or any of those pretty gold ribbons on his sleeve.

'Shouldn't they have given you a medal for it?' she says. Then, 'Why don't you go to your room and change? I'll just finish this rubber, and we'll have a cosy chat.' Giles swings his kitbag full of nutty and dirty socks.

'OK, mater.' He wanders upstairs. If he takes off his Number Ones will he stop being a sailor? Most of the lads have a long trip by train to get home. They dripped about it all the way down the English Channel.

'What's wrong with bleeding Liverpool anyway?'

'Everything, if you ask me.'

'There'll be a bloody sight more wrong with you if I ever get my hands on you, you miserable cockney bastard.'

As they walk down their street, if it's still standing, people will come to the doors of their houses.

'Back from the wars then?' 'Good to see you lad.'

Women wiping their hands on their aprons. Old men wearing slippers and waistcoats and shirts with no collars. When he opens the door of his little terrace house all the family will be there greet him. 'We're that proud of you, son.' Warm embraces; handshakes. Little kids screaming with excitement. 'What you got for me? What you brought me?' The kitbag emptied, contents spread all over the floor. Bars of nutty and packets of fags. 'Ooh, chocolate.' 'Don't make yourself sick now. This is for you Mum, and 'ere, Dad.' When he goes to the pub in the evening the doors swing open to a warm fug of yellow light and smoke and beer and welcome. 'Good ter see yer.' And an arm round the shoulder. ''Ave a pint on me.'

They'd have girls, too. Perhaps he should take out Margaret. But his father wouldn't like it, she's only a maid. Once he's in civvies again he doesn't feel like taking her out anyway. The Simpsons, who are playing bridge down below with his mother, have a daughter of about sixteen. If she isn't at school he could take her out for a meal. He still has most of his pay. He could borrow his father's car. Drive into Plymouth.

When he goes downstairs again it is just as if he'd never been away. He helps himself to a drink, and pulls a chair up to watch the game. Trouble is, the Simpsons' daughter is still away at school. And when his father comes in and he mentions the car, his father says,

'Are you mad? Haven't you heard of petrol rationing?'

Giles frowns. 'Yes, you're right. When you've just seen a big tanker with a hundred men on her go up like that,' he snaps his fingers, spilling some of his drink on his sleeve, 'you feel a bit choked about people at home who wangle extra petrol coupons.'

Most of his leave is like that. His father makes a big effort to be nice, and takes him along to court a couple of times. One case deals with a Maltese who's been selling black market nylons. He gets five years. 'Bloody little foreigner,' says his father on the way home in the car. Another case is that of man who strangled his nine-year-old step-daughter and buried her body under the hen house. The police and a few volunteers had spent the whole night searching for her in the surrounding woods while he warmed himself up a turnip pasty in the oven, ate it, and went to bed. The hens dug up the little girl in the end. Why did he knock her off? Well, it appears her mother was a nurse, and worked nights, and while she was out at work the old man was stuffing it up her daughter. The little girl didn't like it much, and complained to her mother. She told them at the hospital, and begged to be put on days, but they couldn't see their way to doing it, they were so understaffed. During the trial the mother sat in court, looking very tired and wearing a brown hat. On the last day she fainted. She was still working nights. The step-father was an ex-soldier, he'd been at Tobruk. Shell-shock and wounded in the leg. He got five years too.

'They really might have given you your leave at Christmas,' says Giles' mother. 'It's such a pity you'll miss Robert.'

Days when Giles didn't go into the town with his father he'd walk through the woods to the little pub at Trelarret and discuss the progress of the war over a pint.

'Can't last another month, Jerry's finished.'

'What about the Japs?'

'Let the Americans take care of the Japs, them and the Aussies.'

'If they'd let us give them a hand the war would be over a damn sight quicker.'

He went sailing a couple of times with an old chap of seventy-four who'd made three trips to Dunkirk in his fishing boat. It seemed odd to be low down in the sea, smelling the salty air and feeling the gentle shift and chop of the small waves. In a destroyer you were isolated from these small movements of the water by the vibration of the engines, and the smell of the ship often drowned the smell of the sea. Those were the best times of his leave, lying back comfortably with a line trailing for mackerel, and the green woods and grey cliffs so close, swapping tales about horrible deaths and miraculous escapes.

•

He was glad to be back with his mates. The war—well, you saw it differently aboard ship. They were all in it together. It was difficult, when you were at home, to think that you were fighting for the rhododendron bushes, and the Simpsons, and a rubber of bridge, but in the ship you were fighting for each other.

It was good to be home. Good to be back in the old ship. She looked small, perky, welcoming, cuddling up to a ruddy great cruiser like a chick to a mother hen, as the lads made their way aboard, greeted each other, looked eagerly around.

They'd fitted her up with a sparkling new gun turret, and a new, more advanced radar set, and—'fucking hell,' says Skinny Dobbs, 'they've patched that leaky steam pipe in A mess deck. No more Chinese water torture as I lie in my hammock.'

'The Japs'll think up something better for you.'

'Little yellow bastards.'

SIX

Yes it's true this time. The buzzes become certainties as they nose their way out into the Atlantic and into the Bay of Biscay. The Bo'sun pipes 'All Hands to Muster' and the Captain, in his oilskins, and fighting against the wind, tells them that they are going to join the British Pacific Fleet in the Indian Ocean.

'We've had our dose of ice and snow, men, and now it's our turn for a bit of sunshine. And with luck we'll be in at the kill.' The wind howls round them, whipping the words out of his mouth and turning his nose scarlet. Grey clouds race across the sky, waves ten, fifteen feet high bear down on them like juggernauts.

'This is nothing to the seas you can get in the Bay of Bengal,' says Rattler Morgan. 'I remember one storm, it was the outside of a typhoon, these bloody great waves thirty foot high. You'd crawl up them, staggering, trembling, and then fall off the other side, screws out of the water, 'orrible noise they make. Slap down forty feet, like falling onto solid concrete. That shook the teeth out of your head all right. Five days it went on.'

'This'll do very nicely to be getting on with.'

'I don't like the sound of that wind. Sounds like a bleeding slaughterhouse.'

Most of the lads are sicker on this trip than they have ever been on the North Sea. Groaning figures, faces whitish green, hang over the rails or clutch buckets like the breast of their mother as they heave their stomachs up. Every sip of tea or water turns to bitter yellow acid in seconds, and after they've retched that up there is only blood.

The Indian Ocean seems very far away. Outside the possibilities of their imagination. At Guz they have been issued with tropical kit, crisp white drill suits, shirt and shorts. Crisp—hard as a board, in fact. 'Looks like bleeding sailcloth to me.'

'You want to get your kit made out there.'

'Oh yeah, I'll send a wire to my tailor.'

The old hands have had their kit made on previous trips out East. The problem is to keep it from getting stained with dye from their blue serge suits. The dye just pours out of that stuff when it gets wet. Stains their singlets and vests, skin too, so that sometimes in the shower, after it has been raining a lot, they look like a crowd of ancient Britons, covered with woad. When the lockers crash open in a storm and the kitbags spread their contents into the mess on deck it breaks a tidy sailor's heart to see his neatly stowed gear all creased and stained, hours of scrubbing ahead.

Just before they come to Gib the storm abates, the sea calms. The sky is still high and grey though, drizzling rain with a watery sun peering through the clouds at intervals.

They are in Gib for a day and a night, and no one gets a chance to go ashore. Most of the paint they had slapped on the side of the ship before they sailed from Guz had been knocked off by the sea, and the side party are over the side, slapping on some more.

'I don't know why we bother.'

The rest of them are clearing up the disorder on the mess decks. Visions of Spanish-eyed girls and swaying cotton dresses glinting in the sun die stillborn. The rock looks dark and uninviting, and what is the point of buying nylons on your way to the Far East? The harbour is busy, with two large tankers and several other destroyers and frigates oiling, and a couple of troopships and an aircraft carrier also on her way out to the Pacific. They are glad to see her. The old hands, who'd been on convoys in the North Atlantic and on the Arctic run earlier in the war without air cover, are particularly glad.

'Each one of those little bleeders is worth an escort ship,' says Skinny Dobbs with feeling. He'd been in one Atlantic convoy where they'd lost twenty ships out of twenty-four to submarines and enemy aircraft, and he'd spent five days in an open boat.

'Those blasted Jerry pilots,' he said, 'they weren't content with sinking your ship. They'd use up their ammunition strafing the poor blokes swimming in the 'oggin.'

It stops raining the morning they start into the Med, hugging the African coast. Occasionally buffets of a musty, spicy smell hit their nostrils, coming out of Africa. They make their way under a clear sky and through an empty sea between Cape Bon and Sicily, past Tripoli and the Gulf of Sirte. Past Tobruk and Alexandria. There is a flotilla of escorts, a carrier, and a cruiser escorting the troopships in loose convoy. How different from a huge convoy of merchantmen in the Northern seas, where a straggler invites death, and the escorts have to behave like sheepdogs, continually on the watch. The ghosts of old battles hang in the air. They sail peacefully over a blue sea that so many months, so many years ago had been a holocaust, streaming with blood. The fingers of dead men, who might have been their shipmates, who have died for them, cling to the bottom of the ship, scraping on the barnacles. The Mare Nostrum is no longer Theirs, but Ours. That was what they had died for. The ship sails peacefully on, and the men play tombola.

They go through the Suez Canal. Occasionally tanks and jeeps can be seen, stuck in the sand. Some are moving, but appear to be without wheels because of the high banks of sand between the canal and the roadway. Camels, too, look even more like ships of the desert as they sway along on their bellies.

'I don't give much for this,' says Price. 'It isn't a patch on the Manchester ship canal.'

The pale blue of the sky has become deeper. At midday a haze of heat shimmers over the desert. As they come into the Red Sea they really begin to feel the heat. Pale, hairy figures lie on deck during Make and Mend days, slowly turning pink. Sweaters and duffel coats and oilskins are stowed away, and singlets and sandals make their appearance. During the dog watches groups of men sit around smoking in the purple dusk. Their voices carry in the warm air, sounding soft and sweet. Someone begins to sing. White, vulnerable flesh, pale brown armpit hair slicked into points with carroty sweat; toes creeping out of socks and seaboots, coming hesitantly into contact with wood, with air. You feel like a different human being in the heat. Partly you feel different when you can see your own arms and legs. A skinny white arm, hairs down one side, knobs of bone at wrist and elbow, muscles and sinews that twist and bulge as they move—you could almost think your arm has a life of its own as it picks up a piece of cotton waste, turns and twists it into a neat bundle and hardens and stretches to rub the grease off the gun casing—sort of thing you wouldn't notice if that arm was just a tube of blue boiler suit or navy serge. When my mate had his arm blown off by a shell above the elbow he said, 'Blimey, and I'd just mended that bastard sleeve.' Neat job he'd made of it too.

Out of the canal into the Red Sea.

''Ere, where's the lollipop man? There's a camel wants to get across.'

'Never seen such a lot of bleeding nothing.'

'What do they do all day, the poor blokes what live 'ere?'

'Sunbathe. Look at the colour of 'em.'

Through the Gulf of Aden and out into the Arabian Sea. The heat is fierce. It seems to beat them down. No more white bodies, blissfully spread out, sucking up the warmth.

The deck is burning to the touch. They wear sandals, or socks and heavy shoes, and slink around looking for patches of shade. Down below it is stifling. The stokers stream with sweat and gasp for breath. There is always someone dripping on about his feet or his sunburn.

'Give me the bleeding Arctic. I'm coming back, Uncle Joe.'

'Know what this is? The Sailors' Graveyard.'

It gets worse. Their eyes ache. There is nowhere they can look. The heat presses down, stifling the sailors out of existence until they are only tiny patches of black shadow. Pools of sweat steaming in the sun. The land, while they can still see it, is dark brown, rocky, empty. No life. Life is in the sea. It teems with it, like a kettle full of eels. Dolphins dive in and out of the foaming wake and leap for scraps of food. Flying fish make midget rainbows as they jump. When the sun sets, sky and sea glow blood red, and the sea snakes shine with eyes of fire. The sailors bathe in blood. Their hands drip with it. They sigh with relief as the heat fades, and scratch their burned and bitten skin, and stare with disgust into the living, undulating soup beneath their ship. The ship itself is full of insects. Cockroaches grow fat in the heat, and double in size. The deck is littered with grasshoppers. They crunch underfoot, they stick to your sweat, they get into your food.

'Bloody 'ell, why did we ever want an Empire? Let's go 'ome.'

The ship fries in the heat. Day after day the sun rises, a perfect round red ball over a sea as smooth as milk. The sun and the ship sail serenely on, each alone in an immense and silent circle, their paths forming a cross.

At night the men sleep on deck, under the heavy, brilliant stars. Their voices are hushed, their movements slow. Hypnotised by the sea-serpents they forget the war again. This time the sun is their enemy. It sucks their souls. The only signs of their passage are trails of black smoke and white wake, which separate with infinite slowness and dissolve into blue.

They put into Diego Garcia, and stir a little from their sleep. The ship is fitted with awnings, fans, ventilators. They drink long draughts of lime juice and exhale a long, slow breath. They stare at each other like men who wake from a dream and see in front of them the same faces that were in their dream. Then once more they cross the crawling sea. This time their path is the same as the sun's. They perform its hidden semi-circle. We sail towards you as you rise. You sink behind us, and while you are hidden we move together towards the same horizon.

Soon after dawn one day they pick up an SOS from a sinking merchant ship. She has been hit by two torpedoes from an enemy sub, and is going down fast. The buzzer goes, and the men close up for action stations. The ship is suddenly alive.

'Japs?'

'Dunno, hope so.'

Their eyes sparkle. They have come to themselves again. They remember what they are here for.

'This is more like it.'

They are still alone in the middle of a perfect universe of blue, but they feel the ship rattle and shake in the wind of her own speed, they handle the guns longingly. Warm bully beef tastes good, and apricots eaten out of the tin, the juice trickling down your chin. They stay closed up for action for seven hours before they see a raft. A black speck on the immense, glittering sea. No sign of the ship. Spawned like gods in the belly of the ocean the Australian merchant seamen clamber aboard, gasping, bleeding, not one who isn't wounded. One, in fact, blood congealing from a hole in his throat, covered with insects in spite of the efforts of his mates, dies choked in a rush of his own blood as he is lifted carefully, tenderly, aboard.

How strange it is after the silence, the emptiness, the burning heat, the dazzling sheets of light, to be in the small world of a ship again. The great world, because it shuts out the other. The clang of metal, the sound of men's voices not hoarse with thirst and fear.

'Steady on, matey.'

'Thanks, cobber.'

The smell of men's bodies, soap, disinfectant, instead of salt, oil, blood. Cool milk on their cracked tongues. Hands gently bandaging their smashed bones and ruptured flesh.

'Bastards. Little yellow bastards. They machine-gunned the rafts. Sank one of them.'

'Murdered my cobbers in cold blood. Just wait till I get at them.' The leading stoker leans his blackened cheek against a bulkhead and weeps.

The men of the *Patusan* are eager for battle. They grit their teeth and clench their fists. They are silently determined to avenge their mates.

•

Seven hours. The sub could be miles away by now, or it could be lurking underneath us, waiting deep in the water for aid to come to the stricken ship, using the wounded survivors as bait to lure another juicy prize into their trap. The boys are spoiling for a fight. Our eyes scan the horizon ceaselessly. The Captain decides to make a couple of wide sweeps before pushing on eastward. But to our disappointment there's no sign of the enemy. Not until the next morning, that is, when Nippon does not signal his presence by a creamy line of foam in the water, a silver fish streaking silently towards our tail, as we had feared he might, but by a faint smudge of smoke on the horizon. Then another. At first we aren't certain whether they are ours, but they make no answer to our recognition signal. There is a flash, and half a minute later a huge waterspout rises into the air and splashes back down on top of us. We are still more than eighteen thousand yards away, well outside the range of our guns. We have run into a couple of Jap destroyers. Jimmy, the First Lieutenant, lets loose with a stream of curses. We start to zigzag. We could have turned and fled, but there isn't a man on board that wants to. Their next salvo goes way over us and to starboard. The two enemy destroyers start to separate. On our zigzag course we will be sailing straight for one and two guns will be able to bear on the other. The old ship is racing, roaring through the water, screws thrashing, but it'll still be a good one and a half minutes before our guns come within range. The skipper knows better than most, though, what it's like to wait, with nothing that you can do. Away to port he sees a flash from the second enemy destroyer.

'Open fire!' he calls down the voice pipe to the director, and immediately the director layer pulls his trigger. A and Y guns fire together, but as the guns recoil, before we can see the splashes made by our own shells, a huge explosion slams into the *Patusan,* rocking her like a toy boat in a child's bath. We must have bought it. But no, a great wall, a cataract of water hurls itself down on deck, sending men and spent cartridge cases staggering, flying to the far rail. We gasp, shake our heads, stare at each other, blackened with soot, streaming with water.

'Blimey, that was a near one!'

'Are we hit?'

We run back to the guns. Waterspouts rise from the sea all round us, white flowers on huge, muscular stems. On each zigzag the change of course puts the director off its target and sets Halliwell furiously turning his handle to bring his sights into line again. Another crack, flash, recoil from the guns, and next time they'll be within range. Look out Nippon, here we come. We dart through the enemy salvoes like a fish, like a bird, we are invincible, we have a charmed life. Oh. With a shudder, with a jerk the ship slews round. What a punch. What a series of punches rammed home into the belly. One has whistled through the galley and one explodes between decks. The damage party run below. The galley is a ruin. Bully beef is plastered over what is left of the walls. Is that part of Cook too? One of the seamen sticks a finger into the stuff on the wall and licks it. The cook is all right. He was watching the fun, standing on top of the hatchway. But is he? He takes his hand away from his belly with an expression of dismay and his guts fall out, spilling over his apron.

B mess is a shambles. But as the smoke clears away a shriek goes up from B gun—one enemy destroyer is on fire. At extreme range they have landed a couple of direct hits right on her bridge. As they watch, clutching each other, yelling with excitement, a cloud of smoke balloons out and hangs in the air, pursued after a moment by flames trying to drag it back, but the purplish grey cloud rises and spreads and the boys on the *Patusan* cheer.

'Oh bloody good, oh bloody good bloody shooting!'

The Skipper suddenly notices that the second enemy destroyer has changed course again and is racing towards her stricken comrade. If they make their zag to starboard a few degrees sharper they will be on a parallel course in half a minute and within fishing distance.

'Stand by tubes,' he calls.

The torpedo gunner comes onto the bridge to adjust the sight. He takes his time about it.

'Come on Guns, we'll be past her in a minute.'

'Fire A.'

Everyone on the bridge is sweating with excitement. Jimmy the One is biting his nails as he mutters under his breath, 'Come on, come on come on come on.'

'Fire B.'

The Nip ship sees the streaks of silver darting towards her and starts to change course. The torpedo Gunner makes some quick adjustments to his sight. 'Come on come on come on come on.'

'Fire X.'

In the rest of the ship we have other reasons to sweat. As Price runs to dump a shell on the loading tray a shell from one of the Nip guns whips through the middle of him, slicing him neatly in two at the groin and carries his torso over the rail, his mouth open to say 'here she comes,' maybe he's actually saying it, but nobody can hear because of the howl and whistle of the shells and the flash and *ker-rack* of the guns, as he splashes into the sea for a nice swim while his legs fold up at the knees and collapse on deck held together by a seam in the crotch of his trousers.

'Fire Y.'

Everyone on the bridge watches the bubbling, creamy death trails in the sea. The first two miss, they pass in front of the destroyer as she swerves. The third one gets her somewhere amidships, the fourth too, and as it hits, the ship disintegrates. 'Oh goal, goal!' She flies in the air, shaking the pattern of men and metal and reassembling in the form of a cloud of smoke, thin in the middle, a huge flash, then dense volumes of black smoke spreading themselves in the air from no visible source, and a concussion that is more of a thump in the eardrums than a sound. This one we've got in the magazine.

'Take that, you bastards!'

We scream and dance with glee. The first Jap destroyer is still very much in the battle though. She has her fire under control now, and is scoring regularly. A shell from one salvo accounts for the main switchboard, striking forrard and a few feet above the water line and shrieking across the torpedo-men's mess deck on the way. Another explodes on the breech of A gun, killing four of the crew instantaneously, and smashing various parts of the other three. Splinters from the gumshield get Jimmy in the chest and slit his throat for him, they also scoop out the Skipper's right eye. Blinded by his own blood, with no response from his First Lieutenant, he shouts for a smoke screen. Has anyone heard him? Luckily someone else has had the same idea, and a cloud of smoke rises up as another shell hits us amidships, causing the little yellow bastards to think that they have done for us, while we limp away out of range. Luckily too they are badly enough damaged not to decide to chase us to make sure. Three more shells hit the *Patusan* before she is safely out of range, but they miss the boilers, and the engine room, and the magazine. The ship is still in one piece, though as full of holes as a sieve. She still has a Captain, though he's only got one eye, and she still has most of her crew.

'That was a fair dingdong battle,' says one of the Australians appreciatively. We have twelve dead, and fifteen wounded. We've won a blinking great victory.

Water is pouring in through two large holes on the water line, but as it becomes clear that Nip is not chasing us we can reduce speed, and the damage control party can shore them up with something more permanent than a mass of sodden hammocks.

They limp on, alone again, across the ocean. They patch, mend, mop up blood. Giles swabs down the deck. Blood's congealed already. You can't get it all up. Price's legs are stuck to the deck by the drying pool of their own blood. Giles empties out the trouser pockets before putting the legs aside for a Christian burial. The smell of blood mixed with crap is sickening. Still, once you start something you've got to finish it, that's one lesson the Navy teaches you. He scrubs away with his stinking cloth, picking great scabs and trails of dried blood off the deck with his fingers.

'OK lad, get yourself some tea.'

The violence is over. Nothing remains except the blood and a certain numbness. Pains here and there. Comradeship among those who are left. Let down after the high pitch of excitement. Pride, of course.

The ship settles down once more into a familiar routine. The men speak gently to one another, their ears still ringing with the commotion of battle. The Captain wears a black silk scarf tied rakishly over his empty socket. They eat biscuits dipped in tea. Bully beef from the store. They are heroes. They are tired. They have done what they came to do. They have fought. They have been willing to die. Have they? Price, are you willing to die? Not on your . . .

Chance has mercifully taken the responsibility for deciding who shall die. Giles sleeps on deck. His hammock is still damp. He pillows his head on iron and paint and blood and mashed insects. His ear is crushed uncomfortably. The iron plates hum and reverberate beneath it. He holds in his mind the image of half Price flying over the side clutching a shell and finishing his sentence. It would be interesting to be conscious while your body is cut in half, while you fly through the air in the course of duty, sinking in a misty cloud of blood and fragments of flesh through the clean turquoise water, and sharks with a powerful smooth thrust glide towards you, this feast, here, here are my entrails, still warm, my hands like trailing petals let the shell fall, a star somersaulting down, they gather up my own, my beloved red flesh, stomach, duodenum in the rich sauce of my blood, this dish has taken twenty years to prepare, and much loving care. You are my most valued guest, shark, as you open up your carrion mouth, you alone shall taste my tender white arms, my soft stomach, my bosom, the smooth muscles and the bones, strong and well made. My mother slaved to make me. I am milk for strong teeth, and greens, and bread and dripping and bully beef. Tin after tin of bully beef saved from the hungry civilians for me and for you, my guest.

Giles' body is all present as he lies on the hot iron deck, part of a blanket beneath him, his back turned to the stars. Bodies lie like ghosts, confused at their own life, relieved by sleep. Behind each pair of closed and twitching eyelids the battle roars and shrieks again. Men struggle endlessly through the same efforts. The images of the day, hard and bright, drag through their dreams like a loose end of film chattering through an empty spool.

The moon comes up over a blackened weary ship, toiling over a black sea, smooth and velvet soft as oil. The moon turns this velvet surface into a mirror. It contains the light perfect and unbroken until it spills into the phosphorescent gleam of the *Patusan*'s wake. The twitching eyelids grow calmer. The dreams of lifting, loading, ramming, gasping at the flash and smack of the recoil, fade. As the moon's light grows those who can sleep sink deeper into their refuge.

This is their baptism of the East. Under the fiery eye of the sun they do their duty as they had done it by the wall of the eternal arctic ice. The sailors' dreams soften into the round full bosoms of dancing girls, glittering with sequins. Tiny waists. The navel a deep pit in this golden fruit into which they can plunge soundlessly.

They contain the East in their dreams, and the East contains their ship as she crawls on towards Trincomalee. But the ship, that contains their lives, is England.

They see surf hissing onto white beaches, and palm trees rising diagonally over huts made of leaves, and naked brown fishermen throwing nets in a silver circle. They see thick green jungle growing down to the water's edge. Sometimes they can even hear the shriek of parrots and see monkeys swinging in the branches. They can smell the smell of the land, spicy, like warm buns. They turn their eyes away. They look at each other and talk of home. They are ignorant. They are wary. They have had too many sensations.

In Trinco they are back again among the familiar dockyard sounds. English officers stride purposefully on the soil of this strange land. There are other English ships. Matelots greet each other with friendly cries, and swap stories.

'Three Jap destroyers and a sub . . .'

'Oh yes, and I sunk the bloody Turpitz singlehanded.'

Bronzed sailors over the side slap on paint and whistle. Cockroaches with a new coat of battleship grey scuttle across the decks. In the Naafi they can drink warm beer and eat peanuts and listen to Vera Lynn. The dancing girls fade. They're good lads, kids a lot of them, wouldn't know what to do with a dancing girl. The women they see in the streets are graceful and dressed in beautiful colours, but the sailors never get to speak to them. It's their men, fawning and bowing, who ask, 'Dhobi, master?' Men who serve them huge plates of noodles and vegetables when they occasionally venture into one of the little restaurants, a few tables set up under a bamboo awning, that line the streets. It's the men who walk hand in hand, or with their arms twined round each other's necks. You'd think the whole blinking lot of them were fairies. Bloody wogs. Most of the lads are happy enough with their mates in the canteen.

The BPF is already on its way to Australia. Because of the time they'll need for repairs the *Patusan* will remain based on Trinco with what is left of the East Indies Fleet. Giles is disappointed. He longs to see the homeland of Maily and Bradman. While the ship is in dry dock the lads are moved to HMS *Lanka,* the base camp. In the afternoons games of cricket and football are organised. The pitch is hard and fast, which makes the game exciting, but not even enough for any really valuable stroke practice. In the evenings there is a sing-song, the cinema, sometimes a big meal. We can protect ourselves fairly well from the strangeness of the East—but there is always the heat and the insects. Nothing to be done about those.

Writing a letter home the sweat drips down not only from your forehead and armpits, running along your ribs, but even from the palms of your hands and between your fingers. 'Dear mother, these are not tears but drops of sweat.' The mother, reading, puts the letter down and wipes her fingers.

Some of the huts we live in are made of brick and some of cadjan leaves like the native houses. Broad brown leaves on a wooden frame. They are used as fences too, shutting each house and garden into its own privacy. Long white dusty roads enclosed on each side by these high brown fences.

Oh, they may bow and salaam and call you 'Master,' but they will never invite you into their houses or their arms. Never hang their arms laughingly round your neck and look you full in the face with their long black eyes. They do not see the charm of our bony knees and shaved necks and ears that stick out, and the cap at a jaunty angle at the back of the head. They know nothing of *Blighty*, or *Lilliput*, and the *Daily Mirror*, and the things by which a man is judged on the Seven Sisters Road.

The lads make forays to the Turkish baths in Colombo where the girl attendants massage you with naked breasts. We venture into the Arcadian countryside haunted by fabulous beasts in whose reality we can never quite believe. That slack grey monster walking with purposeful shambling feet towards a tree, and leaning its forehead against it continuing to walk until the tree in surprise falls over backwards. There is something infinitely frightening about their lack of exertion. Like the huge paths, wide and flat as a main road, trampled through the jungle by the passage of these same beasts. Can this be the meek elephant we have glimpsed through the bars in zoos? Babar? Our cuddly toy with the button eyes and a blue ribbon round its neck? These people live their lives in the midst of such strangeness that it is truly difficult to imagine that they share any sensations with us. What do they know of fear who sit cross-legged on the necks of mammoths and jab them with spears? Who eat dragons? They may say it is a lizard, and harmless, but any reader of nursery tales knows that such a scaly creature, four foot long, must be a dragon. They are surrounded by strange noises. Monkeys shriek and chatter in the streets. Baboons, infants clinging to their bosoms, lollop along the dusty roads beside their rickety buses. Frogs croak all night. Excrement lies around in heaps, and birds swoop down to eat it. Shitehawks, the lads call them.

Quite apart from all the animals roaring around that ought to be in zoos, and the filth and the stink, the real thing that proves they're different from us is the snakes and the insects. Now you don't get bloody great snakes wriggling around in Liverpool or Glasgow. The odd flea maybe. Bedbugs. But not scorpions and snakes that can kill you before you know what hit you. Or about a million bloody mosquitoes per human being. We must have swatted thousands of those things each, but it doesn't make a blind bit of difference.

This is how it goes with the beds. There could be three, four to a hut. You come in. A couple of blokes are lying down. You see a bed that's empty.

'Anyone nabbed this one yet?'

You throw down your kitbag and lie back, hands clasped behind your head, for a bit of a snooze. And right above your head, staring you in the eyes, is a fucking great snake. It's not until you're half way through the door and yelling blue murder that you realise the blokes are laughing.

'It's only Albert.'

'Keep your hair on.'

He's their pet and they love him. It's only Albert winding his slippery green body round the roof beams and peering out between the cadjan leaves with his evil little black eyes. And why do they love him? Because of the rats. He doesn't hurt people, and he eats rats. You get to love him too after you've lived with some of those rats. The cheek of them. At night you wake up suddenly. What is it? The air is stifling. You itch as usual. There are faint scuffling noises, the rattling of dried leaves, frogs croaking, deep sigh of the night outside the hut, and suddenly it comes again. A secret signal, a childish message, let's get up and creep outside into the dark fields while the grown ups are asleep and the world is changed, a sharp tug at the mattress. All right, I'm awake, I'm coming. The tugging continues, becomes fiercer. There is pattering, scuffling, squeaks, the grinding of teeth. Swinging over the edge of the bed your eyes, upside down, meet the sharp red stare of a rat. Sitting back on his haunches with one paw slightly raised, like a character in a Beatrix Potter story, interrupted while eating my bed.

They're made of coconut matting these beds, and not only do they provide nourishing meals for rats, but they make good homes for insects. Every day you have to take the bleeding thing apart and knock out the bleeding insects. Tap it on the floor and out they all tumble. Then you take your blankets and hang them up on lines stretched up outside the hut. Interesting this. You hang 'em up and wait for the red ants to come along and eat all the other insects, fleas and such, that have been eating you all night. Then you knock off the red ants and Bob's your Uncle. When you pull the blanket off the line the ants fly all over the place, and if they land on your arms or shoulders you feel a thousand tiny stings as if you'd been spattered with boiling water.

And all this sunshine. Sometimes you long for a nice drizzle. It doesn't even rain properly here, when it does rain. It's like turning on a bleeding tap. Regular as clockwork down it comes. And then one of their Hindu Gods with lots of arms turns the tap off again and it stops.

Oh, it's all right to get brown for leave, have a bit of a swim; but the lads are chokker after a few weeks. It's pretty. It's like a postcard. But once you've seen your blue sea and your blue sky and your palm trees and your jungle, you've seen them. You start to long for a bit of civilisation. You start to think what you'll do when the war's over and you're demobbed. Can't be long now. Funny. When you're back home doing the football pools you think that's the life, lying on a beach in the sunshine with bugger all to do all day; and when you're there, lying on your actual beach with nothing to think about but whether to have another fag or go for a swim, you're bored. It seems like the best thing in the world to be sitting in a little terraced house with the rain glistening on the grey streets and the gas fire hissing and the same old job to go to next morning. You even find yourself getting nostalgic about those Russian runs, when the war seemed as if it would go on forever, and it was so cold the air froze your lungs as you breathed it in.

Sometimes you bum some V.J. discs from a bloke in one of the carriers and take them off with a couple of crates of beer to one of the islands in the bay. You play football, leaping and panting in the sun. The bay curves gracefully. The water is limpid. Palm trees grow diagonally, and for a shilling little boys climb up them and throw down coconuts. A boy running after the ball takes a flying leap over a ridge of sand and takes off again with a wild cry almost before his feet have had a chance to touch the ground. He hops on one foot, clutching the other leg.

'Scorpions! A whole nest of them!'

He had missed them. It was fear which had pierced his calf to the bone. Against the dazzling white sand their flesh is pale, invisible, even though they have already been out several months and have a richer tan than you'd ever see in Blackpool. In the afternoon they feel a tingling, a prickling along the flesh of their forearms and shoulders. Not unpleasant; as if sand was being rubbed into a scratch as it begins to heal. Is there a faint pattern of pink visible along the nose and cheeks and outlining the pattern of the singlet? This light eats colour. The fishermen, the trees, are only shadow. The water is cool and green if you can find a protected patch to bathe your eyes in under the lee of the boat. But look up, turn your eyes to the sun, and a burning plate of metal turns your lids to blood, no protection for the stricken eyes, whimpering, turning somersaults inside your skull. Drained, pallid, with pain flashing in their heads and beginning to caress their skin with the sharp teeth of a saw, the pleasure party of young men climb back into their boat. They pick up the empty beer bottles. Nausea rises in their stomachs. Their memories of the sounds brought to them by the gramophone are of harshness. The transparent water, making ripples and eddies round their ankles as they push the boat out reminds them of childish games on Northern beaches. But it is too late. Their heels dig into the sand. The sand makes mountains between their toes. The leaning palms and jungle clad hills are black, then reabsorb their colour as the boat chugs away.

By evening those with the fairest skins have swollen into monstrous pink balloons, caricatures of men. Giles, who himself has difficulties in smiling or opening his eyes, remembers in the freezing cold, in the Arctic, a direct hit in the No. 2 boiler room and the way the four surviving stokers looked as they staggered up through the hatchway in a cloud of steam, blind, swollen, faceless creatures, with wavering pulpy hands in the white mist.

Oh to be back home where things make sense. Where you put your hand in the fire and you get burned, but not while you're playing a game of football.

How will things be after the war, when we get back? Will they be different? Will the ordinary bloke have more of a chance, or will the spivs take over? It sometimes seems as if they've taken over already, from what you hear. People complaining about the service in restaurants, bookies getting a special petrol allowance. Are we being the mugs, allowing ourselves to be smashed, burned, our wives left widows, weeping real tears, our children orphans, so that some bright young idiots can dance the night away on some lawn by the Thames? Has the simple offering of our lives made any difference? Does it mean there'll be no more wars, no more Depressions? These are the sort of things the lads are thinking. Giles thinks them too, at least he nods, frowning earnestly, when someone voices them late at night in the stifling comfort and familiarity of the canteen, or lying on their beds in the sudden darkness while the monsoon rain pisses down outside. He cannot come out and say anything openly because he might well himself one day be dancing the night away on a lawn by the Thames. Some of the fellows he was at school with do it all the time. It's absolutely true, spivs shouldn't be allowed to get away with it. And people shouldn't complain about the service in restaurants when other people are dying horribly to bring them food. He sees his mother and father in the Unity Restaurant in Chelsea. He is with them, dressed in a suit, as through the door, from the unmoved King's Road, (it is a summer evening) a sailor staggers, breathing in great rattling gasps, his ear and half his scalp torn off, the white bone showing through, a roast chicken in his hand. His eyes are huge, with half circles of white under the irises, and half circles of red beneath that. He manages three giant steps, knees buckling under him, the chicken held out towards Giles' mother. He sinks to the floor. Yellow foam bubbles out between his lips. A hand with dirty fingernails tries to grasp the tablecloth. The *maitre d' hotel* picks up the chicken, dusts it off, and puts it proudly on the table. Giles thinks he ought to explain the sailor to his parents, but they aren't interested; or his parents to the sailor, but he is dead.

When asked what he is going to do after the war Giles says he is going to be a solicitor. He has always assumed that he will be what his father is.

'My father's a solicitor, you see,' he says.

If you met my father you'd see that even if he thought you were a lot of vulgar unwashed yobs and oiks, you'd see that he was right.

They are impressed with the idea of Giles being a solicitor. They know it takes a lot of education.

In the sick-bay being anointed with soothing lotion Giles feels the burden of responsibility. He feels it when he thinks of home. The others talk longingly of home, he thinks longingly of Australia, and cricket all year round. But he doesn't dwell on the subject, because responsibility is something you must face up to. No use pretending you're free, and can go to Australia and be a sheep farmer, or live in a little terraced house in Liverpool and work in a factory.

The end seems to be within sight. When the ship is out of dry dock they go on patrol, three weeks out, two weeks in, mainly round the Nicobar islands. Little to see. Little to do. The Jap supply line of junks hugs the coast of Malaya. The RAF boys have been taking care of them, bombing and strafing the rows of fragile flat craft, laden with tanks and men. They look too peaceful to be a source of danger, low in the water, with billowing sails, golden brown on blue, hugging the green shore. They're tapering off now anyway. Rangoon is taken in May with hardly a shot fired. The cruiser *Haguro* is sunk in the Malacca straits. We rejoice. Though we took no part in the action we cheer ourselves hoarse when we hear about it. That's a good moment. And V.J. Day's a good moment. It's what we've been waiting for all along. There are fireworks. Some of the lads break into the rum store and set it on fire. Oh, there's shouting and singing and dancing in the streets. But all the while you're aware of the local darkies. They clap their hands, they smile, they wave. But they don't feel the same as we do. It's not their war. In the harbour the British ships let off everything they've got, flares, tracer, showering the sky with light, but on either side of them, beyond the jetty, the brightly painted fishing boats clop and murmur on the water, their colour veiled by the night, and the fishermen, barely visible at first, sit cross-legged on the sand, watching.

There are no Mums and Dads to hold hands with, kids jumping about and yelling with excitement. No pretty girls to lift in the air, their high heels kicking while you give them a big hug and a kiss, because we've all come through it together. There are just a lot of sailors a long way from home, and the only thing they can do is get royally drunk, and that they do, and some of them get a bit wild and set the camp on fire, but they're good lads. Everyone goes a bit wild at times. You can't be surprised after all they've been through.

We heard some pretty strange stories about the taking of Singapore a few days later. Our lads had to disembark among a sea of floating bodies, mainly local people, killed by the Japs as they retreated. They'd already been in the water several days and were swollen and purple, eyes gone, flesh starting to rot off them. The river was full of them. Our lads had to push the bodies aside, rolling over and bumping against each other, their beautifully coloured clothes trailing and spreading out gracefully on the water, before they could climb ashore. They fought their way through the streets, hand-to-hand fighting, dodging round corners, a sniper in each window for all they knew. Make for the Cathay Cinema are the orders. A big white building, fairly high, at the back of the town.

You can't miss it. When our lads get here, breathless, filthy, eyes sharp and bright, fresh blood on their hands and conscience, there in the foyer of the cinema, heavily sandbagged, among the toughest of the Yorks and Lancs Airborne Division, directing operations is the Staff Officer, red tabs and all, wearing rouge and lipstick. Round red patches of rouge and a cupid's bow mouth. Bloody good job he was doing too. Like I said, they've been through a lot, these lads.

There's still sporadic fighting, and a hell of a lot of clearing up to do. It'll be a long time before some of us get home. Those who were in first go home first. The *Patusan* goes home before the end of the year. Giles is left behind. He is sad to leave the *Patusan*, his ship for two years. But some of his chums are still with him. They are sent up to the rest camp at Dieter Lawa for a couple of weeks. It's beautiful up there, not too hot. Huge rolling hills, more like mountains really, open forests for what seems like hundreds of miles. This is the land of the tea plantations, but not many of them are being worked now. There is a WRNS rest camp next door, separated of course by a couple of fences and a space patrolled by dogs. The dodge with the dogs is you slide a shutter through your fence until it touches the opposite one, and when the dog comes up to investigate you slide one through on the other side so you've got the poor bugger nicely trapped and can stroll through to visit your lady friend. Trouble is there aren't enough Wrens to go round. The lads miss their wives and their girls back home. They talk about them, but not as much as you might think, healthy young blokes cooped up together.

There's a lot along the lines of:

'I wouldn't mind being on a desert island with Vera Lynn,' and:

'That Mona Lot, I'd make her moan!'

Giles doesn't miss girls. He's never had one. Never thought of it really. There are quite a lot like him. It's the brighter sparks who stroll off to visit the Wrens, and visit the brothels in Colombo when they're back down in the plains again. While they are in Dieter Lawa an Ensa troupe comes round, a couple of girl singers and a comedian, and that's the high spot for most of the lads. Those girl singers keep them happy for months. And it is the next few months that are the worst.

The war is over. Nobody wants them to fight any more. Nobody knows what to do with them. They are in limbo, commonly known as HMS *Mayina*, transit camp. They don't actually belong anywhere. They've been turned out of their ship. Other sailors, weary and battle scarred, are slinging their hammocks and working parts of ship on HMS *Patusan*. The iron plates of the deck, some of them newly rivetted, all with a fresh coat of paint applied by other hands, the route from the mess deck up the familiar ladders and companionways is being trodden by someone else, as the *Patusan* retraces her path across the Indian Ocean, up the Red Sea, through the Suez Canal and the Mediterranean, no need to hug the coast of Africa, past Gibraltar, the Bay of Biscay, through the English Channel and home. Giles' imagination stops there because the *Patusan* is his home.

•

In HMS *Mayina* time passes. Slowly. In the morning lines
of men make patterns with twig brooms in the dusty road,
and then sweep them smooth again. Zigzags in the best
Royal Navy tradition. In the afternoon they have time to
think about their healing sunburn and their athlete's foot.
There are many cures for athlete's foot, but the best one is
peeing on it. The trouble with the others is they don't work.
There's something very satisfactory about using your own
pee to turn the mushy white mess between your toes into
nice healthy scabs. Waste not want not. They don't even
do their own dhobying. The native johnnies do it. They
bang the clothes with stones in the water. You'd think it
would tear them to shreds, but it doesn't. They use irons
filled with charcoal, and all the time they're doing it they're
chewing betel nut. Filthy habit. They steal you blind too,
if you give them half a chance.

Without a ship you're lost. What do ancient cities and
vanished civilisations mean to Able Seaman Trenchard and
Leading Seaman Bates? Why should they bother to go to
Kandy and see the Temple of the Tooth and a lot of daft
monks in yellow dressing gowns with their heads shaved
prancing around banging bells and waving incense? Leave
that sort of lark to foreigners and blinking officers. Giles,
if he had been an officer, would have gone to see the Temple of the Tooth, and drunk pink gins, and stayed at the
Galle Face Hotel. But he's not an officer. It's all right, he's
still safe. He complains like the rest. They long for home.
He longs for home. Red buses, wet pavements, a proper
cinema, instead of the heat and smell and flavour of the

East. The grey cliffs of Cornwall and rhododendrons in the garden. He's reprieved for a year. For nearly two years. Back to Trinco, where the deep water comes right up to the shore and the big ships are tethered like elephants grazing at the edge of the jungle, and the ants build themselves fairy tale castles to live in, made from chalk, or icing sugar.

There are still jobs to be done. Help the little buggers back on their feet. Distribute food. Ferry across a couple of destroyers for the Burmese Navy. They will be the Burmese Navy. Give it all away. From what you hear about life back home it's about time we stopped giving things away. Started looking after Number One. You get nothing but complaints from poor old Blighty. Wot no coal? No petrol? No butter? Yes, we have no bananas, *te tum te, te tum te, te tum*. And then there's the Government. And the weather. The worst winter for a hundred years, and no coal. It's hard to imagine them freezing and queuing back home as we stroll through the hot and crowded streets, or patrol the camp at night. The camp has no life at night, it's a patch of deadness. But the jungle. Even among these scrubby trees and bushes not much higher than a man, there are pure lines of movement, of vision, of sound. Those who live in the jungle are alive. Their lives reach out to touch or avoid each other. We strain our eyes in the darkness and breathe out fear. We long to bury our eyes in yellow light, our noses in smoke, our ears in the soupy comfort of Vera. Can they imagine the jungle back home? Can they imagine me, standing here, bladder twitching, separated from my pals by a wall and a patch of asphalt, with the life of the jungle breathing on me like the open mouth of a great black snake, one flick of the tongue and I'm wiped away, boots and rifle too?

SEVEN

It's so small, England. It's so fucking small. You feel like bleeding Gulliver. Is that why they called Lilliput 'Lilliput'? You clump around in your uniform, and the girls look at you as if you were some sort of wild man from Borneo. What's it all about, then? We're the boys in blue, lifeline of the Empire. Last time we was back home you loved us, so what's the matter now? You have to be the King himself to get a cup of tea. The rest of us get half of it in the saucer.

'I'd like to see you serve a cup of tea like that on the mess deck in the middle of a force nine gale, my girl. You'd soon hear about it!'

'Don't you "my girl" me. You're not in the Navy now, you know.'

Yes, we know.

Demob clothes.

They sit in the cafe and look at each other. Halliwell, Bates and Trenchard. The tea is pale, tepid, grey. White cups chipped and greasy, with lipstick smeared on the rim.

The bowl of sugar in the centre of the table has a hard crust on top and round the edges. If you dig deep with a spoon the sugar is whiter, and pours more freely. Their minds go back to a thick sweet brew made in a bucket and drunk out of tin mugs. Coming back into harbour after some nasty weather and cleaning up. Sweeping, painting, polishing, stowing away. Making everything shipshape.

The waitress is very young, not more than sixteen. She is very pretty. Like a caricature of a pin up she has a blonde quiff lolling over her forehead, and pageboy curls down to her shoulders. Her cheeks are round and smooth, and her lips a bright red bow. Her bosom sticks out in the accepted manner like twin torpedoes, and her calves are cheeky and round. But she doesn't peer at them under her eyelashes with a come hither smile. She ignores them. Have all these pictures for all these years been lying, then? Doesn't a nice girl like a sailor any more, even in his demob suit? She perches on the edge of a table and buries her nose in a movie magazine. There is a ladder in her lisle stocking and she is wearing a pair of fluffy bedroom slippers that might have been blue several Christmasses ago. Harry Bates rattles the money in his pocket and goes over to the counter where packets of cigarettes and a few bars of chocolate are piled up for sale.

'Ten Players please Miss.'

She slides off the table and comes round the other side of the counter without bothering to look up from her magazine. Her hand feels its way along the counter like a blind man's until it comes to the right shaped pile. She detaches one packet and shoves it across the counter, all without looking up.

'Nutty?' says Bates over his shoulder to the others. He tries to make out who she is so engrossed in reading about. Jimmy Stewart is it? Difficult to tell upside down.

'Wish I looked like Jimmy Stewart.' He doesn't even bother to say it. She wouldn't even notice if the whole place was full of bleeding film stars. She just wants to be out of that caff, and who can blame her?

'And I'll have a tuppeny bar of chocolate.'

Ah, she looks up. Her eyes focus. There's a man standing in front of her.

'Got your coupons?'

'My what?'

It's not a man, it's some sort of mental defective who doesn't know what country he's in.

'Yer coupons. You can't buy sweets without coupons.'

Twenty seven years old and he blushes like a kid at school up in front of teacher for doing something dirty like wetting his pants. He's got a brand new ration book in his pocket, each page divided up into horrible little rectangles.

'I won't bother.' He pushed across the money for his cigarettes and slinks back to the table.

'Better be getting on my way,' says Halliwell. They finish their tea and push their chairs back, ostentatiously leaving sixpence under the saucer for their pin up.

''Ow much are you getting for your next movie, Jim?' asks Bates loudly as they go out the door, but even that doesn't make her look up.

The air is raw outside, and the sky yellowish grey. They pull their collars up round their ears and thrust their hands deep into their pockets. The strings of their kitbags cut deep into their shoulders. It is spring, but lumps of snow, filthy and hard as stone are still lying in the gutters and vacant lots. Opposite the cafe the whole side of the street is rubble, flattened out, covered with weeds and snow, without even a fence round it. Next to the cafe itself is a gap where one house had gone four, five, six years ago. The wallpaper still clings in mildewed strips to the walls. On every floor there is a neat little black grate, and from the chimney at the top, in the wall that is shared with the house that has the cafe on the ground floor, a worm of black smoke ascends. The three sailors stare at the desolation that stretches round them, further than they can see, over the whole of England.

'What this place needs is a bloody good buffer.'

'It's been like this for bleeding years.'

'Get a few thousand matelots on to it, we'd have the place cleaned up in no time.' But nobody asks them.

Halliwell takes a train for Liverpool, Harry Bates goes to see a girlfriend in Croydon, and Trenchard wonders what the hell he's going to do.

He ought to go down to Cornwall. Ought he? Maybe he ought to stay in London. He takes a tube to Sloane Square and walks down the King's Road. The Classic Cinema's still there showing a film with Margaret Lockwood. So's the Unity Restaurant. He goes to see Margaret Lockwood. When he comes out it's getting dark. The houses and shops down the King's Road look small and solid. It must have been grim during the blackout. It's not exactly sparkling now.

He goes into a pub and orders a double Scotch. That's better. That's where the life is. He puts down his kitbag and moves his shoulders uneasily in his brown utility suit. His mother won't like it. She probably wouldn't recognise him now, leaning against the bar drinking his whisky. Only commercial travellers wear brown suits. Her eyes travel over him with no change of expression. She looks round the bar, holding her bag neatly in both hands. Her face looks blank and slightly anxious. She turns round to leave.

'It really is too bad,' she says. 'I come all the way up to town to meet him and he isn't even here. He knows I never go into pubs alone.'

There's a regular leaning on the corner of the bar, drinking a pint of bitter. He is middle-aged, and wears an old army greatcoat. His face is very lined, with reddish patches on the cheeks and nose, and great bags under his eyes. He turns to an old woman sitting on a green leather bench with a bottle of Guinness.

'Where do you think he's come from dear?'

She munches her false teeth and smiles.

'Nice and brown, i'n't 'e?'

'Just come back from Ceylon, as a matter of fact. Trinco.'

The regular opens his packet of Senior Service, lying on the bar, and feels for a cigarette.

'Did you speak to him dear?' he says to the old woman. 'I didn't.'

The packet is empty.

'Have one of mine, sir,' says Giles.

'Sir,' says the regular, taking a cigarette with fingers stained like tortoiseshell, from gold to black with nicotine.

'Sir. We have here a public schoolboy, but not, I gather, and officer. Interesting.'

Giles stays in the pub till closing time. He forms an ambition. The ambition is to become a regular. If you're a regular you have a place and everyone knows you. After closing time they all go with a woman called Margaret to a house where she is staying. It's not her house, but she's staying there.

Giles has in his kitbag a bottle of whisky intended for his parents. Someone else brings several bottles of beer. The house is in Margaretta Terrace. It's a pretty house, with a tree in the front garden and a lot of nice antique furniture in the drawing room.

One of the regulars is a journalist called Stephen. He is very drunk, but before he is sick he has to phone in a story to his paper.

'Quiet everybody, Stephen's on the phone.'

Giles sits beside Margaret on a red velvet chaise longue. Stephen collapses onto the floor and pulls the phone towards him; supporting himself on one arm he dials the number, then he starts retching. For half a minute while the phone rings he heaves, groans with great sucking intakes of breath, gags, and swallows down his bile. The room is otherwise silent. The audience pauses, in arrested motion, arms half raised, breath held, concentrating on the movement of Stephen's diaphragm.

'News Desk please.'

He dictates in a loud clear voice, pitched half an octave lower than his usual speech, two perfectly formed paragraphs, each sentence containing several subordinate clauses, about Sir Hugh Dalton's speech in the House earlier that evening. Punctuation is provided by liquid heavings and rumblings of nausea. The glottal gag. A titanic struggle between the voluntary and the involuntary forces of the body. At the News Desk a young man waits with his pencil raised. No one moves to fetch a basin. When he has finished someone says,

'Bloody good journalist, Stephen.'

Margaret puts her hand on Giles' thigh.

'Are you a fairy?'

'No,' says Giles. He laughs, ''fraid I'm normal.'

Margaret has thick black hair and heavy limbs. The centre of her body is tiny and thin, like a wasp. If she wrapped those limbs round you they would wind themselves round your body like a green and juicy plant, sucking the life out of you. In the bath house in Colombo girls with flat brown faces and naked breasts press and knead your body. 'Please do not touch the attendants,' says the notice on the green tiled wall, half obscured by steam.

They drink the whisky and beer, and play some American records on the gramophone. Stephen and the regular argue for a long time about US Aid to Greece. Margaret and a middle-aged Polish woman argue about art and experience.

'No one who has not experienced the horrors of such a life has the right to express them.'

A man and a girl argue fiercely in a corner. He gets up and looks through the books in the bookcase, making a pile on the mantlepiece, while the girl weeps. Margaret shouts across the room.

'Oh for God's sake leave them alone.'

'I've got to eat,' says the man, turning round in surprise. 'And anyway, what does Francis know about first editions? He won't even notice they've gone.'

The Polish woman says to Giles,

'Why won't he let her have the child? What difference will it make?'

Giles goes into the kitchen to look for some food. In a paper bag under the table there are two onions, soft and brownish, with green shoots growing out of them. Ah yes, here's a cupboard with a pot of Marmite and a piece of stale bread. Margaret follows him. She leans against the door jamb holding a glass of whisky, barring the escape route with her legs.

'I bet you're really a fairy.'

He puts down the pot of Marmite.

'No I'm not, honestly.'

She advances. He leans against the sink. An arm snakes round his neck.

'I say, do you have any marge?'

'Oh blast!'

'Margaret!'

'Don't be filthy.'

The man with the books has thrown a glass of beer over the regular. He picks up the weeping girl.

'Stop blubbing, you silly bitch.'

'What did he say?'

'I'll bring them both round at three tomorrow.'

The weeping girl is led out into the darkness. The Polish woman goes as well. So does the regular, giving Giles a funny look.

'I say,' says Giles, 'I think I've missed my train.'

'You can sleep in here.' Margaret shows him a bedroom upstairs. Next door Stephen is sprawled across an unmade double bed, still in his clothes. Giles is a bit pissed. He's excited. He's back home. The four years in the navy seem extraordinary. He wished his mates were here tonight. He'd show them that the Lord knew how to live. He goes down half a flight of stairs to the bathroom to pee, and then gets into bed. He hasn't slept in a real bed for more than two years. The sheets are by no means clean, and a faint smell of vomit comes from under the pillow, but the bed is infinitely softer than a hammock. His pyjamas are deep in the bottom of his kitbag so he keeps on his vest and pants.

After a few minutes Margaret comes in.

'Honestly Stephen's so drunk. I can't wake him up. He is a bore.' She takes off her nightdress and gets into bed. There's not much room. She puts her hand inside his pants.

'For God's sake take these things off.'

His little willie is standing bolt upright in surprise. 'Jolly good.'

Giles takes off his pants and rolls over on top of Margaret. His willie is between her legs.

'Oh gosh, oh I say, that's marvellous.'

'You didn't even get inside me, you silly idiot.'

'Frightfully sorry.'

She takes hold of his little willie, soft now, and all wet. After a few moments it gets hard again, and he rubs and bounces up and down, but comes again before he can penetrate the hairy fortress.

'For God's sake, what on earth have you been doing in the navy?' She sits up. Giles is lying on his chest, panting.

'You're not much good to a girl are you? Can you do it again?'

'Wait a minute.' Giles is enjoying himself. This is a bit of all right. After a few minutes he tries again, then goes to sleep, lower lip pushed sideways on the pillow. Margaret wriggles out of bed, picks up her nightdress and goes back to Stephen. He's still too drunk, but the bed's bigger.

Giles leaves his kitbag at Margaret's place while he pops back to Cornwall to see the Pater and get a few things sorted out. It is agreed that he shall live with his Uncle Walter in Kensington and go to a crammer's to prepare for his law exams. His father will give him an allowance. His mother gives him money for a new suit. He comes back to Margaretta Terrace wearing an old tweed jacket and a pair of grey flannel bags that he'd had when he was at school. When he rings the bell the door is opened by an elderly man with curly grey hair parted in the middle and plump, drooping jowls.

'Afternoon, sir, is Margaret in?'

The door slams shut.

Giles looks round. The tree in the garden is in the same place. He rings the bell again. The door opens.

'Frightfully sorry, but . . .'

'Margaret does not live here.'

'I left my kitbag here.'

'Hm.' Francis opens the door wider and purses his lips. He picks up the kitbag which is in the hall, opens it and feels inside.

'I just want to see what you've pinched,' he smiles sourly.

'I haven't pinched anything, sir,' says Giles.

Francis slips his hands between the bell bottoms and the rolled up jersey.

'A sailor. You're a nice boy. Come in and have a drink.'

''Fraid I'm normal, sir,' says Giles with a smile.

'Oh go away.' Francis has a headache. He throws the kitbag out and slams the door.

Giles settles in at his uncle's house. The crammers don't see much of him. Nor does his uncle. His cousins work in the city. Hugh is a stockbroker and Nancy a secretary. Sometimes he goes down to Leadenhall Street to have lunch with Hugh and stock up on the latest dirty jokes and shaggy dog stories. Sometimes he takes Nancy to Chelsea in the evenings. Sometimes one of Nancy's friends asks him to a dance. He doesn't learn much law, but he does work hard at being a regular. The only trouble is that it's expensive. You almost always find by the end of the evening that you don't have a bean left. Still, people are pretty decent about standing a chap a beer now and then. He comes across Margaret in the Six Bells quite often, and she's nice to him. She introduces him to an afternoon drinking club in a basement beneath a furniture shop, to fill in those empty hours between three and five-thirty. Sometimes they go to the cinema instead and spend a romantic afternoon with Michael Wilding, Anna Neagle, Margaret Lockwood, Vivien Leigh, in cravats and wigs and flounces, sucking and squeezing each other. There are lots of quiet little alleys where there's a wall or a couple of dustbins to lean against and pull off her knickers and wriggle in. He knows where to go now, no signpost needed.

'Wot no knickers?' says Mr. Chad, peering over the wall. Margaret draws him with a piece of chalk, shrieking with laughter. 'No more coupons!'

•

There were other girls as well as Margaret. There were always girls to be met in pubs or at parties, or even walking down the street. There was a grand freemasonry of the . . . what were they? The young? the free? Those anyway who think that the world has changed, who are not going to be bound by the conventions of the past. Those who are not destroyed by effort and the prolonged weariness of war. Those who can still be jerked into life by alcohol, by sex, by argument. Those who are not absorbed by the antics of the old black cat Socialism, patting with a timid greying paw instead of slashing with claws out and dripping red.

Unfortunately Giles' uncle and aunt see no beauty in this freedom. They are working to rebuild the old world, and they are not weary. Giles staggers down to breakfast at half past ten as usual, after a thick night.

'Really, Giles, this is too bad. You owe your parents more consideration than this.'

Giles tries to focus his eyes on the coffee, but it has been cleared away.

'Mr Freeman rang yesterday afternoon and said you hadn't been in for ten days, and the exam is next week.'

'Yes, I've been worried about that.'

Giles has shaved sketchily, but his shirt hasn't been changed for some time, and his Old Rugbeian tie is a greasy crumpled piece of string. His clear brow furrows with momentary anxiety.

'Trouble is I find it pretty hard work.'

'Well,' says his aunt triumphantly, 'if you'd study a bit more you wouldn't find it so hard. This is the third time you've sat this exam. You never do any reading. You're out every night. I don't know what you do with yourself.'

'You can't work all the time. A chap's got to have a bit of relaxation.'

'Well, I hope you're not going to let your father down.'

Giles sits over his books for a week, and takes the exam. Phew! After that a fellow deserves a bit of fun. They are jolly glad to see him at the Six Bells. There's a pretty girl called Laura who giggles at everything you say to her. Giles takes her to eat at a place called the Magic Lantern, where there's a pianist with a bushy black beard and pictures on the walls of dogs wearing clothes and sitting up on bar stools with glasses in front of them.

'Rather a super place. I'm celebrating. Just passed my law exams.' Giles asks the pianist to play 'Open the Door Richard,' and hums energetically. They have rabbit *fricassée* and treacle tart and custard. Laura is only sixteen. After dinner they go back to the Six Bells. Margaret is there with a new boyfriend.

'Come on,' she says, 'we're all going back to Tim's place.'

Tim's place is a house off Belgrave Square. It is mostly one large room. Tim has his own boat, and smuggles brandy across from France. He is beautifully dressed in a pale blue jacket with padded shoulders, and an American button-down shirt. He hands Giles a large glass of brandy.

'Rugby? I was at Eton.'

'Actually it was Borstal,' says Margaret. Tim smiles. At half past twelve he leaves. 'Make yourselves at home.'

Laura is asleep on the floor, curled up on her side. Several people are arguing about the morality of smuggling, getting more heated as they finish one bottle of brandy and open another.

'You've got to give the Government a chance.'

'Bloody war's been over for four years.'

'Well, frankly if someone's got the guts to get hold of bananas and nylons when people are absolutely dying for them, and people have got the money to pay for them, I don't see what's wrong.'

'Or brandy.'

'He's a spiv. He's an absolute spiv.'

'He's divine.'

'The thing is, it's against the law.'

'Who the hell cares about the law?'

Francis and a young sailor are having an argument in a corner. Francis puts his head on one side, coyly. Soon it's nearly three o'clock. Margaret turns out the lights and says, 'I'm going to bed.' She puts a coat over Laura. Giles stretches out on the floor. Someone else is on the sofa. When the lights are out the large arched window in the far wall shows pale, if you don't look at it directly. Tim still isn't back, so Giles thinks he will go and look for Margaret. He feels his way through the dark room, bumping his shins against the coffee table.

'Blast.'

The lino of the passage is cold under his feet. He's taken his shoes off. He creeps upstairs, but someone has got there before him. A voice says,

'Come on, you bitch, use your tongue.' It sounds like the regular. That's funny. Giles had always thought the regular was queer. He creeps down again. Laura is still curled up like a baby, deeply asleep. Her body turns over but her head lolls back with an inarticulate gurgle. He explores the girl on the sofa, whose name he does not know. She wakes up with a giggle. 'Sh.' He finally manages to push her skirt up and undo his trousers. She's jolly hard to get into. She must be a virgin. But he does it in the end.

Trouble is, the celebration was a bit premature. Giles has failed his exams again. His father is coming up to London. They are going to have lunch at the old Judge's club, of which Giles' father is a country member. It is a beautiful day. The sky is blue and the air clear. Stone and asphalt are a warm, pleasant grey. The details of buildings clearly etched. White clouds sail briskly across the sky. Red buses trundle along their familiar routes. Giles strolls down Pall Mall. He is a gentleman. He is going to have lunch at the club and discuss his future with the Pater. He is a few minutes early. He climbs the steps and pushes through the glass revolving doors.

'Morning, sir.'

'Morning, White; I'm going to meet my father.'

'Shall I tell him you're in the bar, sir?'

White is in his mid-fifties. An NCO during the war. Giles knows the way. He's been here before. The hall is marble, with an imposing staircase that divides into a Y halfway up, decorated with the busts of judges. Giles makes for the small bar on the ground floor. It is quiet, almost empty. The barmaid is new and Irish. Giles leans over the bar, rich reddish brown wood, polished by elbows and skivvies. The bottles make a halo round the head of the barmaid.

'Double whisky please.'

'Are you a member?'

'No. but my father's coming in a minute. My grand-father was a member here for years. Old Judge Trenchard.'

'Oh yes, I've heard of him. Didn't know him myself.'

Giles carries his drink over to a table. He picks up a copy of the *Times*, and turns to the crossword. He takes out his pen.

Austin Trenchard has several people to see in London. He would prefer to forget about his son. While he was in the navy it had been quite easy to forget about him. You've got a duty to your own children, though. He comes into the bar adjusting his collar and planning his method of approach. He has promised the boy's mother he will not be too hard on him.

His son is there before him, sitting deep in a leather armchair, with one leg crossed over the other, the *Times* folded on his knee, and a large whisky at his elbow, like a caricature of a clubman. His shoes are cracked and dirty with the laces trailing. His hair an uncombed bush, his shirt collar undone, and his tie a chewed string. He looks up and smiles with boyish exuberance.

'Hullo, Pater.' He jumps to his feet, putting down the paper. He has underlined several of the clues, but not pro-gressed any further with the crossword.

Mr Trenchard orders a tomato juice, and pays for both drinks.

'Good to see you, sir. How's mother?'

'You look like a tramp. How dare you come to my club in that state.'

Giles passes his hand over his hair. 'I'll get a haircut this p.m.'

'You would make your mother sick. You look disgusting.'

Giles tried to think of something that would make her feel better. 'I'm sorry about the exam.'

'So am I,' says his father. 'I understand that you wasted your time here just like you wasted it everywhere else.'

'I should do better next time,' says Giles. 'I think I'm beginning to get the hang of it all now.'

'Next time you'll take it from home. You'll be articled to me, and I'll see that you work.'

Giles swallows down his whisky. He realises that he has upset his father. They go in to lunch. To get to the dining room they have to go past the kitchens and up the back stairs. The front passage is still out of commission through bomb damage. Even if you could get the materials or workmen for repairs the club couldn't afford it, with money so tight these days. The back passage is damp and dark. The carpet is so soaked with grease that it is almost shiny. The walls are stained by years of cooking. They haven't been painted since well before the war. The cooks move lethargically, pallid and unshaven, hands and forearms unnaturally white. The layers of smells remind Giles of the *Patusan*, and he smiles at the cooks in fellowship, but they do not smile back. They walk up one flight of stairs beside the ancient openwork iron lift; dust lies half an inch thick on each cross piece. This is the unwiped arse of the establishment.

The dining room is huge and cavernous. Great pillars support an ornate Edwardian plasterwork ceiling forty feet above the heads of the diners. In an effort to make them appear more friendly the pillars and parts of the ceiling have been painted pink. Not many people are eating lunch. Men sit alone in dark suits, chewing steadily with a paper propped in front of them, or two or three at a table, talking in low voices. Through the huge windows, slightly open, comes a breath of sweet air, and the sounds of traffic, and movement. Because of the manpower shortage there have been waitresses instead of waiters for the last several years. The *maître d'* is an Italian ex-prisoner of war. The waitresses are mostly middle-aged and cheerful. It is surprising to find them there, so tiny in the immense, pompous room, with their bright blue overalls and dyed blonde curls, and frilly white caps and aprons. They are never without their lipstick and a friendly smile. Quite a few of the club members know all about their grown up sons and daughters. They're ever so lucky. They earn three pounds ten a week and get to meet all sorts of famous people. Not that anyone she knows outside the club has actually heard of them, but the other members tell her they're famous. Betty stands beside them, her lipstick smudged by an early lunch of shepherd's pie and tapioca pudding.

'The steak and kidney's good, sir,' she says. Mr Trenchard pushes the menu aside.

'Bring us some *hors d'oeuvre* and a plate of cold beef,' he says. He doesn't order any wine.

'Your mother said I wasn't to be too hard on you,' he tells his son. 'But you're a disgrace to the family. You made a mess of school. You didn't even get a commission in the navy, and now look at you.' Giles takes a mouthful of egg mayonnaise. There is a dark yellow rim round the edge of the dish, and the mayonnaise has started to ferment.

'But lots of people fail their law exams, Pater. A chap I met at the crammer's had failed thirteen times.' His father grinds his teeth and drinks a glass of water. He swallows half a hard-boiled egg.

'You are a miserable worm.'

From half way across the room they look a fine couple. A distinguished middle-aged man having a heart to heart talk with his son. Decent looking young fellow, with a pleasant open face. He'd never forget to give you a smile and a thank you.

'I've met some jolly interesting people while I've been in London,' says Giles, seeking to retrieve ground. 'Journalists and people like that. It's been quite an education.'

In Cornwall journalists are part of the audience at the bar of the Imperial Hotel. They print witticisms that are made in court, so long as they're not made by the defendant or the witnesses. They are eager to report the doings of the Under Sheriff of the county, who might occasionally buy them a drink. The editor is a friend, and he is invited to dinner. Nobody could get much education from them. In London they're probably all layabouts and Reds, the fact that they associate with his son only goes to prove it.

'Your brother was Captain of the Rugger team, and a Prefect.'

They'd been doubtful about sending Robert to Rugby after the farce with Giles. They had been afraid that he would suffer for it. But things had worked out fine. They had just about forgotten his elder brother after four years, though they remembered him later.

'I thought I might play a bit of cricket while I'm at home,' says Giles. 'Try to make the county team.'

'Hmm.'

The beef is very good. Tender and underdone. One of the members has a farm in Scotland.

'I've stopped your allowance. You can pack up your things and drive down with me tomorrow.'

Farewell the King's Road. Farewell the Six Bells. Farewell Laura and Margaret, and the regulars. I have been neglecting my responsibilities. I must take them up again. It would be nice to get in some more cricket this summer. Giles had spent several afternoons at Lords the previous summer, when he could drag himself away from his books, or Margaret, or the cinema, but he hadn't been able to do much playing. Lunch is over. Coffee is served downstairs.

'Jolly good lunch, Pater, thanks.'

Mr Trenchard has a splitting headache. His hands shake slightly. He imagines himself at the wheel of his Triumph, scorching down the road with bared teeth. He sits at the bar and drinks double brandies while Giles goes back to Kensington to take leave of his aunt and uncle. In the evening he takes leave of the regulars.

'Had lunch with my old man today. He was jolly decent really. Offered me a job.'

He lives in Cornwall. He works in his father's office. He is not satisfactory. He is hardly ever seen there. When he is there they don't give him much to do because he'll probably mess it up. During the summer he spends most afternoons playing cricket. He feels his father's hostility breathing at him from the darkness of hotel bars as he makes a beautiful stroke to leg. He practices at the nets as long as he can find anyone to bowl for him. Here father,

I offer you this beautiful straight bat, this supple twist of the body, this rich, pure and resonant sound as the ball hits the wooden bat and soars on its truncated flight to freedom. Again and again my red bird, my heart, flies up into the blue sky, and is snatched down, wrapped and embraced, its purpose killed, its freedom destroyed by the brown net. Brown net in which I am imprisoned like a fish. I turn, I twist, I leap, beautiful and pure in my motion, infinite in my demands, my body turns, my bat points up, I am white, I am perfect. My movements are silent and secret. My language is the language of a fish. No one can hear what I say. I am desperate. I am divine. I am impenetrable.

In the afternoons his mother's room is empty, scented, dull. A film of powder lies on the dressing table. A thin woollen scarf with yellow and mauve flowers on it smells of powder. The carpet is cold. The air is cold. The mirror on the dressing table has two wings which can move backwards and forwards. In them can be seen a young man with a string of pearls in his hand. He holds them against his cheek. The window is open. A breath of warm air and the smell of cut grass come in from the garden. He holds the pearls to his face. His skin is lightly tanned, his eyes greyish blue, with fine lines around them. His lips are not sensitive. They are too muscular. Their expression is pleasant. They are the lips of a young sportsman, friendly and straightforward. His mother accuses the maid of stealing the pearls. 'You have to lock everything up, can't leave anything lying about.' Later they are recovered from a shop in Plymouth. The whole affair is hushed up. They have difficulty in getting another maid.

Giles is in a difficult position. He doesn't have quite that forward momentum that his brother has. Robert is going out to Australia before doing his National Service. He thinks seriously about his life. Each alternative is weighty, and to be considered. Giles is puzzled. He sits on a bench holding his tennis racquet in both hands and looking at the ground. He had desired Australia, but he had not been free to consider her. It is difficult to understand Robert's greater freedom. The life of the household revolves round his decisions.

Their father can no longer look Giles in the face. In the office he never speaks to him. He is given the work of an office boy. His mother can often be caught staring at him with a look of bewildered surprise. She offers him food in a loud voice, with her head turned away.

'I'm afraid there is no more butter, dear. Only marge for the rest of the week.'

He is tested for Cornwall and selected. It's not first class cricket, but if he has a good season there might be a chance of playing for Somerset next year. His parents do not consider cricket a serious way of life. If Robert played cricket it would be serious. He is mentioned, though, in the local press; and his name comes up at luncheons.

'Lovely straight bat that boy of yours. Navy, was he?'

His parents come to see a home game, against Devon. Nothing has ever been said about the pearls, stolen and then recovered, or the maid, falsely accused. His mother has not worn them since the incident, though she looks at them often in the blue leather jewel case. The white figure of her son moves purposefully across the green grass. He leans forward as he walks. The pads make his legs look prehistoric, giantlike. He swings his bat jauntily. Small boys change the number on the scoreboard. The concentration demanded is continual, but not too intense. It allows time for handstands, and Sharps toffees. Trenchard 1. Oh the freedom and exhilaration of the bat slicing through the air, and the firm step forward with the whole weight of the body and the ball sailing towards the pavilion for six and a spattering of applause. The batsman flexes his shoulders and his neck, moving his head from side to side. His arms are strong, the muscles move freely. The head is firmly balanced on top of the spine, the joints of the shoulders move smoothly in their sockets. All shipshape and pusser fashion. A lovely piece of work. By the end of the afternoon it is Trenchard 73 not out. He is the hero of the day. His parents do not see his triumph, because they left after tea to have drinks with some other local bigwigs. They might have said, 'That son of ours looked well on his way to getting a century. Probably would have done if it had been a two day match.' But they didn't. His mother admires his picture in the paper though.

'Darling, you look so handsome in your whites. You did awfully well.'

She smiles at him. She gives him a kiss on the cheek. She has forgiven him for the pearls. He's her dear boy. He didn't mean it.

•

The summer is good. There are plenty of pubs, and girls and beer. Beer tastes good after a long day's work, when your head rings slightly from the sun and the air, and the sweat is raw on your skin. Girls taste good too, behind a hedge or on the beach. They are the girls he meets in pubs, eager and pert, in gangs of three and four, so that they have to be pursued in gangs too. They reinforce and protect each other. They smoke cigarettes provocatively, their red lips leaving kiss shapes on the cork tips, their glasses, the air. They breathe forth a scented cloud of sexuality. He never takes out the daughters of his parents' friends. Their hands are cold, their voices apologetic. When he is with them something nags at his mind, probably the office, where he shows up occasionally in the mornings. It does seem a bit wrong that he should get a pay packet on Fridays, just like the others who have been sitting there every day all through the week. On the other hand it also seems a bit wrong that he can't spend as much time as he'd like practising his hook and pull shots, both strokes where he can compensate for his lack of stature by his speed, and mastery of which might make all the difference when he tries out for Somerset next year. Some of his friends have much the same problems.

'My Pater's not too keen on cricket.'

'Nor's mine.'

'Trouble is, I can't do anything else.'

'Nor can I.'

Nobody has much money. Not many of them have cars, or if they do they can't use them because petrol's still very scarce. The summer's all right. The winter's bad though. Whenever he comes into the office he feels out of place and guilty. His father looks at him and says nothing. His mother wrinkles her forehead and puts her hand on his arm.

'Why don't you do some studying darling? Your father would be so pleased.' Giles stares at his law books, and they stare back at him.

During the Assizes his father arranges for Giles to be his Junior in Court, and have lunch afterwards with the Judge. Giles forgets, and spends the morning in a pub with a cricketing acquaintance.

'Great place, Australia. I spent a couple of years there during the war. Not much cricket then of course, but we got in a few scratch games. Beautiful ground, Sydney. Most beautiful cricket ground in the world.'

After that he thinks he'd better go to London. He borrows some money from his mother's bag. He bumps into Stephen, the journalist, in a pub, and dosses down at his place for a few days. Stephen's place is a flat in Paddington, shared with two other journalists. Even Giles notices that it is dirty, but with relief. He is to sleep in the sitting room. When he opens a cupboard a mountain of filthy shirts and underclothes falls out. The dirt has more life than the cloth, and is devouring it. There is a cold, metallic, suffocating smell. Stephen has led a pampered life. He has never discovered the various processes by which things that have become dirty are made clean. He is a little surprised by the filth that surrounds him, but hopes that eventually it will go away. On the piano is a half-eaten tin of cat food and a loaf of bread. Stephen's lunch. Giles admires Stephen very much. He and his friends talk for hours about America, and the Marshall Plan, and India and Pakistan. They know a tremendous amount. Giles listens, without saying much. Sometimes girls come round. One of them has short black hair, and is in love with Stephen, but marries an Earl instead. They eat sausages, and spam sandwiches, and porridge, and drink enormous quantities of beer. After a couple of weeks Giles has run out of money, but luckily he has a chequebook. The landlord of the pub down the road cashes him a cheque. So does Stephen. They both bounce. Stephen says,

'Don't worry old chap, pay me back when you've got some money. But you'd better not stay here any longer. Friend of mine is coming over from India. Splendid fellow. We put him in prison for five years before the war.'

'I was afraid of it,' says the family doctor over dinner. 'Even when he was a small boy. He's no good.'

'He deserves to be shot.'

'He's got such a sweet nature.'

'I'm not having him in the county.'

'The main thing is, what are you going to do with him?'

The law, it is felt, is a dangerous choice for Giles. He does not seem to understand which side of it he is meant to be on. In the end a job is found for him in Hampshire. An old friend of his father's, for whom his father had once done a favour, has an estate agent's business in Romsey. Stratton and Ferry, in the Market Place, by the Abbey.

Giles decides to turn over a new leaf. Start a new life.

'It's just that I wasn't suited for law. Never was any good at exams.'

His mother gives him five pounds and kisses his cheek reproachfully.

'Do try not to let your father down dear; he's so disappointed you're not going into the firm.'

Part of the burden has been lifted from his shoulders. Romsey is pleasant and grey and slow. He doesn't mind going into the office. Mr Stratton is friendly, and helps him find digs in a little Georgian house in the High Street.

'Mrs Boone'll look after you.'

He shares an office with a very decent fellow named Dawney, a local farmer's son, about his own age. Dawney loves horses and sailing, and keeps a small boat down at Bucklers Hard.

He drinks Strong's beer in the White Hart and the Dolphin. He tells weary ladies with small children and tentative elderly couples that there are no modern three-bedroomed houses close to a good bus route on their books, and drives them out to see pretty, damp cottages with the roof falling in, that might soon be on the mains. In the summer they quite often buy them. It's pleasant getting to know the surrounding countryside. Being able to put a name to someone in most of the villages you drive through. Holding the key to other people's houses. Having the right to knock and be let in. It's pleasant shuffling through old brown leaves on a crisp morning in early spring, puffing one's breath into the cold air, towards the white sun gleaming through the clouds. Being at home momentarily, in a strange village, a strange house, as people gaze abstractedly at breakfast not yet cleared away, and make mental patterns of furniture, and wonder about keeping hens.

Dawney has a car. His family lives well on their own bacon, eggs and butter, though they flog most of it on the side. Giles often has lunch there at the weekends. He could be said to have settled down. His mother thinks he's settled down. He's probably happier than he has been since he left the navy. Being pleasant and polite to people, involving yourself in their needs, that's not difficult. Giles finds it particularly easy to identify himself with the needs of his clients. Both with the couple who have to get out of their picturesque, damp, rotting hovel because they can't stand another winter there, and want at least £1500 for it, and with the couple who are equally desperate to find a place before next winter, and fall in love with it, nestling among the trees. It should make him the perfect estate agent.

Mr Eveling, his immediate boss, is pleased with him. Mr Eveling has twinkling eyes decorated with a pair of National Health wire spectacles, and a grey toothbrush moustache. As a sign of his approval he takes Giles on a guided tour of the Abbey.

'There's a pair of house-martins been nesting in the top of that drainpipe for years. Look, d'you see them? There they go. Come back every year.'

The main trouble with his new leaf is that the steam has gone out of Giles' cricket. He doesn't have a chance of playing for Hampshire. He goes back home to play for Cornwall as often as he can. Mr Stratton is pretty decent about it. But he doesn't even try out for Somerset. He couldn't get in enough practice.

OK, abandon this desire for excellence. Abandon this pursuit of your own natural skill. You're the same bloke whether you're on the cricket pitch or the office. The thing is to settle down. Fit in. Blend into the background. You're bloody lucky to have such a good job. Lots of fellows coming back from the war can't settle down. Not enough excitement. After never knowing what's going to happen in the next half hour for four or five years, it's pretty hard to adjust yourself to planning ahead for thirty years. The other side of the same coin is that it's hard, when you've been used to having every decision made for you: what you're going to eat, wear, think, where you're going to go, what you're going to do for every hour in the bleeding twenty four, made for you all those years, it's hard to have to suddenly decide all those minor things for yourself. You've been looked after like a baby, and then you're suddenly thrown out into the cold hard world. Giles suffers again, in retrospect, the loss of the *Patusan*. It's better to forget about ambition, and play what cricket comes your way, and when you can't play drive down to the New Forest with Dawney and a couple of girls, and end up at a pub, and go for a walk under the trees, picking up acorns and beech nuts, and trying to persuade the girl down onto a heap of dry leaves, being careful not to pick one under a holly bush.

Dawney has a fine, high colour, with a yellow down over his face that thickens into eyebrows and whiskers and hair. Giles is paler, the shadows on his face greenish and transparent. They are a fine young couple of Englishmen. By the second summer they go sailing most weekends. Up the woody waterways of the Beaulieu River, the water murky brown and deep green under the rhododendron, or out towards the Solent where the blue reflections widen. It's too far to go home for a game of cricket.

In liquid diamonds of flesh he slips through the net. Drop by drop. He doesn't change. It is still the golden afternoon. Soon he will fall through the rabbit hole into a world of perfect logic. But there's a bit of time yet.

There are still some London dances, deb dances. Dawney is not invited to these, where golden and greenish brown bloods with loud voices and thick fingers pee out ten minute streams of champagne through organs twelve inches long. In the backs of taxis their limbs, like tree trunks, fall across young girls, lifting soft and formless tits out of strapless dresses, and thrusting themselves in with a hearty laugh through layers of petticoats.

Cousin Nancy is pursuing, as a rabbit pursues a snake, the thick tipped penis of a young Guards officer. Over *Sole Veronique* and *Poires Belle Hélène* she pursues him, at the Dorchester, Grosvenor House, Hurlingham, and to disguise her desperate longing she makes up a party and invites other girls, not too pretty, and safe young men like Giles. Over the tinned peas and the *Chicken à la King* she flirts with Giles, saying as her shoulder strap slips voluptuously down her biceps, love me, love me, see I am Madame de Pompadour, I am Mary Martin, ignore my lumpy nose, my drooping shoulders, my mousy hair, the blackheads on my chin, and see the passionate riches of my nature as I throw back another glass of wine and wind my arms around the neck of my current lover, whom I would throw aside like an old glove if you would only look my way. It is the foreskin of the thick tipped penis that is thick. The outer layer of epidermis on the balls of the fingers and the lips is thick. The tongue, as Nancy finally captures it in her thin pale lips, is slack and soft. The fingers brush together like a fat woman's thighs. What excesses of emotion under her green taffeta are now unfulfilled. That is the process of learning. The matching of reality to expectation.

Giles has always struggled gamely to fulfil the expectations of others. He has none of his own. He takes Nancy to a nightclub, and holds her numbed hands and kisses her rigid cheek.

'Have some more champers, Nance. Make you feel better. Terribly thick sort of bloke anyway. You're worth ten of him.'

Stephen has decided to propose to the girl with black hair, who, not content with being the future wife of an Earl, is the daughter of a baronet. She lives in a baronial hall, in a park, in the country. Stephen, being an Englishman, and shy when it comes to matters of the heart, needs support in this mission. He and his supporters drink several pints in several pubs before they feel prepared to embark, and by the time they get on the train it is ten thirty. Luckily someone has had the foresight to slip a bottle of the hard stuff into his hip pocket. By the time they arrive at their promised land it is nearly midnight.

'Taxis? No, there bean't no taxis 'ereabouts. Them as comes 'ere walks. It's four miles by road, but if you was to go over the fields that'd make it about two and a half. Follow the path, you can't go wrong.'

Like blind men they stagger and grope their way through the shuttered streets and over the stile into the field. Their feet sink deep into the soft mud. There is the squelch of water and the smell of dung. The shadows of the hedges watch them out of the darkness. Clumps of grass scratch their ankles. Shouting with laughter they hurl things into the air to prove that they are not cowed by the darkness and the hidden spaces and the vegetation. Giles pulls his foot out of a long, sucking embrace and cannot find his shoe. They follow the path, and come to a farmyard, and go down a lane and into another field. There is no way out. There is only one gate. Unknown animals stir restlessly in the centre of the field. They creep with exaggerated caution round the outer edge of the field again, clinging onto one another's clothes and whispering loudly. After a colloquy on the far side of the field they scramble over the wall into a bed of nettles. There is a house looming not far in front of them, silent and black. Curtained. Sleeping. By someone's luminous watch it is one a.m. The party scatters to reconnoitre, then comes together again.

'No light. Must have gone to bed.'

'Is it the right house?'

'Dunno.'

'Let's knock them up and see.'

'Do you suppose, Stephen,' says someone lugubriously, 'that it will predispose her in favour of your suit to be woken up in the middle of the night by a band of mud-spattered ruffians?'

In the end it is decided that courtship at a distance is the best bet, and a few stanzas of 'A Frog He Would a Wooing Go' and 'My Heart's in the Highlands' are sung in harmony, being the only songs of which anyone can remember the tune. They walk back to the village. They get lost several times, and are attacked by the soft muzzles of cows and unexpected briars. The station is shuttered and silent. They have to wait several hours for the train, and sleep uncomfortably on the platform.

But this was all after the affair of the safe. If only Great Uncle Arthur had died six months sooner. At one moment there was Giles, despised and rejected of men because there was fifty pounds less in the safe than when Dawney went on holiday; losing his job, threats of the police, father bailing him out—all jolly unpleasant. And a few months later there was Giles with over a thousand pounds to his name thanks to Great Uncle Arthur having popped off and left him the aforementioned sum in his will. Pretty decent of the old bugger when you consider that he hadn't seen his godson and great nephew since infancy. Our parents in their infinite wisdom plan for these eventualities from the day of our birth. Anyhow, here is Giles at last able for a few months to live in the way in which he has been brought up; according to his station in life; in the manner to which his parents are accustomed. And if you can't try to emulate your parents, then who on earth can you try to emulate? The trouble is that life moves on. That Uncle Arthur having died once will not die again. And that one thousand pounds, though a solid and reasonable sum, does not last forever.

While Giles is rich he stays in Hampshire. He hires cars and goes to race meetings, and buys dinners. When his money runs out he gets odd jobs. He works as a packer for Woolworth's, and in a rice pudding factory. He borrows. He writes cheques, when he can get hold of a cheque book. It is summer again. He goes back to Cornwall and breaks into his parents' house. He creeps through the empty rooms of his home and takes all the money he can find. Then he takes the train to London. In London he stays at hotels and spends the money in pubs. But it isn't enough. He needs more. He comes down to Cornwall again. I want more, Mother, Father, I want more. He takes cameras, jewellery, cigarette lighters. Anything disposable he seizes. Secretly, silently he tiptoes off with his booty. His parents feel the blow. Blow after blow he deals them. His mother lies back gasping, her eyes rolled towards the ceiling, only the whites showing. His father's blood thickens and rises up in his veins. They are silent. Their mouths are stopped with disbelief. They are martyred. They are made mock of by the secret, hidden greed of their son. For the third time in this summer Giles comes home.

He wants to straighten things out with his father. He has sold the camera, the jewellery, the cigarette lighters, but hasn't even bothered to spend the money. He comes straight home to Daddy. As the battle lines are drawn up, how do they read? You are a disgrace. You are the black sheep of the family. If you would only let me I would like to forget that you ever existed.

I would like to fit in. I'm perfectly willing to fit in. I do whatever is asked of me. Here I am, of my own accord. A son getting things straight with his father. What more can a father ask? The resolution, this slight shift in positions which in fact is not shift at all, is that the father who would prefer to forget the existence of his son, whose body shivers and becomes rigid to prevent him from bursting out in a fury of loathing when they are in the same room, demands that the son stay at home again, and study to pass his law exams. He is in a cleft stick, an untenable position. If he cuts the boy off without a penny then bouncing cheques and pilfered possessions will follow him all the days of his life. His eyes glitter with the desperation of a strong man trapped.

Giles on the other hand, is innocent. His gaze is clear and straightforward. Give him a life to lead and he will lead it. He asks for nothing that is not the birthright of every human.

Giles stays at home until the middle of August. He plays a little cricket. He can't be said to do much studying. As his father, and his father's friends see it, he never learns. Chance after chance he's been given.

'Lot of trouble Austin's having with that eldest boy of his.'

Hard to know what to do with him. You could, of course, stop protecting him from the consequences of his own misdeeds and let the law take its course. But then you'd bring disgrace on the whole family. Make his mother the laughing stock of the town. And the boy behaves all right, on the whole, in public. He's scruffy. Doesn't seem to notice the difference between clean and dirty. But he is well-mannered.

EIGHT

In the middle of August, however, the uneasy truce comes to an end. Giles comes to London again, and this time he meets Jenifer. What trophies does he bear away with him from Cornwall? Nothing? Has two months in the bosom of his family been enough?

The King's Road in August is dead. No one is in London. There is a sleepy warmth in the streets. The pubs are half empty. Strolling down the road in the sunshine with the familiar sounds and sights tinkling at the edge of your senses is like being in a foreign city. Everything is strange. Mouths open, and there is a pause before they produce a voice.

It is in the White Hart that Giles meets Jenifer. In fact it is she who notices him first. She is sitting under a window with her mother, drinking a glass of lemonade. Her hands are clasped in her lap. She is like a squirrel with a hoard of nuts. She and her mother are great friends. They only have each other.

'Oh Mums, do you see that young man over there? He looks terribly nice.'

'You may wonder,' says the mother at a later date, 'why I allowed my daughter to frequent public houses. But she doesn't like dancing, and where else, in Chelsea, was she to meet young people?'

The mother, if such a thing is possible, is a double widow. She is the widow of a bomber pilot, and an RAF chaplain. She had hoped to marry her daughter off from the haven of a country parsonage, but her plans were destroyed, together with her second husband, during the last few days of the war.

Beside them, on a bench, is sitting a Chelsea Pensioner. With his round smiling face and bright red uniform marking him out as one of the chosen few, a hallowed part of the local scene, he is a safe compromise between the shame and disappointment of sitting alone, and the hazards of talking to just anyone in a public place. He enjoys their company and is flattered by it. They are plucky little ladies.

'Oh, Penny, do you know that young man over there, the good looking one with the curly hair?'

'I've spoken to him. A very pleasant young gentleman.'

'You forward little minx!' Her mother takes another sip of pink gin and giggles. She is bright. She is eager. She never gives up trying. The bags under her eyes are marked by deep black lines. She is always attractively dressed in spite of the limitations of the time.

'Shall I bring him over?' asks the elderly cupid. Jenifer shrugs her shoulders. 'I don't mind.'

She and her mother become engrossed in a conversation about clothes.

'Oh, I think a dirndl would be really sweet. As full as possible.'

Jenifer is small and plump, with brown hair softly waving. She has a high forehead, and round cheeks, and a pursed mouth. She has beautiful hands, with tapered fingers and no bony knuckles. Queen's hands. Suitable for rings.

Like sweet spiders the mother and daughter suck in the young man. They combine, they separate, they dance a minuet of joy around him. They are poor. They have no connections. Jenifer, though as charming as any other nineteen-year-old girl, is not invited to deb dances. Two families have slipped through their fingers. They are adrift, and anxiety underlies all their pleasures.

Giles, you can tell at a glance, is a young man from a good family. He has charming manners. He's not a bit snobbish. He buys them drinks. He finds this web of femininity delightful. He basks in it. He has never known a mother and daughter who are really friends. They think he is witty. They think he is charming. They think he has led an exciting life.

'You really played for your county?'

'Only thing I'm any good at, actually.'

Starved middle-class minds imagine gracious lawns and trees and a life of beautiful relaxation. They think his father must be very distinguished. Giles wishes his father could meet them. The Chelsea Pensioner accepts several bottles of Guinness and his rosy face becomes rosier.

Giles visits their flat in St Leonard's Terrace. They dance down the street and smile over their shoulders beckoning him in. They throw the room at his feet as they open the door. They lay everything before him.

'I say, what a pretty flat.'

There is only one decent sized room. The rest of the flat is a long passage with two tiny bedrooms opening off it, and a kitchen and bathroom. The sitting room is warm and light, with lots of pictures and rugs and cushions, and small objects placed lovingly on shelves. They sit him down. They offer him coffee and biscuits. On Sunday they will invite him to lunch. It will become a regular habit. If Giles invites Jenifer out to dinner what shall she wear? Where will they go?

She wears a blue and green strapless cotton dress with a bolero jacket over it so that she can appear demurely at a cocktail party or an ordinary restaurant in the early evening, but be prepared to throw her jacket to the winds and bare her milky shoulders if the evening should lead her to the romantic darkness of a nightclub. Giles takes her to the Magic Lantern. It's his favourite restaurant. The pictures of dogs sitting up at the bar with drinks in their paws and the pianist with the bushy black beard make him feel happy. They make him feel happier still when Jenifer is there.

'What a wizard dress.'

Jenifer is not like the other girls he has taken to the Magic Lantern. She closes her small mouth with its Cupid's bow upper lip. She folds her hands in her lap. She knows a secret. She contains a secret, cupped in her soft, neat hands.

'Don't you think the poodle with the tutu and the champagne glass is absolutely killing?' The young man smiles boyishly. Jenifer lowers her chin and looks at him from under her eyelashes.

'Men are such children,' her mother says. Jenifer is not even really disappointed that they didn't go to Quaglino's. In St Leonard's Terrace her mother is waiting up, listening to the wireless and making a woolen dress for the autumn. On the way home Giles is so full of *joie de vivre* that he tries to climb a lamp post. He does not even kiss her. Her rosebud mouth fascinates him. He sways in front of it like a daffodil in the wind. He waits for her permission. Jenifer is triumphant, but she is also a little annoyed. She is triumphant that Giles has fallen in love with her and she can take him in hand. But she is also a teeny bit annoyed that someone who doesn't need taking in hand shouldn't have fallen in love with her. Someone who could immediately raise her up to his own level, where she naturally belongs.

Giles is a captive to Jenifer's charms, no doubt about it. He's like a puppy dog rubbing his stomach along the floor and banging his tail, gazing up at his mistress with adoring eyes. As their power expands the women can allow themselves to become critical. Even the smallest bit patronising. Not too much, because everyone knows how fragile the emotions are, and so rapid and violent a storm of love may well blow itself out before anything can come of it. Before he has known her two weeks Giles has proposed marriage. He has only kissed her once, clumsily, on closed lips. He is her slave. The women take stock of this galleon that the fortunes of war have landed on their shores.

'Oh, Giles, you really shouldn't drink so much; it isn't good for you.' Jenifer knows better than her mother how much he drinks, since they spend every evening together, in pubs or restaurants. Giles does not become wild or angry when he is drunk. Just desperately serious. His face is whiter than ever. Sweat appears on his temple and upper lip. He holds Jenifer's hand.

'I can't tell you how much you mean to me. I don't care about anything in the world except you.'

Who wouldn't be flattered? Jenifer doesn't commit herself yet, but in her mind she constructs plans for marriage. Her mother cannot prevent herself from designing wedding dresses. The relief, after years of lonely struggle, is fantastic. Because Jenifer—a mother's got to be honest—is not exactly a raving beauty. Pretty, yes, and sweet. But life is so difficult these days. One thing that it's rather difficult to discover is what exactly Giles does. He has mentioned to them that he is studying law, to become a solicitor and go into his father's office. But he never seems to do any work. He's always available to go for a walk in the park or a trip on the river, or to take them to the cinema.

'Aren't you worried about your exams, Giles? You never seem to do any work.'

'Trouble is, I just can't seem to get interested in law. Don't want to upset my father though, so I keep on trying.'

Aha! Here is the core of the problem. With a wave of her magic wand the understanding woman can solve it.

'But if you really don't like law it's silly to do it. You can't spend your life doing something you hate, just to please your father.'

'He won't pay my allowance though, unless I study law.'

'Get a job then. You could do all sorts of things. You don't need to be dependent on your father.'

By Jove she's an extraordinary girl, Jenifer. She's marvellous. She's absolutely right.

They take him in. They absorb him. They introduce him to their little rituals, their treats, their friends. Sunday lunch is served on the round table by the window, with the sunlight streaming down onto the square outside. The women have laboured all morning to prepare the food. Giles has been drinking in the pub for an hour, but he has not forgotten the time. There is another guest for lunch. Also a young man. Very young. He has not yet left school. What monstrous establishment could harbour such a nauseating little twerp? He is some sort of a second cousin of the deceased chaplain. Giles sees with horror and despair that he too has been initiated into the little rituals of the household. The glass of dry sherry savoured in tiny glasses. The real coffee. The special peppermint creams with bitter chocolate that are so expensive and difficult to get hold of. He watches the bowing and pirouetting before masculinity, the heightened colour, the flashing eyes that he had previously assumed to be aimed only at himself. It is not much more than two weeks ago that he first met Jenifer, but already the attitude of the women towards him has changed. He has become, insofar as his relationship with them is concerned, a known quantity. He can be played with.

The twerp, the sprog, the nonentity, is daring to suggest that Jenifer should accompany him to Twickenham in a month's time. A friend of his is getting up a party.

'Funny thing,' says Giles, 'I've got a couple of tickets for that too.' Lucky Jenifer, whose company is desired by two young men. I'll have plenty of time to run her up a long dress. You must have fun while you're young and can enjoy it. As to who she goes with, it doesn't matter really, does it?

The monstrous interloper goes back to the country. He'll be safe in school again in a couple of weeks. Giles is once again the undisputed centre of their attention. They have decided that he needs smartening up. Mrs Wynne pops into Sydney Smith and buys a pair of leather patches.

'Now, Giles,' she says as the young couple come back from the cinema in the late afternoon. 'Take off your jacket.'

He sits in his shirt sleeves in the dusk, filling the room with the musky smell of sweat, while the sewing machine on the round table in the bay window buzzes round the elbows of his jacket. It is greasy and solid with dirt around the neck and down the lapels.

'Don't you have another jacket?' asks his would-be future mother-in-law.

'All my clothes are down in the country.'

'Darling, you are too scruffy for words.' Jenifer sits on the arm of his chair and leans her cheek against his hair.

'You must get your parents to send them up. You can't wear the same jacket day in day out.'

She scrubs at it with hot soapy water, and while it is drying they eat fish stew with onions and tomatoes.

'Mums is such a super cook.'

No one expects young men to be clean, or to remember to change their shirts, or their underclothes, or get their shoes mended. They need someone to look after them. Neat hair, and a shave, and scrubbed fingernails are the most you can expect of any man. There's something charming about a man's unwillingness to have a bath, like a small boy not wanting to scrub behind the ears. If a girl smells of sweat she's revolting and vulgar; but sensitive nostrils are anaesthetised in the presence of an eligible male.

'We must get you organised, darling,' says Jenifer, running her finger gently along his eyebrows. He shuts his eyes. The pleasure of her caress is so exquisite that it gives him pain.

'You must write to your parents and tell them that you don't want to go on studying law, but are going to get a job and support yourself. And ask them to send your clothes up. You can't try for any job looking like that.'

'Will you marry me then?' asks Giles without opening his eyes.

'We'll see.' Jenifer, who contains so many gifts and secrets, smiles.

If he shuts his eyes, and refuses to let go of Jenifer, and allows no changes, Giles can share their dream of marriage, a house, a job. Eternal protection. Actually to try and get a job, to tell his parents he wants to get married, would put it all in jeopardy. He cringes back against the floor, protecting his head with his arm while his father's contempt whistles through the air like an arctic wind. Jenifer belongs to his internal life, the life of his emotions. She has taken it over. And yet she, as herself, belongs to the world of weddings and taking clothes to the cleaners. Can she, miraculous Goddess, unite these two worlds in one person? Each day spent chatting in the White Hart to their friend the Chelsea Pensioner, going to the cinema, walking in the park, talking in the sitting room of her flat, with Jenifer's hand in his, or his head leaning against her knee, is salvation to Giles. He quotes poetry to her. They write their favourite poems in a notebook. He kneels at her feet and stares into her face. Her hair her forehead her cheeks her nose her lips her eyes. He learns her feature by feature. No part of her must escape.

Break, break, break,
On thy cold grey stones, Oh sea!
And I would that my tongue could utter
The thoughts that arise in me.

He stares into her face. His eyes are grey like the sea. Her eyes are blue like the sea.

Break, break, break,
On thy cold grey stones, Oh sea!
And I would that my tongue could utter
The thoughts that arise in me.

'That's beautiful,' says Jenifer. 'I learned it at school too.' Carefully, with one arm round Giles' shoulders, she copies it into their book.

Sometimes in the evening when they have been drinking and are walking home from the pub he is overwhelmed with sheer delight, and out of animal high spirits, leaps and shouts and pulls up manhole covers, staggering for a few yards with a Roman shield, and clanging them on the pavement like cymbals. He clambers up lamp posts and unfurls himself like a flag. Jenifer watches fondly, feeling part of the gay life of London. Each day is unbelievably perfect because Jenifer is with him. But as a sign of doom his clothes become more and more filthy and dilapidated. He does not look at himself. He has never looked at his body, why should he look at his clothes? At night he throws them on the floor, wherever he happens to be dossing down, or doesn't bother to take them off at all. His tie is a twisted and greasy rope. The knot is never undone. He slips it down to make a loop large enough to pass over his head, and then pulls it up tight to rest snugly under his Adam's apple. His shirt has lost most of its buttons, and the cuffs and collar are dark grey. Jenifer is not ashamed to be seen with him, because after all he is very good looking, and not really at all a bohemian sort of person. She doesn't quite dare take the clothes off him and wash them, she doesn't really know him well enough to rip off his shirt and underclothes (she and her mother have a fit of giggles). But she does go on nagging, in a womanly way.

'My parents are sending them up,' promises Giles. 'They should be here any day now.'

As his garments disintegrate and his love for Jenifer becomes more secure his own promises begin to operate on Giles' mind. His parents are sending his clothes. Or if they don't he will go and get them. He will also ask his father to give him a better allowance. Jenifer is not the sort of girl who can be expected to live from hand to mouth. It's ridiculous, in fact, that he should be treated in this way. He tells Jenifer.

'My parents don't seem to have got the message, I think I'll go down and fetch the clothes myself.'

Jenifer doesn't see this.

'It's silly,' she says. 'Surely your mother can pack up a parcel with a suit and a few shirts and socks? It'd be much better if you got yourself settled in a job before you went down to see them. Then you could present them with a *fait accompli*.'

'No, no,' he shakes his head. 'I'd better go down myself.'

Jenifer is a little annoyed. She sees trouble ahead. Their romance is progressing from the stage of delicious intoxication towards a serious relationship, when you begin to see the drawbacks in your loved one's character. Still marriage itself is a serious relationship. You can't play all your life. She feels very old and worldly for nineteen. She has long discussions with her mother. Should she marry him? He's obviously not a very strong character. It's usually decided that she herself is a strong character, and that she should marry him.

'Because he obviously absolutely adores you, and believe me, darling, that's the most important thing in a marriage. Far more important than a good job.'

Giles announces his departure and puts it off. He does this several times. He cannot tear himself away. But the weekend of the Twickenham rugger game and dance is approaching, and he has no money to buy the tickets. He has promised Jenifer that he will take her, and if he doesn't the teenage twerp will. He sees it as his father's duty to provide money for him to take Jenifer to this dance. No other money will do. He decides to hitchhike.

He arrives home on a Sunday evening. His parents do not leap for joy to see him. They look at each other. They are not surprised. In his absence they have discussed their eldest son, and have come to the decision that he will not in future be protected from the consequences of his crimes. Better have the family name tarnished by a son in prison, feels his father, than continue to be blackmailed by him. It is the sheer malice of these thefts—always his mother's favourite jewellery—that sticks in the gullet of Mr Trenchard. His mother would like to weep quietly to herself, but cannot think of any good reason for doing so. Of course she is a bit upset that Giles should steal her pearls, and her engagement ring, and the cameo brooch and gold locket on a chain that she wears all the time, rather than the diamond spray or the square cut emerald ring which are much more valuable, but which she hardly ever wears. But then she's used to being a bit hurt or upset. It's almost a permanent condition of her life. It's Austin who's taken it so much to heart. She can still see his face when he said, 'he's stolen your pearls again!' Outraged. He was outraged, it was almost comic.

He comes in late on Sunday night, just before they go to bed, looking like a tramp. Austin just says,

'So you're back, are you?' and goes off to bed.

His mother makes him a mug of cocoa. She would like to take him aside and whisper in his ear that he must be careful. But she looks over her shoulder and doesn't.

'I didn't have much trouble as far as Taunton,' says Giles, warming his hands round his mug, 'but it took me four hours to get from Taunton to Exeter.' The shoulders of his jacket are damp, and his shoes and socks muddy. It has been a cold, drizzling unpleasant day.

'Didn't you have a coat?' asks his mother.

'That's what I came home for. I want to pick up my coat and some other clothes. I want to get cleaned up. Start a new life.' He looks down at his cold hands, and the bubbles of undissolved cocoa floating in the mug. He blushes. In his mind he says,

'I've met this girl, . . .' His mother leans her cheek against his hair and says, 'Oh, darling, I'm so glad. The love of a good woman will save you.' He thinks he will tell her in the morning. He finishes his cocoa and they go up to bed. His mother says,

'Try not to annoy your father, dear,' as they go up the stairs. 'Try to do as he says.' She really means, 'Don't steal anything else, because this time your father will go to the police.'

He hangs around for a week, writing long letters to Jenifer and phoning her every evening. Mr Trenchard's blood begins to throb in his head at the thought of the phone bill, but his wife restrains him with a little expression which means, 'Let him talk to her. This is something new. Giles has never been really serious about a girl.' Quite early in the week Giles has made his demands clear. He needs some money. Though it's not exactly money he needs, but simply that he must be able to take Jenifer to the dance next weekend, and he needs some clothes so that she shall not be ashamed of him.

'I can't take her out like this,' showing his threadbare jacket. 'Not a girl like Jenifer.' Austin Trenchard gnashes his teeth with jealous rage. What has Jenifer got that we haven't got, that our son should not want her to be ashamed of him? He gets lost in the convolution of his own sentences. They are all in his mind. Why the bloody hell shouldn't she be ashamed of him? She bloody well ought to be, if she's got any sense. Austin Trenchard doesn't think much of Jenifer. Giles usually chooses to ring her up from his father's study, just before Dad gets home from the office. He sits hunched over the phone for half an hour, a glass of his father's whisky by his hand, scattering cigarette ash all over his father's comfortable armchair and leather-topped desk. Jenifer, bright and girlish at the other end, cannot understand why Giles doesn't just pack up his clothes and come back to London.

'But you said you were only going to be there for a day and then come back.'

'My father's got some business he wants me to do in London over the weekend.' Giles taps his cigarette purposefully towards the ashtray. 'I think he may let me have his car.' It's odd, but Jenifer doesn't seem to care much about this one way or the other.

His father has delivered an ultimatum.

'If you want any money from me you must stay at home and study. If you do that I'll continue your allowance. Otherwise I wash my hands of you. You're twenty-six. You should be able to look after yourself.'

Funny. Maybe his father and Jenifer would get on after all. They both seem to have the same ideas. Most of his friends think that's much too generous an offer.

'You spoil that boy, Trenchard. I've known people like that before. A few years' hard labour is what he needs.'

On Friday things become really rather urgent because of this wretched dance the next day. Over lunch, which is cold ham and salad, Giles asks,

'Is there any chance of my having the Triumph tomorrow?'

His father does not answer. He breathes heavily. He thinks that if this son, who does not seem to understand what is said to him, does stay at home, he Austin Trenchard, will probably have a heart attack. He takes a last mouthful of ham and mustard, wipes his mouth and gets up. As he leaves the room he says,

'I have already made myself plain about what you may and may not have.'

Mrs Trenchard gets up too, and stacks the plates.

'I shall be back quite late, dear,' she tells her son. 'Do you think you could do the washing up and peel the potatoes for supper?' She is off to a Conservative Women's Meeting.

Giles is alone in the house. He has a headache. The house is empty and silent. He goes upstairs to lie down. Outside, but a long way away, under a sky of high cloud, the sea is sparkling and bright. Giles takes four aspirins. His headache gets a little better. The sharp pain becomes a muzzy throbbing. He thinks a drink might help, and goes down to his father's study. There is an open bottle of whisky in the cupboard, almost full. As a matter of fact, just being in the study makes him feel better. He goes into the kitchen and fills a jug with water, climbs upstairs again to find the book he is reading, and settles down comfortably in the leather armchair with his book, and his glass of whisky and water. The book is called *Randall and the River of Time* by C. S. Forester. It is about a simple, ordinary, suburban young man who is inveigled into marriage by a widow older than himself. Randall is a soldier. One of the young heroes come back from the horrors of the trenches. He's an inventor, and he's good at that, but otherwise he's not very good at managing life in peacetime. He can't manage his wife at all. She takes a lover; a stocky dark-haired Captain with one leg. When Randall catches them together, in his shock and horror he rushes at the one-legged adulterer, and pushes him through the window. He didn't exactly intend to kill him, but there he is, dead and naked in the front garden. Well, at the trial he gets off with manslaughter, and the wicked wife gets her comeuppance and none of his money, and at the end of the book he is ready to go off and start a new life in America.

Giles has read the book before, so it holds no surprises for him. He is reading the beginning again, about the innocent young man and the older woman to whom chance alone gives the appearance of innocence. He begins to feel much better. Quite cheerful in fact. And his headache has gone. By about four-thirty he has drunk a fair amount of whisky, and the water jug is empty. He goes into the kitchen to fetch some more. Through the window he sees the friendly old gardener digging over a flower bed. Several times during the past week the gardener has posted Giles' daily letter to Jenifer in the pillar box at the top of the road on his way home. There are some bottles of beer in the larder. Giles flings open the window and calls,

'Come and have a drink.' He pours out another whisky for himself and a beer for the old man, who stands outside the window to drink it, holding the glass delicately in his earth-stained hand.

'Not so cold, is it?'

'Looks like rain, though.'

Silence.

The old man's head and shoulders only just appear above the window frame. You have to go up some steps into the kitchen. A smell of warm, damp earth and weeds comes in from the garden. The old man swallows down the last quarter of a pint in one smooth gulp and hands the glass back through the window to Giles. He touches his cap, and wipes his mouth with the back of his hand.

'Thank 'ee, sir.'

Smiling, Giles goes back to the study. He looks at his watch. He thinks he'll have a go at the *Times* crossword puzzle and then phone Jenifer. His father usually does the crossword in half an hour, but Giles finds it pretty difficult. He frowns over it and manages about half before he gives up. It's nearly five-thirty, time to ring Jenifer. Jenifer is rather upset. Is he coming up or isn't he? Will he take her to the dance or won't he? She simply wants to know. She bursts into tears. She has told Freddie she can't go with him and now he's probably taking someone else, and Giles doesn't even have the tickets so it doesn't matter if he comes up or not, anyway what's the point of him coming in his father's car, he'd only have to take it back again. She rings off. She cries on her mother's shoulder. Her mother says,

'I know it's disappointing, darling, but you've got to look at it in perspective. What's one dance beside your whole life?'

'But everyone will be there and it'll be such fun.'

'Someone who loves you is more important than everyone. Now what did Giles say he was going to do?'

'He says his father is sending him to London to see to some business, and he wants to drive up tonight. But he doesn't even have the tickets.'

The mother brings out a clean handkerchief and wipes her daughter's eyes. 'Now you ring Giles back and tell him to come here for breakfast. He'll be tired after his long drive.'

'I could ring Freddie and see if he's got anyone else yet.'

'Don't bother with Freddie. You ring up Giles, there's a good girl. He needs you.'

Like a dutiful daughter she rings up Giles and tells him he can come to breakfast. Giles says he will phone again after supper, when his mother and father are both in, just to make sure that things will be all right with the car. But from what his father said at lunch he thinks they will be. He feels very business-like. It is dark now. He turns the wireless on loud so that he can listen to Radio Newsreel while he does the washing up from lunch, and peels the potatoes for supper.

Whisky's wonderful stuff; it can do more for a headache than any amount of aspirins. He lifts the cover off the Aga hotplate and puts the potatoes on to boil. As he opens the larder door to get some sausages he sees the lights of a car through the scullery window. He goes out to open the doors of the garage. It is his mother in her Standard Eight. She's tired, and sighs as she gets out and slams the door. The light in the garage just comes from one uncovered bulb, and it makes her look quite old. She pulls the scarf off her hair.

'Did you have a good meeting?'

'Yes thank you, dear.'

'I've put on the potatoes.'

'Oh good.'

She pauses in the door that leads from the garage into the scullery.

'Here comes your father.'

Giles holds open the garage door, flattening himself against it.

'If you're tired I can go and put the Simpsons' cat out.'

'Thank you, dear,' she calls from the kitchen, her voice drowned by the engine of the Triumph as Mr Trenchard aims his car accurately into the gap between his son and the Standard Eight. He gets out, slamming the door with a brisk, hollow clang. He walks round to the bonnet of the Standard and opens it up.

'I'll just check your battery while I'm here.'

Giles hears his own voice saying,

'Any chance of my having the Triumph to go up to London tomorrow?'

His father doesn't move or react in any way. His father is immovable. He picks up a piece of iron piping that is on the floor and hits him over the head. He still doesn't say anything. His hat falls off. He slumps forward over the bonnet of the car. Giles hits him again. He rolls slowly over the nearside wheel until he is sitting on the floor leaning against the running board. There is still a piece of flex in his hand. Giles goes into the kitchen. His mother has taken off her coat and is tying on an apron. Her back is towards him. He hits her on the head. She falls down. Her brown hair is beginning to go grey. There is a large patch of red, and in the middle of the red some greyish pink. The potatoes on the Aga are bubbling furiously. On the wireless Ronnie Renald is whistling like some insane, voluptuous bird. His mother likes Ronnie Renald. He stands still in the middle of the kitchen for quite a long time wondering what to do with the piece of iron pipe. In the end he puts it down on the table. The kitchen clock says eight-fifteen. He ought to phone Jenifer and tell her it'll be all right. He goes back into the study and turns down the wireless. He looks over his shoulder into the kitchen. His mother is lying on the floor. For the moment he can't quite think why she is there. He telephones Jenifer in London, forcing himself to be cheerful.

'It's definitely OK about the car. I should be up about six.'

'Well don't wake me up then will you,' says Jenifer. She has got over her disappointment about the dance. It's childish. Her mother's quite right.

'Will it be all right if I have a wash and shave too?' asks Giles.

'Of course it will, darling. And I'll cook you a lovely breakfast.'

She makes the sound of a kiss down the telephone.

'Smashing!' He returns the kiss.

'Drive carefully.'

'I will.'

He goes out of the front door and round into the garage, without going into the kitchen. In the garage his father is no longer leaning against the Standard, but on all fours between the two cars, moving his head from side to side and making strange inarticulate noises like an animal. Dash it, Giles had forgotten about his father. The old man lumbers to his feet and comes toward him with hands out-stretched and blood running down his face. Luckily there's another piece of iron pipe on the floor. Giles picks it up and aims a careful blow. His father's temple is smashed right open. He pitches forward on his knees. That should keep him quiet. Giles pushes the body to one side, takes the keys out of the waistcoat pocket and backs out the Triumph.

Hmm. The petrol tank is only half full. He'll need some more if he's going to get to London. He turns the car carefully in the drive, so that it's pointing towards the gate, and gets out, leaving the keys in the ignition. His feet crunch on the gravel, and a rhododendron brushes against him in the darkness. He goes back into the house to get some clean clothes. As he passes the kitchen he glances in and sees that his mother has moved. She is sitting up and holding onto the table. With the other hand she is making little reaching gestures like a kitten with a ball of wool. Her eyes are shut. Giles picks up the iron bar he had left on the table and hits her again. Blood is pouring out of her head and making a sticky mess all over the floor and down her blue angora jersey. As he looks round the kitchen he sees blood everywhere. On his hands and on the table and the floor. The maid will clean it up. It's her day off. She'll be back about ten. If she sees all this blood she'll ring the police and then he'll never get to London.

His mind is fixed on Jenifer. She is the magic talisman that can resolve everything. He considers his mother, lying on the floor still pumping out blood. He drags her out through the scullery and leaves her in the darkness on the gravel. There is a wheelbarrow in the shed, among the comfortable smells of rope and sacking. It's quite difficult getting her properly balanced in it. Her head lolls from side to side. He pushes her down the path, through the back gate, across the lane and into the field. Whew! It's hard work. He sits her down for a moment and wipes the sweat off his forehead with a rather grubby handkerchief. The ploughed field stretches away in grey and black ribs to the sky. It's not absolutely dark. There must be a moon somewhere behind the clouds. The field is ploughed almost to the edge of the cliff. Then there are a few gorse bushes, then a hundred foot drop. At the bottom the sea washes restlessly against the cliffs. Giles cannot remember whether it is high tide or not. One leg of the wheelbarrow is resting on his mother's hand.

'Sorry.'

He lifts it off and puts the hand in her lap. It has been drizzling on and off for the last few days and the earth is very soft. It is incredibly difficult to push the laden wheelbarrow through it. He has very little control. The wooden wheel plunges awkwardly into each black furrow like an overloaded ship into a heavy sea. The field stretches, slightly up hill, for a hundred yards to the end of the point. You can reach the cliffs sooner if you turn to the right, but Giles, with Herculean strength, straining and gasping, pushes his mother on her one twitching wheel to the very edge of the land. He tips her out and drags her through the gorse bushes to the lip of the cliff. The gorse spikes tear at his hands and ruin his mother's stockings. He pushes her over. It's impossible to hear anything. There's no cry, or thump, or splash. It's impossible to see anything. There's no line of foam visible, down on the beach. The cliffs overhang a bit. Giles feels his arms slowly rising like the wings of an angel as his muscles relax. They expand and lighten like a sponge squeezed dry.

But his purgatorial journey is not yet over. He trundles his three-legged machine down to the house again, full of sweet scented leaves to make a funeral pyre for his father. The old man lies in the garage like a dead bull in a pool of his own blood. He is black and heavy. Giles requires a brightly coloured horse, dressed and blinkered like a paper crusader, to prance out of the ring dragging this black death easily behind him. It is a monstrous labour to lift him into the wheelbarrow. And once he is in, with his chin sunk on his chest and his feet dangling stupidly, lifting the two wooden arms shifts the weight so dangerously that he almost topples out again. It's lucky that Giles has strong arms and shoulders, because they have to bear the weight—fourteen stone or so, a good four stone more than Giles himself—of his father, but they have to control and steer the wheelbarrow too. It was a miracle how he did it, several people later agreed. His father does not believe in making things easy. No good spoiling the boy. Twice, after a particularly violent lurch, he falls out of the wheelbarrow into the soft mud, and twice his son, a struggling figure silhouetted against the sky, a medieval woodcut of sin and effort, manoeuvres him in again. But to take him right out to the end of the point to join his wife is too much, even for Giles. In the end he is dragged on his back, one hand under each armpit, to the nearest point of the cliff edge and tumbled over. The wheelbarrow follows, flying down light and free.

Before he finally lets go of his father Giles takes five pound notes out of his wallet. He had not forgotten, either, to relieve his mother of her pearls and rings.

Giles learned in the navy that once you have started a job you must do it properly. He wants to start off for London, but you have to be methodical. He has enough money for petrol now, but he needs—he opens the kitchen door, yes, he needs to clean up a bit, or the maid will see right away that something is wrong. He gets the mop and bucket and starts washing blood off the floor. It's just like being back in the navy. Any minute he expects the Buffer to peer round the bulkhead and say,

'Brace up there, Trenchard, use a bit of elbow grease.'

Half Price flies through the air carrying his shell and winking. He batters desperately with his fists at a closed door, shouting and screaming. The noise in his head is very loud, but he cannot tell whether he is really making any sound or not, because nobody moves or turns round and the door does not open. He takes the scrubbing brush to a recalcitrant stain under the table, and then thinks he's done enough. He wrings out the mop and leaves it back in the cupboard. He sluices down the garage with a couple of buckets of water and the yard broom. There. At least you can see he tried.

Of course there are still his clothes. But he's eager to be off. He takes a suitcase from the hall and runs upstairs. Jacket, shoes, trousers, what else? A couple of shirts. OK. He goes through his parents' room. There's some more money in his father's overcoat pocket. Good. And this time he might as well take the diamond spray and the emerald brooch. He stops in the middle of the room. He puts his hand to his head and turns round in a long, slow fall. He is clasping the body of his mother as it floats through the air. She is anxiously holding her pearls. She turns her head from side to side. His father's body falls more quickly. Nostrils stuffed with earth he plunges down into the blackness. Giles is standing in the kitchen. The clock says eight-fifteen. A feeling of horror touches him. His veins open and the floor beneath his feet is an old string bag over a black pit. There is a piece of metal in his hand. He looks at it; turns it over; puts it down on the table. He thinks that he has killed his mother and this is the last time he will see Jenifer. It is time to start. Jenifer will be waiting. In his mother's dressing table drawer is a bottle of sleeping tablets. He puts them in his pocket. As he leaves the house he sees a piece of metal on the kitchen table. He picks it up and throws it and the suitcase into the back of the car.

NINE

He has always liked driving his father's Triumph. One of the best looking cars ever designed, as elegant as a Rolls and streamlined as a sports car. It's fast, too, and there still aren't very many of them about. When he gets to Fenny Bridges he feels a little safer. He stops in the carpark of a pub which slopes down to the river. It's after closing time and the place is deserted. He feels his jacket and trousers. The blood has dried by now and they're both pretty stiff and uncomfortable. They have a bit of a sickly smell too. He changes the jacket and trousers and feels a lot better. He throws the old clothes into the river with the bit of iron pipe. His shoes are so covered in mud that he can't tell whether they've got blood on them or not, but they are awkward for driving, so he throws them in the back and puts on the other pair.

He swoops through the night in his father's powerful car. He feels at home in it. Somewhere near Ilchester he sees a couple of hitchhikers. Their backs and the weary gestures of their hands glow in the headlights. He hasn't passed another car on the whole of this Roman stretch of road. He stops to pick them up. He knows what it's like hitchhiking when nobody stops for you. It's nice to have company too, when you're driving at night. He drops them at Chelsea Bridge about five a.m. It's still pitch dark. He parks the car fifty yards down the street from Jenifer's house, and crawls into the back seat to have a nap until eight o'clock.

Jenifer sleeps. Like a log outside her door Giles sleeps. He has reached her after overcoming insuperable obstacles. Climbing mountains on his belly. Shifting seas with his cupped hands. Witches, laughing, have struggled to prevent him. Kindly figures have turned into monsters, gnashing their teeth, but by the power and purity of his love he has overcome them. He alone with his sword has slashed away the undergrowth and slain the wicked giant, and lays himself down now, outside the castle gate, to wait for the morning, and his Princess.

She is there. At the magic hour of eight the door is opened wide, and the Princess, and her mother the Queen, welcome him into the palace. They are wearing flowing robes of scarlet and gold, and sunlight dances in their hair.

'Goodness,' says Jenifer, yawning and stretching, 'You're punctual. I've only just woken up.'

Giles would like to lie back in the armchair and close his eyes and abandon himself to the smells of coffee and bacon, but his fingers tingle and he cannot keep still.

'I've left the car in the garage,' he says, walking up and down the passage so he can talk towards the kitchen and bathroom at the same time.

'I've got an appointment at ten o'clock, this bit of business I'm doing for my father. Perhaps we could meet after that.'

Not a word about the dance. He's obviously forgotten all about it. He was jealous of Freddie, poor dear. Rather flattering really.

'Why don't you come back to lunch here, and then perhaps we could all go to the cinema.'

'Are you sure it would be no trouble?'

'Of course not.'

He eats like a wolf. He eats mountains of bacon and eggs and toast and marmalade. He must be tired from driving all night. His clothes don't look much better than they did before, in fact his shirt is filthy. But still, it's nice to have him back.

After breakfast Giles keeps his appointment, which is with a jeweller in Piccadilly Circus where he sells his mother's jewellery for fifty pounds. She would be very upset, because it's certainly worth more than that. Keen nose down, the earpieces of his deerstalker trailing along the ground, Detective Inspector Lamprière is hot on the trail. Giles books a room at the Regent Palace Hotel, and goes upstairs to have a shave. He remembers the bottle of sleeping tablets in his pocket and puts them on the dressing table. If he takes them all now there won't be any unpleasantness. But he has half promised Jenifer's mother he'll be back for lunch. He goes downstairs to telephone, although there's a phone in the room. But he thinks he'd like a drink at the same time. He tells Jenifer's mother that he won't be back for lunch; but she's very much looking forward to going to the cinema.

'Oh, do let's go and see *Limelight*, we've both been long-ing to see it.'

'Where's it on?'

'The Odeon, Leicester Square.'

They arrange to meet at two o'clock. Journalists in the West Country are licking their pencil stubs. Their eyes glitter. The maid had stumbled for two miles across the fields to her cousin's house when she came back and found the kitchen smeared with blood. The wife of the Member of Parliament says,

'It's a miracle that I'm alive at all. I nearly went home with poor Alice Trenchard, and there that monster was, waiting in the shrubbery with an axe.'

Mrs Wynne and Jenifer look so pretty walking down the street towards the cinema. Giles goes to meet them, and kisses them, and takes one arm of each.

'How lucky I am to be taking two such beautiful women to the cinema.'

Jenifer is wearing a bright green coat with a fur collar, and her mother a smartly tailored black. The blue angora jumper, unfortunately, is past saving. Charlie Chaplin, the Prince of the Screen, the Tramp with a heart of gold, saves Claire Bloom, the beautiful Princess, from a sad death. They all shed a tear. Giles holds Jenifer's hand. He feels very humble. He really shouldn't be allowed to sit next to Jenifer and hold her hand, but he does love her so much.

'Everything I've done I've done for her,' he thinks. And then again, 'She wouldn't like it.' He holds her hand very gently. He is aware of nothing but the softness of her flesh and the delicate whorls of her fingerprints. He is sitting in the cinema between Jenifer and her mother and everything is all right. They will live happily ever after. If time could stop right now they would live happily ever after. His parents don't mind any more. I don't know what came over me. I don't seem able to connect me in the cinema with Jenifer and me in the kitchen with the clock saying eight-fifteen and the potatoes boiling on the stove and my mother lying on the floor. I was desperate. I was desperate to get to Jenifer. I love my mother. I would never hurt her. I know I would never hurt her. He clutches Jenifer's hand so tightly that she gives a little squeak of pain. He begins to believe that he is in one of those nightmares where something terrible has happened, and he is responsible, and nothing will ever change it. But he shakes his head. Come on, snap out of it. Be sensible.

They emerge, sighing, into the dusk. Jenifer's mother gives Giles a kiss on the cheek.

'Thank you, dear. That was lovely.'

She trots off to Regent Street to do a bit of early Christmas shopping, before the rush starts and the prices go up. Giles and Jenifer wander hand in hand down to the Embankment to look at the river until the pubs open. Giles is hungry, so they walk back through Trafalgar Square to the Salisbury to have a plate of cold beef and salad and a piece of apple pie. It's just like any other evening except for Inspector Lamprière, busy on the telephone, spreading his net. And the maid, lying on the sofa in her cousin's front room.

'I can never set foot in that house again. Not after what's happened. Not if you paid me a thousand pounds.'

The MP's wife has been talking to the other members of the Conservative Women's Association, and they are huddled together in small groups all over the county, heads bent, short sharp sighs, voices echoing like a whisper in church. The sanctity of the family has been immensely reinforced. The women preen themselves, puffing out their breasts. One of their number has been attacked in her sacred function as a mother. Her defenceless body, her unmuscular limbs hurled over a cliff. And the father too. A certain gleeful triumph is apparent as the women grasp each other by the wrist, saliva gathering at the corners of their mouths, their voices becoming harsh. The father too, whose dignity must never be questioned, has been bashed over the head, transported in a wheelbarrow and tossed down onto the beach by his no-good, worthless, puny son. It would have been better if it had been a daughter, but still it is rich and full of savor. Secretly they cackle with laughter and rub their hands. They bow down until their sharp noses almost touch the ground. Together they swing round. Together their movements are graceful, supple; they raise their hands to the soft grey sky.

'What a terrible thing!'

'Such a fine man!'

'Such a good woman!'

'They did everything for him.'

'Such a lovely house.'

'They had everything.'

'Of course you know he drank.'

'The purest chance that I didn't go home with her, and there was that monster lurking in the shrubbery.'

•

Jenifer might have had a more amusing evening if she could have heard all of this. Giles is not in one of his gayer moods. He drinks steadily, and holds her hand, and stares at her with doglike devotion.

'To be married to you,' he says, 'is all I'll ever want.'

It's extraordinary how quickly doglike devotion can become a bore. Jenifer feels that she is meant for higher things, like going to the rugger match at Twickenham, and the dance afterwards. She looks round the pub, the second or third since the Salisbury. Here are all these people with nothing better to do. She has something better to do, but she has given it up for love. She looks at Giles and sighs impatiently. It's all very well for him. He's obviously quite happy to sit and stare at her all night. She knows you sometimes get bored with the person you're in love with, but maybe she's not really in love at all. Maybe she'd rather marry Freddie. All right, he's only sixteen, but people do marry people three years younger than themselves.

'Shall we move on,' asks Giles. The pub is a gay little oasis in a quiet cobbled mews. When they get outside he says,

'Jenifer, I've got to tell you something. I killed my parents last night.'

'Oh don't be so silly, Giles. Come on, let's get a taxi and go to one of those pubs in the East End where they have singing.'

It's still only nine o'clock. They find a taxi quite easily. Maybe Jenifer is right not to believe him.

'I don't want to mix you up in it.'

The cab that she is riding in is going to be paid for by his father's money. He really ought to have got a job as she suggested. Well, perhaps he can now. This time he's really learned his lesson.

'You're the only person in the world that I care about. I just couldn't help thinking about you down there in Cornwall. I just felt that if only I could get back to you everything would be all right.'

Jenifer is furiously angry when he tells her that he has killed his parents, He's just trying to make himself interesting, she thinks. Well I'm not going to play his game. In the East End pub, where a large blonde woman sings with a voice like Paul Robeson's, they meet a couple they know slightly from pubs in Chelsea. At the time this couple are not very thrilled to bump into Giles and Jenifer, but later they have cause to be grateful as they dine out on the story for several months.

What did you feel when you did it, ask various people later. Policemen, lawyers, psychiatrists. He tries to remember. The only thing is that he didn't do it. So how can he remember what he felt like when he did it? The part of him that did it was a desperate infant suddenly grown strong, marching back out of the past. Not this light-haired young man with the candid grey eyes and nice manners kneeling on the floor of the cab with his head on Jenifer's lap.

'I've done a dreadful thing, Jenifer. I must have had a brainstorm. I may not be able to see you again.' The two things don't seem to have any connection. He has drunk a tremendous amount. He feels muzzy and hollow, as if he's going to be sick. His arms and legs feel as if they're waving aimlessly in a pool of oil. He stares at the ridged red rubber mat on the floor of the cab, and the ground-out cigarette butts on it, and feels Jenifer's warm knee and the tweed of her coat against his cheek.

'I wish you wouldn't talk like that, and honestly if you go on drinking so much you'll get DT's.'

Sometimes he almost grasps it.

'I think I must have killed them. . .' But then he knows that Jenifer is with him, feels her hand in his and her knee against his cheek, he reaches up and clasps his arms around her waist.

'Oh and I killed Queen Mary,' she says impatiently, pushing his arms down again.

'Did you take your father's car without permission? I had a feeling you'd done that. You are stupid. You'll get into the most frightful trouble.' Maybe he'll go to prison. She'll wait for him faithfully; after all, he did take it to come and see her.

They've reached St Leonard's Terrace. The taxi stops.

'This all right?'

There's the most fantastic sum on the meter. He tries to kiss her. His breath smells of alcohol and tobacco. She turns her head away.

'Do you love me?'

'Of course I love you. But I love you more when you're not so drunk.'

'I'll always love you. Always. Even if we have to part.'

She runs up the steps, feeling in her bag for the key. She doesn't notice the police car that pulls out smoothly from fifty yards down the street, waits till the door shuts behind the young lady and the taxi starts up again, and then swerves in front of it, forcing it to stop.

''Ere, what the bloody 'ell's going on?' asks the taxi driver in astonishment. But Giles says,

'It's true. I did it. Let's get everything cleared up with as little fuss as possible.' And,

'I don't want Jenifer brought into it.'

It all seems rather an anticlimax. It's difficult to understand what all the fuss is about. In one way, yes, he does understand. He's done a very terrible thing, and he's got to pay the penalty. Here he is in a cell with no tie or belt, and the rest of his fifty quid in a brown envelope somewhere, and all the policemen being very polite and giving him funny looks out of the corners of their eyes. But he doesn't feel much different from how he felt last week or the week before. He'll miss Jenifer of course. He wonders if he'll be able to see her tomorrow.

The bed is hard and narrow, with only one blanket. He is reminded of the air-raid shelter at school, and of the navy. He is very tired. The hardness and narrowness of the bed comfort him. He goes to sleep.

The drama is all outside. There's none at all in Giles, nor in the empty bodies of his parents. As far as they're concerned it's all over, might as well be forgotten.

Their photographs seem to feel differently, though. They stare up purposefully from the desks of policemen and journalists. Alice Trenchard is sweet, grey-haired, apologetic. Just like all our mums and all our wives.

You've got to protect her. She's the little woman, all right! You don't take much notice of her while she's there, but attack her, and by God we'll defend her to the last breath. Austin Trenchard, now he's no beauty with his thick neck and scrubby moustache. He looks a bit apologetic too, but when you read the blurb underneath you realise that he's a pillar of our way of life. Under-Sheriff of the county. Built his own house, the way we'd all like to do. Had a no-good son. Bad luck. Could happen to anybody. Why do we care that it happened to you? Why do we care more about this bloke being knocked off by his no-good son than we care about a nine-year-old girl being raped and strangled by her step-dad? Well of course we care about the little darling, might have been one of my own kids. Yes, well. One nine-year-old girl more or less . . . But you get kids going round thinking they can knock off their dads especially when Dad is not just anybody, but like I said, a pillar of the establishment, head of the family, why, that's a bloody revolution. That's upsetting everything. It doesn't even matter so much knocking off your mum. Well, in a way she's asking for it, isn't she? But Dad. That's going too far.

As to Jenifer's reaction, that can be imagined. What price Twickenham now? Her cheeks flush pink, and her eyes are a deeper blue. Her mother almost faints. She runs to the bathroom and is sick. It is too much to accept that this charming and eligible young man, whom she was already looking on as her own son, should have cold-bloodedly murdered his parents. She is raw with insult. How can one plan for the future of one's children when things like this happen?

Jenifer rustles out to the kitchen to make coffee for the detectives. She slips into her room to put on a touch of powder and a dab of lipstick. Circumstances have made her more adult than her mother. She is the centre of real life. Her mother retreats. She lies in a darkened room with a wet flannel on her forehead.

With what skill did Inspector Lamprière extract from the old gardener the address of the young lady to whom Giles had written so many letters! What a stroke of luck that his simple Cornish mind had retained it. It is sweet to know that there are men at your command. That a word on the phone will summon armies of trained men in belted raincoats with felt hats pulled down over their eyebrows to melt into the surroundings of St Leonard's Terrace, waiting for the monster to return to the hinged trap. When they see the Triumph parked half way down the street they know that intuition and painstaking labour have paid off.

'I am familiar with the criminal mind,' says Inspector Lamprière, removing his pipe from his mouth. 'And what I always say is, *cherchez le femme.*'

It wasn't difficult as a matter of fact. There she was at the bottom of the cliffs. The tide never reached her at all.

Jenifer is a celebrity. She had always known she was a woman of destiny.

'I'll do anything for you.'

'I love you so much I'd be willing to die for you.'

People die for all sorts of things. Men could be said to die for you when they go to war. And to kill for you. But Giles killed for her by name. He has risen up and killed two grown up people for her sake. And he has told the world that it was done for her, Jenifer Wynne. She walks proudly down the King's Road in her green tweed coat. Her plump cheeks and pretty mouth are composed in a serious expression. She will not abandon the poor boy now. A detective accompanies her to visit him in his cell. The police have impounded the suitcase in the back of the car. After some heart searching, they have decided that the shirt he is wearing, the collar and cuffs of which are crusted with some brown substance, might be of use to them in their investigations. They unpack a clean one, and order him to change.

Giles looks unusually smart. He is pale, and has a hangover, but the long sleep and a mug of strong tea have revived him a lot. He feels better than he has for ages. The concrete walls of his cell are a pleasant grey, soft and relaxing. It's very quiet. The occasional clang of iron and the smell of urine remind him of the ship. The uniformed men reassure him. It's unbelievably lovely to see Jenifer for a brief moment, her green coat glowing in the shadows, her face soft with tenderness. She reaches through the iron bars to clasp his hand. Perhaps it's the happiest moment in his whole life.

'I'm afraid there's going to be a hell of a lot of unpleasantness,' he tells her. 'I think it would be better if you tried to forget all about me.' He sees their happy life together, in a house at the edge of the sparkling sea.

•

What do the other members of his family think, his uncle and his brother? Uncle Walter chokes on his supper of macaroni cheese as he hears the news over the telephone from Inspector Lamprière. His face turns red, then purple. He puts his hand to his neck. With bulging eyes he stares at his children as they eat their supper from a trolley in front of the fire, and argue about who they will invite to a cocktail party. Nancy's fork, dripping with cheese sauce as she takes a second helping, points like a dagger towards his heart. His wife pats him on the back.

'Choke up, chicken.'

He shrugs her off. He puts down the telephone. Takes a drink of water. Pushes his plate away.

'What on earth has happened?'

It's all bloodily in his mind, in the important voice and preparatory cough of the Inspector. He too, is dragged, heels kicking, into Real Life, eagerly followed by Hugh and Nancy, who are mentally rehearsing what they will say to their friends.

'I say, do you remember that fellow Giles, our cousin who used to stay with us?'

'Rather a terrible thing's just happened in our family.'

You'd be hard put to find a better story than that.

'Poor Alice and Austin, how frightful.'

'I always said the boy was, was . . .'

Walter has a good heart. He is suddenly responsible for a criminal nephew. His older brother is dead. His father is dead. He is all alone. He tries to remember what his duty should be. He hires a lawyer.

Some people know what they ought to be doing in a situation like this. That's the advantage of the police and the law. They have machinery. They are not rushed dizzily to the station, and the morgue, and the scene of the crime, or left alone in a cell, or just wondering at home. They move along their routine, punctuated by cups of tea. They are slow, pleasant men, also husbands and fathers. What a relief when your murdered brother and yourself have become part of the machinery.

Robert, in Australia, decides to leave well alone. What is there to come back for really? It must have been a horrible shock to get out there on those sunny beaches. The plains are scarlet and the trees are blue. Laugh cookaburra. You can't blame him. Sometime later he claims the estate through a solicitor.

The golden afternoon is over. The long fall through the rabbit hole is over. It is time for the trial to begin.

Ha! There is the Judge. An old woman with long grey curls sits on the bench. She is a coquette. Her curls are arranged in ringlets. She twitches at her scarlet robe. When she enters the room the people rustle to their feet. She bows to right and left. They are her servants. The people in the courtroom are dull, passive, sheep-like. They obey the ritual of the court. They are preparing themselves. A meal is about to be set before them. They must say a silent grace. Purify themselves by fasting. They are going to be satiated.

In the town and in the country rumours run and stir. They pass in waves from one group to another.

'You know she was still alive when he threw her over the cliff?'

'No!'

'The pathologist's report said so!'

Heads turn in the cafe. Voices are lowered in the pub. The jury carries a heavy burden. So do the witnesses. Their serious, frowning faces indicate that they are anxious to do their duty. The second nurse, now a married woman living among the claypits, knows that she holds the key to her charge's life in her hands.

'Ever such a nervous little boy. He never was normal. They expected too much of him.' To her and the people who listen to her the parents appear inflexible, granite statues crushing their child. To the family doctor on the other hand they are infinitely fragile and vulnerable. Alice's hair is soft under his hand. She bows her head onto his shoulder. And Austin drunk, or pale and shaking with the cure, is putty in his hands. All the power is in the son. His is the power of the irrational. The power of the unexpected. The power of evil. Born with a silver spoon in his mouth he spits it out. He was offered Rugby and he spurned it. When every natural law demanded that he become an officer he remained an Ordinary Seaman. What treachery was brewing in his heart during those years with people who were not his kind? The doctor strides through the town in a black coat and grey trousers. He is an avenging fury. He moves from drawing room to drawing room. The feeling of the people is with him. Revenge must be taken for this shameful act.

•

The young man sits in the dock making no movement, not even stirring his head, staring straight in front of him. Looking at him, so young, healthy and clean-limbed, and knowing what you do about him almost makes you doubt your own senses. You might almost think, that's the sort of son I'd like to have. Not tall, a little over five and a half feet, but broad shouldered, with such an honest, reliable, open English face that you've half a mind to put an arm around his shoulders and say, 'that's as fine and promising a young English lad' . . . then your arm draws back as if you'd touched a snake. It recoils in horror and drops to your side. If he were my son . . . The image rises in your mind.

We look at him blankly, Master Giles. Some of us who knew him always did think his father was hard on him. But even so, what he did was too much. There's plenty of fathers bully their sons, but they don't all go around throwing them over a cliff! It's funny to think of him without his parents. It was always, 'poor Master Giles, he's in trouble with his old man again.' Or, 'poor Mr Trenchard, what a time he's having with that no-good son of his.' 'Of course, nothing ever came out about his stealing things, but I knew because I've got a cousin in the police. His father's friends would have known about it, some of them. He had influence, you see. So nothing ever came into court. I expect if he was alive now he'd wish he hadn't covered things up. If Giles had come up before the courts and had to serve a spell in prison it might have made him pull himself together. Given him a bit of a shock. I suppose he felt he could get away with anything. Serve him right really, old Mr Trenchard. If he hadn't been so keen to cover up and protect the family name he might be alive today.'

DINAH BROOKE

•

Some of the lads from the *Patusan* read about him in the papers. Bits from the letters he writes to his fiancée are published in the *Daily Mirror*. Nice looking girl; girl-next-door type. Nothing outlandish. Shows how little you know about people. Never have thought he was that romantic. None of them write to the lawyers or the papers though. Never enters their heads. What would they say? He seemed a decent enough bloke. Who'd have thought he'd do a thing like that? It makes something to talk about in the pub though.

Jenifer has come down to Bodmin for the trial. She is fêted. Her mother has recovered enough to accompany her, in case the strain should prove too great. She is famous throughout the town. As she comes down the shallow steps from the street into the foyer of the Swan Hotel, waiters and porters take quick, appraising glances. The chambermaids are disappointed.

'I thought she'd be more like Rita Hayworth. Bit of glamour.' It's an affront to their whole system of values. You don't commit murder for a round-cheeked girl with a prim mouth and no figure to speak of.

'Trouble with you lot is you can't appreciate a lady,' says the head porter.

During the lunchtime recess and in the evenings she can often be found in the King Arthur, an ancient, low-beamed pub across the road from the court house, drinking with the journalists. A red-faced, quick-witted, hard-drinking lot they are too, with some rare stories to tell. Jenifer has a rare story to tell too. She tells it often. They take down every word she says, and sometimes put it in the papers. They hand her round from one to the other, and buy her drinks. Photographers are sent to take her picture. When they have heard everything she has to say several times they tend to forget her. The *Mirror* reporter takes charge of her. He finds her a bar stool and stands with one hand on the back of her neck while he talks to his cronies. Every day she receives a letter from Giles. He has written her at least one, every day since he has been in prison. After all, he doesn't have very much else to do. She never forgets to write back, either. Sometimes, if the letters aren't too personal she shows them to the reporter from the *Mirror*, and he puts bits of them in the paper too. Then she puts them with the rest into a special box where she keeps the exercise book with the poems in it and a photograph inscribed—'their memory is forgotten, also their love, and their hatred and their envy is now perished.' She tries not to think about what might happen to Giles. Sometimes he says in his letters that he thinks he might be sent to Borstal. Other times he tells her that it would be best if she forgot about him. The journalists don't talk about what might happen to him either, while Jenifer is there. They cough and change the subject, and insist on buying her a drink.

As a matter of fact Giles does not have all the time in the world in his cell. He's moved about a lot, from prison to prison, and people come to see him. Solicitors and lawyers and psychiatrists and priests and relatives. He's moved about between places like Exeter and Bristol for various tests. For the trial itself he comes down to Plymouth and is driven all the way down to the court in Bodmin every day.

'Quite the social round,' says one of the warders, ushering in yet another psychiatrist. Some of them ask him whether he feels any remorse. What he does feel is that now he'd like to settle down and get a job and marry Jenifer. He's sure things would be much better now. He wouldn't drink so much. He wouldn't need to hang around pubs now he's got Jenifer.

Giles is not in possession of his murder. His murder takes place in a dream. The poetry and justice of it is a dream. How can you perform such an action and not be freed and transformed by it? The world is full of us, haunted by dreams of violence. Swaying like figures hanging from huge balloons filled with heat and air, blind to everything but the murders we commit in our imaginations, over and over again. You have committed your crime, destroyed those who have power over you, and now you are empty and dull. Your life is gone. You are of no interest. I wish you were dead. There's something too single-minded and logical about that perfect Oedipal crime, leaving out nothing, not even the mother, the agent, the function that was not fulfilled. Why can you not be a true murderer? One who finds his apotheosis, his fulfilment in his crime? Whose passions flower in the white serrated petals of his act? You stand there as a young cricketer. An ex-public schoolboy, an Englishman. Those images are more powerful than your despair.

That was the image in which your wretched soul was formed; you destroyed those that formed you, but you did not succeed. They are still stronger. You have done nothing. Your life is wasted, and your crime. You have murdered, but you have not changed. I love you. I wish that I was you. For many years I have been you and you have been my life. Nothing about you is strange to me. You are the measure of my disappointment. You commit the perfect, the absolute crime, but in secret. You deny it. You do not understand it. You are not present. You commit the crime that could have freed us all, and you are not present in it. You deserve to die. You do not understand what you have done. I wish that I had your neck between my hands so that I could shake some knowledge into you. But your eyes still remain blank and innocent. I hate you because you have exposed the secret. You have laid it in front of us. And yet you see nothing.

There is a game going on in the court. Birds of prey are perched round the dark brown panelled walls, watching. Their heads don't move, only their eyelids flicker as they shift their weight from one clawed foot to the other.

The Counsel for the Prosecution, a severe gentleman with grey hair in a pigtail and a black gown, opens the bowling. He glances round to check on the placing of the field, he feels the weight of the ball, positions his middle finger on the seam and prepares to send down the first ball. He has a square red face and flashing glasses. The creases round his mouth form a square too. He takes a few deep breaths and moves his chin from side to side to loosen the muscles of his neck. Gnashing his teeth and shrieking with laughter he sends ball after ball down towards the impassive batsman. Loathsome crime, planned for days, low moral character, disgusting, vicious, degraded, criminal. The batsman stands there still, unchanged, though spattered with mud and slime. For a change of pace the Prosecutor brings on Dr Hood, who sends down a few lethal off-spinners, utilising the natural prejudices of the jury. Despicable little waster, worthless, black sheep. How often has he made his mother weep? One of the best women that ever lived. Cold blooded slaughter of this most virtuous couple. They must be avenged. He weeps. There before the court, tears drop to the ground like crystals from this grey and dedicated man. This is life as it can be understood. We retain our sense of order. Politely the birds of prey nod and clap.

There is a recess, a pause, heads bow together, possibilities are exchanged, hotels compared.

Now it is the turn of the Defence. Compassion. Passion rings round the court. Heads turn. Eyes swivel back again. The Under-Sheriff rises to his feet. He points his finger. He utters a loud cry and falls to the ground. The Judge withdraws her skirts. Who will carry out this pinstriped hulk? Dr Hood bends over him in the cool marble lobby, clasping his hands and wailing, 'Ai, ai, ai.' His hat is by his side. So is his bag. Instruments, rings, eyeglasses, glitter and fumble. The men in uniform who have carried out the body of the Under-Sheriff flex their muscles and straighten their caps. There is not much room in the public gallery. People mill around in the lobby smelling of wet mackintoshes and shaking their umbrellas. Journalists point their pencils at the Under-Sheriff. He is dumb but not dead. He has had a heart attack.

The Defence is under way. We are unctuous and apologetic. We do not want to offend anybody, certainly not the dead. A gentle psychiatrist is lobbed down and easily dismissed by memories of Dr Hood. We all know about idle little wasters. The question is, is he crazy. Well, you've only got to look at him. Of course he's not crazy. On the other hand, anyone who did what he did must be crazy.

The birds of prey giggle hysterically, the ruff of feathers shaking up and down on their scraggy necks. The defence captain decides to bring on a new bowler. He has developed an interesting variation on the googly, which skittled the prosecution at a recent trial in America. The boy was suffering from a sort of fit brought about by not having enough sugar in his blood. Poor starving child. Anyone can have a fit. In the gallery feet and fists are clenched. Toes, and muscles tighten in the bum. Don't say he's going to get away with it. Why, I could strangle him myself, with my bare hands. Ah no, relief is at hand. This bowler is dismissed with a contemptuous flick of the eyebrow. How, we twirl the end of our moustache, could he be suffering from hypoglycaemia when he had just eaten a large lunch and drunk half a bottle of whisky? Greedy little pig. Drunkard. Eating his parents out of house and home. Drunken beast.

Mouths half-open with the effort of concentration, the jury stares at the judge. It is time for her to sum up. She smiles

and gazes at the canopy of clouds above her. She clasps
her hands over her bosom. Once upon a time there was
a King, who ruled over a small but beautiful kingdom.
He has a son, and to prove his fitness to inherit the son
is forced to go through several trials. He fails them, and
his father, unwilling to admit to the people that his son
is not satisfactory, sends him away to another city, where
he becomes famous as an athlete. After several years he
comes home and is given a great welcome and installed as
the Crown Prince. But he gradually deteriorates again, fails
his father in intelligence and cunning and other princely
attributes, and degenerates into a shadow prince, despised
and mocked by everyone. One day this polite and pliant
Prince kills his father and the beautiful Queen his mother,
and the people of the town turn on him and tear him to
pieces. The jury exhales. They want to do their duty, and
now they know what it is.

The Judge pulls the clouds down upon her head and
spreads her hands in a gesture of beauty.

'You will be torn to pieces.'

'Amen,' says Giles. 'I will scatter my body among you.'

He is taken to a place of safety, whence he may be torn
at the time appointed. Those who are full of sorrow weep
in silence. Giles does not weep. He would like to know
whether England can retain the Ashes this year, but a com-
passionate world will not let him live so long.

The Under-Sheriff pops up again. He rubs his hands
with glee. I will jump on your body and piss on your
remains. Afterwards I will drink a glass of brandy with
the Prison Governor and then have breakfast. He leans
forward and whispers into the hooded ear,

'You may not borrow my car to go and see your little whore.'

His dark grey shoulders move up and down in wheezy laughter. He undoes his fly and pulls out his motor car. With this weapon I will thrust you down into the bowels of the earth. The Pierrepoint publican pulls the handle. Giles' body plunges down into the starry blackness. The shark with blunt teeth drags at his legs. His neck stretches like an elastic band. The vertebrae pop. The spinal cord is ruptured. Shit, piss and semen are sucked into the shark's mouth. His head remains above, like Alice's peering over the top of the mushroom. A fair, young, English public school face, with the eyes full of blood and the tongue sticking out.

The Test match ends in a draw.

McNally Editions reissues books that are not widely known but have stood the test of time, that remain as singular and engaging as when they were written. Available in the US wherever books are sold or by subscription from mcnallyeditions.com.